The Detective and the Baroness

The Duke's Bastards
Book 1

by
Karyn Gerrard

Text by Karyn Gerrard
Cover by Dar Albert

Dragonblade Publishing, Inc. is an imprint of Kathryn Le Veque Novels, Inc.
P.O. Box 23
Moreno Valley, CA 92556
ceo@dragonbladepublishing.com

Produced in the United States of America

First Edition February 2025
Trade Paperback Edition

ARE YOU SIGNED UP FOR DRAGONBLADE'S BLOG?

You'll get the latest news and information on exclusive giveaways, exclusive excerpts, coming releases, sales, free books, cover reveals and more.

Check out our complete list of authors, too!

No spam, no junk. That's a promise!

Sign Up Here

www.dragonbladepublishing.com

Dearest Reader;

Thank you for your support of a small press. At Dragonblade Publishing, we strive to bring you the highest quality Historical Romance from some of the best authors in the business. Without your support, there is no 'us', so we sincerely hope you adore these stories and find some new favorite authors along the way.

Happy Reading!

CEO, Dragonblade Publishing

PROLOGUE

Late October 1898
London, England

"DETECTIVE SIMPSON!"

Mitchell groaned, straining to open his eyes. He heard a woman's voice, one somewhat familiar. His bewildered brain tried to place it because the sound of the breathy voice sent frissons of pleasure through his aching body.

"Sergeant, please wake up!" The lady gripped his arm and gave it a vigorous shake.

Mitchell's mind was a haze, struggling to understand what had happened to him. The revelation that the late, loathsome Duke of Chellenham was his birth father had left him reeling these past weeks. As a result, he'd found himself caught up in the lives of certain aristocrats, even ending up agreeing to act as a backup in an intricate plan to retrieve a kidnap victim from the Notting Dale slum area.

The thief and kidnapper, Jedidiah Danaher, was unpredictable. Mitchell knew that made him particularly dangerous. So Mitchell stayed close by with a small contingent of constables as his friends went forward with their plan. Mitchell closed his eyes tight, reliving the event. It unfolded in his mind as if in slow motion. When he heard gunshots, Mitchell and his constables entered the fray, and during a scuffle, Mitchell saw Danaher point a revolver at his friend, Viscount Tensbridge. He pushed him out of the way only to be shot instead.

After that, Mitchell did not remember much else. Someone transported him to the house of his half-brother, the new Duke of Chellenham, where they called in a doctor. But Mitchell distinctly remembered this lady's voice through his numerous fever dreams, as he slipped in and out of consciousness. He recollected her soothing touch as she'd laid a cool cloth on his forehead when he'd been burning up and covered him with blankets when he felt cold. The lady had told him that all would be well, that he would recover.

Not that he had genuinely believed it.

"Mitchell!"

The sound brought him more fully awake. He groaned and placed his blurry gaze on the owner of the frantic voice.

His vision cleared, and when Mitchell saw who had awakened him, a powerful yearning tore through him—just as it had the first time he'd seen her a few weeks ago.

Lady Corrine Addington, Baroness.

The Honorable Corrine Edgeworth, the only daughter of Viscount Rothley. The recently married bride to Travis Addington, the new baron. Travis Addington was a distant cousin to the recently passed old baron, Gilbert Addington.

He might be sick and injured, yet Mitchell still could pluck out relevant facts stockpiled in his organized police detective brain. At least, that boded well for his recovery. Why was Lady Addington here? Then he remembered something else. Of course. Before she'd married, she had been a nurse. His friends had told him so. It made the baroness all the more fascinating. "I am glad you are awake, Sergeant. Do you remember me?"

Remember? How could I forget?

"I was at the Galway Investigative Agency when you came looking for Viscount Tensbridge and Miss Ellingford. We met again when I assisted in nursing Miss Ellingford's injuries."

Mitchell remembered it all. He recalled locking gazes with her, and the potent blast of awareness and arousal that had gripped him tight—just like now.

"I heard that your injuries resulted from a police raid, so I offered my medical services."

"How long have you been here, my lady?" Mitchell croaked.

"Since your friends brought you here five days ago."

Five days? "What about the baron, your husband?"

"What about him?"

"Isn't he wondering where you are?"

The baroness shrugged. "I highly doubt it. We are separated, at least temporarily."

Already? Weren't they married only a few months ago? Why did the prospect of her estrangement from her husband fill him with hope? It was inappropriate, particularly since Mitchell had only met Lady Addington.

"I must tell the others you are awake."

"Others?" he rasped.

"Your family and friends. I will fetch them."

Family? He had no family. His parents died years ago.

There was Damon Cranston, his recently revealed half-brother, and the new Duke of Chellenham. Why had he been brought to Damon's residence instead of a hospital? Still, he'd probably received better care here—a duke could afford top-notch medical attention. What did it matter where he recovered? The fact that he had been shot was the paramount occurrence.

His thoughts and emotions were chaotic and had been for a few weeks. Discovering he was the bastard son of a duke was just one of the shocking twists and turns Mitchell's life had taken lately. But learning he was one of possibly dozens upon dozens of illegitimate offspring from that same late duke was particularly shocking. Then he'd received his recent surprising but welcome promotion to sergeant. Now, this injury on top of it all? Before he could reply, Lady Addington departed, leaving an enticing aroma of vanilla and roses in her wake.

Damon Cranston stepped into the room, closing the door behind him. Unfortunately, the utterly alluring baroness did not return with him. And damn it, he'd never thanked her for her care.

"I am relieved," Damon said, exhaling. "It was touch and go there for a few days. But still, you must be careful. Why don't you stay here as long as it takes to recover?"

"Thank you," Mitchell replied quietly. "The baroness, why was she here?"

"Lady Addington volunteered once again to offer medical assistance."

Right. She had said that. But why was the baroness meeting with the ladies who ran the Galway Investigative Agency? And multiple times? The questions he longed to ask were piling up. Although, how tempting it would be to have Damon call her back into the room so he could enjoy her comforting presence. "Where am I, Clarendon Place or the Duke's house at Queen Anne's Gate?"

"Clarendon Place. The duke's residence is in the last weeks of its renovation. The children wish to see you, but I said you were still too ill for company. And by looking at you, that seems to be the case." Damon smiled teasingly. "No offense."

Children?

Mitchell had only met his assorted much younger half-brothers and half-sister a few weeks ago. Yes, he had more 'family' than he knew what to do with. All of them were the progeny of the detestable Edward Cranston, the late Duke of Chellenham. But Mitchell wasn't ready to deal with them now.

"Thank you. But I cannot see the children in this condition. Not for a while. Is everyone well? Tensbridge and the rest? Is Danaher dead?"

"A body was discovered in the burned building. The police allege the corpse to be Jedidiah Danaher but state that, scientifically speaking, it will be difficult to know for sure. Everyone is well. I don't suppose you can talk about what happened."

"No. It is not my story to tell. Certain aspects—I was sworn to secrecy."

"Say no more. And as far as seeing the children, I surmised you would not be up to having rambunctious tots skipping about your room. By the by, your supervisor, Inspector Stanhope, came to see you, but you were not yet conscious. He wanted an update on your medical condition."

Mitchell's blood chilled. "Why?" A sickening feeling settled in Mitchell's guts. Stanhope would take immediate steps to replace him if he weren't up to co-running the F Division Lancaster Station near the Notting Dale district.

"Doctor Drew Hornsby will relay that to you. He's been seeing to your care." Damon strode toward the door, opened it, and waved in the young doctor. Once Hornsby arrived, Damon left them alone.

Mitchell tried to move his injured leg but couldn't. Panic tore through him, and he elevated his head and looked down the length of the bed.

Oh, thank Christ. He still had his leg. A wave of relief overtook him.

Doctor Hornsby stood by his bed. "Awake at last, Sergeant Simpson. I will be blunt: we almost had to take the leg. Sepsis started to settle in the wound, but I used carbolic acid on the bandages, and luckily, the danger passed."

Sepsis? Wasn't that derived from the Greek word *sepo*, which translated to 'I rot.' His late adoptive parents ensured he obtained a good education, which came in handy more than once. Mitchell flared his nostrils. Thankfully, there was no putrid smell. "And what is my diagnosis?"

The young doctor pulled the chair closer to the bed and sat upon it. "It will be several months before you can return to duty, Sergeant. I am sorry."

The crushing disappointment moving through him was potent, indeed. "If at all?"

"I believe with a sufficient recovery period and rehabilitation exercises, you will regain full use of your leg, at least enough to return to work. Your inspector said he will come by tomorrow to discuss your sick leave."

Mitchell groaned. Payment received while on medical leave for the Metropolitan Police was barely sufficient for basic survival. How in hell would he live? His savings were for his retirement. He really didn't want to touch that money, if possible.

"You will have to use a cane in the interim. And there may be sporadic pain," the doctor continued. "But with focus and determination, you shall recover. I place my reputation on it."

"In other words, don't wallow in self-pity and get on with it," Mitchell growled, allowing himself a moment of temper for his unfortunate fate.

Hornsby pushed his spectacles further up his nose. "Yes. That is the gist of it. I believe your brother intends to ask you to stay with him as you recover."

Oh, no.

They hardly knew each other, and besides, Damon was to be married. The duke didn't need a grumpy older half-brother wandering around the residence like a restless beast.

"I can make my own arrangements. And Chellenham is my half-brother."

"The duke guessed you would say exactly that, so I have another proposition. You can stay with me. That way, I can assist you in your recovery. I live in a large flat not far from here."

Mitchell blinked several times, shocked at the suggestion. "Why would you make such an offer to a perfect stranger?"

"Well, it turns out we are not *exactly* strangers—in the biological sense."

Mitchell stared at the doctor in disbelief.

No. Not another one.

Damon's father, the old duke, was a miserable, egotistical excuse for a man who held a deep conviction in eugenics. Edward Cranston believed he possessed a superior bloodline and ensured he spread that lineage far and wide. It was a complicated tale, not one Mitchell wanted to discuss right now. But observing Hornsby, he could see it: those tell-tale sky-blue eyes, the light-colored hair, and the tall frame. Almost all of the Duke's offspring had the same physical attributes, himself included.

"How and when did you find out?" Mitchell whispered.

"Only recently. My mother passed when I was nine, and Tremain Hornsby, Viscount Hawkestone, adopted me shortly thereafter. On her deathbed, she told my adopted father, then a vicar, who my birth father was and made him swear never to tell anyone. But when Edward Cranston died a few months ago, my father decided to inform me of the truth. You see, my mother and I had been living under a false name—she was hiding me from Cranston. Quite the sordid story…"

Mitchell could not be more shocked if Hornsby had smacked him across the head with a pine board. "Have you told Damon?"

"Yesterday. Chellenham promptly invited me into his club. And more generously, into his life and family."

That sounded like Damon. The club in question was The Rakes of St. Regent's Park. "He invited me, as well. I'm thinking about joining."

"Perhaps we can join, but maybe later. For now, let us form our own group. I appreciate the duke's offer considering their charity work, but I would like us to focus on another purpose." Hornsby reached into his coat pocket and pulled out a piece of paper. "This is the list Damon's mother gave him that started him on his journey of discovery. It contains the names of all the illegitimate children the duchess knew of. I say we find these people, taking on one name at a time."

Mitchell was on that list. He had no idea what to say.

"I'm overwhelming you. I do apologize," Hornsby said softly. "I'm still trying to digest the news myself. I did not expect this turn of events and I cannot explain why I feel compelled to seek out these people. It is not for family's sake, as I have a loving family with the Hornsbys, as you did with the Simpsons. Damon told me of the particulars."

"We were fortunate to be taken in by good people," Mitchell murmured.

"Yes. But how many on this list were not? What say we work together and form a support group of sorts. Do good works for those who need it, whether on the list or not."

The idea began to germinate in Mitchell's mind. He liked Damon more with each passing day, but joining his half-brother's exclusive club filled with aristocratic and wealthy members did not appeal to him, even though they were honorable men. "Let me see the list."

Hornsby handed him the paper. Ten names. Eight males and two females. "There is a ledger full of names beyond this list. We just have to find it."

Hornsby nodded. "The duke told me about that and the foundling home."

Yes, the foundling home—Chellenhome. And another discussion to add to the mounting agenda. The late duke sold his illegitimate offspring, as well as those of other wealthy men of business or the peerage, for profit. When he'd discovered he had been sold to his adoptive parents—like a piece of merchandise—it had stung. But he didn't blame the Simpsons, not at all. No, he blamed the late duke for taking advantage of a couple desperate for a child, charging such an exorbitant price, it decimated their savings. Mitchell returned his attention to the paper. The next name on the list—Liam Hallahan, pub owner.

Following through with this idea would be like ripping off a bandage and exposing a better left-alone wound. But this quest would give Mitchell some purpose while he recovered. He was a detective, after all. There was no reason he could not do some private investigative work on the side.

"You need to think about it. I understand," Hornsby said solemnly. "Take all the time you need. Though I may not show it outwardly, I'm still reeling from finding out who fathered me. I'm sure you are as well."

That was an understatement. It had shaken the very foundation of Mitchell's life. "It was bad enough to find out I was a duke's by-blow, as society calls it, but discovering he was, in essence, a Dickens's villain, selling children, including his own? Yes, I'm reeling." Mitchell exhaled. "Look, Hornsby. I don't need time to think about your offer. I'll be damned if I'm going to lie around and bemoan my fate. Doing good works was the reason I considered joining Damon's group, but your proposal intrigues me more."

Hornsby nodded. "Good. Why not offer assistance to those who share our unfortunate bloodline? Why not do good, not just for the names on the list but for anyone in the periphery? What better way to expunge Edward Cranston's loathsome legacy than banding together and rising above it?"

"Well said. I say we forge ahead," Mitchell declared firmly. "And I have just the name for our group. The Duke's Bastards."

CHAPTER ONE

Early December 1898
London, England

MITCHELL GAZED OUT the window of the hansom cab that carried him to his first case as a private investigator. How ironic that it was Baroness Corrine Addington who wished to hire him. He had not seen the lovely lady since she had awakened him six weeks ago. At times, especially late at night, he swore he could detect her enticing scent, a mixture of vanilla and roses, and feel her soft, silky touch on his forehead as she soothed his fevered brow. Since he found her attractive, he should have declined the appointment outright, but curiosity got the better of him—and he longed to see her again.

Much had transpired since Mitchell had departed Damon's residence. First, he moved in with Doctor Hornsby at Gloucester Square. After settling in his comfortable room, he stopped by Damon's and told his half-brother what he and Drew Hornsby planned to do. Damon balked, believing the past best left alone. But as Mitchell succinctly pointed out, that was easy enough to say when brought up in privilege as the legitimate heir to a duke.

Ultimately, Damon came around to their way of thinking, and agreed to give Mitchell—and Hornsby, for that matter—some space. He quickly realized that they needed it. Their lives, like Damon's, had been thrown into turmoil because of recent revelations.

Mitchell and Drew had agreed to follow the names on the list in the order they were written, and now that Mitchell was recovering, they intended to put their plan in motion. One name at a time. First up was Liam Hallahan. Through letters Edward Cranston had sent the duchess, Mitchell had learned that Hallahan's tavern was in the East End. The evil man had boasted about his offspring and kept tabs on them.

But back to the matter at hand: Lady Addington.

The hansom cab pulled up in front of a Wimpole Street residence in Marylebone. The dwelling resembled the white stucco town house where he lived with Drew Hornsby on Gloucester Square, only this one was more modest and only had the white plaster on the main level. The other two stories were light sandstone.

Slowly, he exited the hansom, paid the driver, and, leaning on his cane, used the door's brass knocker. At least there weren't any stairs to climb to reach the front entrance. Mitchell had enough trouble navigating Drew's home in Gloucester Square. He and Drew lived on the top floors of a large four-story residence recently renovated into flats.

His prior residence was two rooms at the rear of Lady Ainsworth's Kensington home. The kindly older widow insisted he stay rent-free until he fully recovered. But that would not be fair, as she should lease the rooms to someone who could pay the entire rent. Better he recovered under the watchful eye of a doctor.

His insides were in knots as he waited for someone to open the door. No woman had ever had him in this muddled state before. The door opened, and Lady Addington stood before him, dressed in a floral tea gown of light blue silk with a gold and red rose overlay. Her beauty took his breath away. With her auburn hair, blue eyes, and alabaster skin, she was everything bright and glorious. And the bold way she stared at him made his insides turn to absolute mush.

"I am so glad you agreed to meet with me, Sergeant Simpson.

Do come in." She stepped aside, revealing a footman standing nearby. "Jonathan, bring the tea tray to the sitting room."

The footman bowed slightly and made his way down the hall.

"Right in here, Sergeant." The baroness led him to a luminous room caused by the sun's rays pouring in through the sheer draperies—and her brilliant and potent presence.

Good God. I must get a firm grip on my wayward emotions.

But Mitchell could not help it. His insides roiled like mad. He could not stop staring at her. Mitchell looked about the room for a distraction from his inappropriate reaction. The oak furniture, in overall good condition, showed decades of wear. It looked like a peerage residence, with the trappings of wealth, however modest, evident with the art in gilded frames and expensive trinkets scattered about the room. After unbuttoning his wool coat, he sat on the sofa and set his cane and homburg hat beside him. The baroness sat opposite.

"I did not have the chance to thank you, my lady, for your care and competent nursing. I appreciated it very much."

She flushed slightly, making her all the more striking. "I was glad to do it. And I'm pleased to see you up and about. Is there much pain? Forgive me. It seems I cannot stop being a nurse."

"I don't mind. There is pain now and then. I'm staying with Doctor Hornsby, and he is monitoring my situation, insisting that I do his daily rehabilitation exercises. All I can do is take this situation as it comes."

"How very sensible of you. Well done. Is your leave from the Metropolitan Police temporary?"

"I'm hoping that will be the case, my lady. Although Doctor Hornsby states it may be some months before I'm able to return."

"I saw the wedding announcement of the Duke of Chellenham and Althea Galway in the paper," Lady Corrine said.

"Yes, it was a small affair with only a few people in attendance, my lady."

"And you were one of the attendees? Of course, since you are friends with the duke. You recovered at his home."

Mitchell nodded. He did not wish to get into the details of his newly formed relationship with his recently discovered half-brother—at least, not now. Luckily, the footman picked that moment to enter the room. He placed a large silver tea service before the baroness. Small, perfectly cut sandwiches and a few biscuits sat on a platter.

"Thank you, Jonathan. Please see that we are not disturbed."

"Yes, my lady."

With the departure of the servant, they were alone once again.

Lady Addington poured the tea. "Cream? Milk? Sugar?"

"No sugar and a little milk. Thank you."

She passed him the cup. "I wish to hire you, Detective Simpson. Althea Galway informed me that you were open to taking on some of their clients while you recover. I wish to be the first."

Mitchell sipped his tea, then reached for a beefsteak sandwich. He couldn't stand those fishpaste ones that were often served in upper-class parlors.

"Taking on a few customers is only a temporary sideline as I have every intention of returning to the police force as soon as possible. But in the meantime, why are you engaging the Galway Investigative Agency?" He stopped, realizing how forward he was acting. "Sorry, my lady, that is none of my business."

Lady Addington sipped her tea thoughtfully. "I genuinely like the ladies working at the agency and have come to know them a little since meeting them at a tea party. I was going to hire Miss Ellingford, but she is taking a temporary leave to get married."

"And my name came up?"

"Why yes, it did. Do you mind?"

"Not at all, my lady," Mitchell replied.

"I can't blame you for wanting to get involved with them. The last time I visited Althea, I offered to assist her by moving about society and gathering information on any of their cases when needed. They haven't used my services yet, but I stand at the ready. You see, I'm not one for sitting about parlors sipping tea all day, although there is nothing wrong with that. Since I have more invitations than I can handle, I might as well put that to good use. The sisters have their duke husbands to gather information among male peers. I simply offered to gather any information among the ladies."

No, he couldn't imagine all that sparkle contained within a stuffy parlor setting. "Good for you. I admire that. But why do you wish to hire me, my lady?"

Lady Corrine sighed. "I need you to follow my husband and report his activities to me. He's presently staying at his old residence, the one he lived in before becoming Baron Addington. Travis has been there for nearly a month. He owns the Camden Town property. I will give the address before you depart."

Mitchell placed his half-eaten sandwich on the saucer, then retrieved a notepad and pencil from his side pocket. "You can give it to me now, my lady."

"Seven Carol Street. Does this mean you are taking the case? I haven't told you the particulars as yet."

"After what you have done for me—and my friends—I-I will gladly take your case."

I would do anything for you.

He had almost said those words. How disturbing to find it was the complete truth. No other woman had caught his attention like this. It bloody well rankled that she was married.

Her ladyship smiled warmly. "Thank you, Sergeant. So, as to my situation... Like most marriages in the aristocracy, ours is a business arrangement, pure and simple. Travis was one of the presumptive heirs to the barony but never expected to take on the title since the old baron had a son. Unfortunately, the boy drowned when he was sixteen. A second cousin was next in line but he, too, died before the old baron. Next in succession was Travis's father, but he passed ages ago."

"So your husband moved to the top of the list."

Lady Addington nodded. "Yes. He felt it his duty to find a wife, or so I assume. Travis is forty-one and claimed he didn't wish to look for a bride amongst the younger, eligible ladies. We had an acquaintance but hadn't seen each other for years. So, he sought me out. He knew how to entice me to consider marriage. Money."

Mitchell stopped writing and looked up at the baroness, who watched him closely over the rim of her teacup. "That would be an inducement for anyone, my lady."

"My family has lived on the edge financially for years, so I took up nursing, as it was one career open to women. My younger brother works at a bank. I wanted to give my family financial security. So Travis settled a substantial amount on me, and I agreed to marry him. There were a few conditions."

Mitchell frowned. "If your family desperately needed money, why didn't your brother marry one of the many American heiresses haunting London ballrooms? After all, he is the heir apparent to a viscountcy. That would be quite an inducement. Why should it be left to you to take care of your family?"

Again, he knew he'd overstepped the bounds, but if the baroness wanted to hire him, he had to know all the facts.

Lady Addington reached for an iced biscuit. "I recently turned thirty. I had no illusions that I would marry for love—or at all. But I want my brother, Jeffery, to fall in love before he marries. As he is only twenty-three, that may take time—which we did not have."

Somehow, Mitchell had thought she was much younger than his thirty-two years. He turned the page on his notebook. "And the conditions? It may be relevant to the case."

The baroness thrust out that enticing lower lip. "It is also very personal."

"You may count on my discretion, my lady."

"Yes, I know I can. Besides the money, I asked that we try for a child. Travis did not keep up his end of the bargain. At all." The baroness's cheeks flushed as she popped the rest of her biscuit in her mouth and chewed furiously.

What kind of man would not want to bed her? My God, her

beauty took Mitchell's breath away. But it wasn't only that; it was her confidence and how she was so vibrantly—alive. Also, he admired her frankness. What to say to such a pronouncement?

"I now realize I made a mistake," Lady Addington continued. "So I need grounds for a possible divorce. I have tried to talk to Travis about this. But that only resulted in him returning to his former residence. Something broke between us, not that there was much to start with. We could stay married and live apart as so many have done before, but I want more. Being a baroness is not important to me—not enough to stay in an untenable situation. So I want to know if I have grounds for divorce." She sipped her tea. "I *am* sorry, Sergeant. That was too much information. I have a habit of prattling on longer than I should."

"I understand." What else could he say? He couldn't comprehend such upper-class arrangements. Mitchell always thought such emotionless marriage transactions were strange and coldly cynical at their core.

The baroness shot him a look. "Do you?"

"No, I do not understand since I've never been married. As you say, it is an untenable situation."

"And I have been far too outspoken. But you need to know that this isn't some whim of a spoiled peer. I did not want you to think, 'She's got her money, and now she is kicking the baron to the cobbles.' I'm unsure *why* I care what you believe, but I do."

"The thought never crossed my mind, my lady," Mitchell replied softly. And it hadn't. "Can you give me a description of your husband?"

The baroness stood and smoothed her gown. "Travis had his portrait done when he became the heir apparent. It is in his study. Follow me, Sergeant."

They entered another room that had book cases filling nearly every wall. Again, the furniture was old but in good condition. Mitchell stepped before the portrait. It was of a man of middle age with thinning brown hair with shots of gray at the temples and bushy side whiskers—pleasant-looking, neither ugly nor handsome, with a determined jaw and kind eyes. But then, portraits were not always accurate when capturing a subject's true essence.

"I will start immediately, my lady."

"Will twenty pounds suffice as a retainer, Sergeant?"

More than generous. "Yes, it will. Thank you."

The baroness pulled a small roll of pound notes from the side pocket of her gown and held it out toward him. Mitchell tucked his cane under his arm, took the money, and placed it and his notepad and pencil in his side coat pocket. The money was certainly welcome.

Mitchell was never sure how to act in such social situations but decided to mimic what he had seen his half-brother Damon do. Once he leaned on his cane, he held out his hand, and Lady Addington's fingers brushed his palm, igniting a roaring fire within. It swiftly rumbled through him. That slight touch of skin, that barely-there contact as she rested her hand in his caused his heartbeat to thunder in his ears.

Gulping, he gave a slight bow. "Good afternoon, my lady." How he managed to keep his voice steady was a miracle.

"Good afternoon, Detective Sergeant Simpson."

Slowly, he retracted his hand, and her fingers trailed across his skin again, giving him another jolt. "I can find my way out." He turned and exited the room.

Pausing outside, Mitchell raised his hand and looked at the one she had touched. It burned with an almighty heat. Clenching his fist, then flexing his fingers repeatedly, he continued down the hall, collected his hat and gloves, and headed toward the exit and away from the temptation of Baroness Addington.

Chapter Two

CORRINE LET OUT a shuddering breath as she plopped into the oversized chair behind Travis's desk. She hadn't expected to experience such a physical reaction to the detective. *That is not wise at all.* She had decided to hire him, not only for his competence, but to see if that initial spark she had experienced when she first saw him some weeks past was merely an anomaly.

But it hadn't been. That spark had flamed to life, causing a maelstrom within her. Every nerve ending pinged with awareness. All from a slight touch of his hand. How shameful! Yes, Corrine felt shame—for entering into a loveless arrangement with her now husband, taking the money offered, and making a demand concerning children. Obviously, she had spooked Travis. Did he prefer men? If so, why did he not say that upfront? She wouldn't have cared. They could have negotiated another proposal that benefited them both, perhaps leading separate lives. Corrine should have traveled to Camden Town and confronted him today, but she had already tried that. It was the reason Travis had fled.

She'd had three marriage proposals in the past decade, but all her suitors had been as impoverished as her, and none had caught her interest, either physically or intellectually.

Until Mitchell Simpson. How tragic that she'd met him after she had married.

When Corrine was fifteen, her mother died, throwing the

family into chaos. While her father had wallowed in grief, they'd sunk deeper into debt. She'd had to take control even at a young age, which meant letting some of the servants go and selling her mother's jewels and the family's treasured artwork to keep food on the table. Borderline destitution had worn her down, borrowing from one person to pay another, scrimping and worrying.

Worn down. Weary. Exhausted. Discontented.

Nursing had taken its toll as well. Witnessing such grinding poverty while employed at a workhouse infirmary reminded Corrine that her hardships were trifling compared to those who had neither a home nor a crust of bread to their names. It certainly put things in perspective and made her work all the harder to assist those less fortunate.

When Travis Addington approached her with his proposal, Corrine had had enough and urgently needed a change for sanity's sake. Being a nurse made her well aware of when a person was near the breaking point. And she had arrived at that juncture. Accepting Travis's deal meant she could aid her father and brother—all the better. Travis offered the money, and she approved the deal. Her arrangement was not shameful, as it was standard procedure in most aristocratic marriages. No, she would not feel guilty for taking the money.

Corrine had met Travis years before at a ball—couldn't remember which one. He claimed he had never forgotten her, which Corrine doubted because he hadn't he sought her out before. She had never asked Travis that vital question, and she should have. The sudden reacquaintance caught her at a particularly low ebb in her life, and without giving his proposal the careful thought it deserved, she had said yes to his business marriage plan.

A categorical mistake.

The butler, Thomason, entered the study. "My lady, a man is at the door and insists on seeing the baron. He will not go away."

Corrine stood and strode down the hall toward the front

entrance. If this stranger did not leave, she would ring the police. Travis had had one of those telephone contraptions installed before moving into the old baron's home.

Corrine flung open the door. A man stood before her wearing a long cloak, a hood obscuring his face.

"May I help you?" Corrine demanded in an inauspicious tone.

"I need to talk to the baron. Now." The voice was deep and scratchy, sending a jolt of unease along her spine.

"He's not here at the moment, but you may leave your name and address with the butler, and I will ensure he gets back to you."

"And who are you, then?"

"Baroness Addington."

A sharp bark of cynical laughter left the strange man. "That old goat remarried? Trying for another heir, is he? He has more gumption than I thought."

Another heir? Old goat?

Then it struck Corrine what the stranger meant. "You must mean Gilbert Addington. He died five months ago. My husband, a distant cousin, is now the new baron."

The man's head snapped up briefly, as if shocked by the information. Corrine could see scarring on the left side of the man's forehead. He lowered his head and stepped back. "Then I'll seek out the new baron. I'll be back. And soon. Tell him to expect me anytime."

Corrine wasn't about to inform a stranger that her husband had temporary living arrangements elsewhere, for there was something deeply unsettling about this man.

With a flick of his long cloak, he turned and hurried down the walkway. Corrine closed the door, locked it, and swirled about to face Thomason, who hovered nearby. "Did you give any information to this stranger?"

"None, my lady. All I said was that the baron was not available. He became insistent, saying he'd had an audience with the baron on other occasions."

"Did you recognize him? You were with the old baron for twenty-five years."

"No, my lady. I did not see the man's face or recognize the voice. When I tried to close the door, he stuck his boot in it and spoke in an insistent manner. I thought it best that he hear the information from the lady of the house."

How curious. "If he comes to the door again, let me know immediately. We may have to involve the police."

"Yes, my lady."

Corrine returned to the sitting room and sat by the fire with her cold tea.

"Shall I fetch you a fresh pot, my lady?" Thomason offered.

Corrine visibly started. Her family had not had a butler for years, and she had forgotten how much they silently moved about a residence.

"Yes, thank you."

Thomason took away the tray and left her alone. What possible business could that stranger have had with Gilbert Addington? The man had lived alone in this house for years and had hardly ventured out after the death of his only son and, soon thereafter, his wife, which was why the furnishings were decades old. The baron had left a healthy bank balance for his heir—even after Travis's settlement on her, tens of thousands of pounds were still available. At least, that was what Travis had mentioned in passing shortly before their wedding.

As far as Corrine knew, Travis hadn't spent any significant amount since their marriage. Perhaps all this change and upheaval had been hard for Travis to comprehend. It was also problematic for Corrine to take in.

Travis had initially agreed about the children aspect of their arrangement, yet balked when it came time to consummate their marriage—and every time since. The rebuff had hurt Corrine, and so, she had decided to hire Sergeant Simpson to see if divorce was an option.

At some point, she would send a note to Travis and ask him

to come for a heart-to-heart discussion. They must have it out before she took the final step of ending their tenuous union. But first, Corrine had to allow the investigation to continue. As Sir Francis Bacon had said centuries before, knowledge was power. The more information she gathered about Travis's doings, the better. She would mail the note once she had evidence of…anything.

As for Mitchell?

Yes, she thought of him by his first name. Embarrassment filled her for finding a man not her husband—fascinating. She knew it would be wise to keep the association between them professional, but Corrine was aware that Mitchell returned the interest. She wasn't sure if it was instinct or just wishful thinking, but there was a definite reciprocal spark when their hands had touched.

Mitchell was around six feet tall and had wavy hair the color of golden wheat. His azure eyes, rugged physique, and handsome facial features were mesmerizing. But as tempting as the detective was, Corrine would never break her marital vows, no matter the circumstance. Maybe that was another reason she wanted a divorce. To be free and allow these heated sparks to flourish and grow. But Corrine would deal with that obstacle later. Right now, more complications loomed on the horizon. What about the settlement? Would she have to return it? Part of it was already spent keeping her family afloat. She was getting a headache just thinking about it.

Thomason entered with another tray and placed it on the table. When he departed, Corrine prepared a fresh cup of tea and carried it to her desk. Once seated, she pulled open the drawer. Locating note paper, pen, and ink, she composed the letter she intended to send to her absentee husband.

MITCHELL IMMEDIATELY HEADED to Camden Town, where the baron had taken up residence. The house had a white stucco main floor and two light brick stories above it. A small wrought iron fence blocked off a greenery area, complete with assorted shrubberies, before the entrance. There hadn't been much snowfall the past few winters, and it seemed this one would be the same. Only a sprinkling of snow clung to the leafless branches, all that remained of the light flurries that occurred overnight.

How should he approach this?

Did he wear a disguise and watch the residence for Addington's comings and goings? It was not a pleasant prospect, regardless of the sporadic moderate temperatures. The official start of winter was a few weeks away, so the weather would grow colder, making outside surveillance difficult.

It would be prudent to uncover a little background first. Was the new baron a member of a club? Did he attend the House of Lords? Mitchell could have asked the baroness those questions, but considering his jumbled emotions, he thought it best to leave immediately. He could enlist Damon to ask a few questions about the baron, discreetly, of course. But no. He'd told his half-brother he needed space. Mitchell would have to discover this information on his own. Besides, Damon needed time to get his new life off on the right foot. Their young half-siblings were coming to live with Althea and Damon on the first of the new year—a ready-made family. Damon had confided that he had always longed for a large family, and now he was getting it.

Where should he go now? Perhaps, he should check out another place since he was already in the cab. Mitchell banged on the roof, and the hansom's top hatch slid open. "Yes, sir?" the driver asked.

"Head to Old Montague Street." Mitchell didn't know his way around the East End, as all his police work had taken place in the West End, and his parents brought him up north of London, but he mentioned the one street he knew of. It wouldn't hurt to ask around about Hallahan before heading home. Not only did he have Corrine as a client, but now, Hornsby as well.

Corrine.

He shouldn't be thinking of her by her given name, but hang it all, all this overwhelming yearning had taken him by surprise. Mitchell did not possess a vast romantic history. There had been no intense affairs of the heart or even casual encounters beyond some in his twenties.

Some? Try four.

And there had been nothing for the past five years. Work had become his entire life. Routine and discipline guided his every move—until three months ago, when he'd discovered he was the bastard son of a disreputable duke. Since then, Mitchell's life had been cut from its moorings, drifting in all directions, taking unexpected turns. And it certainly showed in his recent decisions, such as taking on cases for the Galway Investigative Agency, moving in with Drew Hornsby, and creating a group with him to find the other bastards. But he'd be damned if he would sit and brood over these upheavals. And the beautiful baroness was indeed part of that turbulence.

The hansom stopped; Mitchell paid the driver, gingerly exited the cab, and then slowly strolled along the street. He noticed many synagogues, as the Jewish population of London lived mainly in the East End. It was hard to believe ten years had passed since the unsolved Jack the Ripper murders, but the area remained scarred by the incident. The discrimination toward Jews at the time of the murders and even to this day turned his stomach.

Whitechapel Mortuary, where the Ripper's victims had been kept, was gone, and laborers were hard at work erecting a new school in its place. Mitchell stopped and watched as several men dug, exhuming graves in the burial ground next to the mortuary. He pondered over where the remains would wind up. Not coming up with a satisfactory answer, he continued along the street, passing tailors, furriers, and shoemaker shops.

After walking for several minutes, Mitchell entered a pub, The Old Commodore, and located a table in the corner. Groaning from discomfort, he sat, relieved to take the weight off his leg. The pain was bad, but at least it wasn't mind-numbing or disabling. *There's a mercy.* Grabbing his cane, he laid it on the table.

A bearded man with a bar towel slung over his shoulder approached him. "What can I get you, guv?"

"A pint of bitter—and some information. I'm not a copper but a private investigator." Mitchell looked about the primarily empty pub. "You're not busy. Surely you can spare a moment."

"Aye, that I can. I'll fetch your drink." The older man hurried away, waited on another customer sitting at the bar, and then returned with Mitchell's pint. The man sat across from him. "What do you want to know?"

"I'm trying to locate someone. The man in question's family hired me. One particular member is very anxious to find him." *That is not exactly a lie.* "The last information I was given was that he managed or owned a pub in the East End."

"Blimey, mate. Do you know how many pubs and taverns are hereabouts? There are half a dozen just in this section alone."

"I have my work cut out for me then. Still, perhaps I'll get lucky. The name of the man is Liam Hallahan."

The barkeeper sat back in his chair and shook his head incredulously. "Well, you just got lucky, mate, for I know of the bloke. He owns The Crowing Cock on the corner of Brick Lane and Chicksand Street. Just a few streets over. You can't miss it."

What were the odds of finding him that easily? It had to be luck—or fate.

"What can you tell me about him?" Mitchell asked between sips.

The barkeeper shrugged. "Not bloody much. The blighter keeps to his territory. Big Irishman with coal-black hair. And piercing blue eyes, much like yours."

That statement about the eyes caught Mitchell by surprise,

causing a swift pain around his heart, as if someone had slipped a blade between his ribs. It reminded him, once again, that there were serious ramifications to heading down this road. And one of them was to make him relive his own shock and distress at learning of his duke father. Perhaps looking for the duke's bastards was not a wise idea if it meant he'd experience this reaction with every revelation.

"It's a bigger place than this one," the man continued. "He ran a brothel upstairs up until six months ago. It's a pub and nighttime gaming establishment, mostly cards. He fancies himself a chef, if you imagine. He's branching out into lunches, teas, early suppers, and the like, trying to lure in a better class of clientele. Good luck to him and all. One thing—you don't want to cross him."

"Oh, why is that?"

"He nearly murdered a man who slapped around one of his girls. I think that's when he gave up flesh peddling. Not worth the trouble and strife." The barkeeper stood. "That's all I know about the boyo."

Mitchell held out several shillings. "You've been very accommodating. For the pint and some extra. Have one for yourself, as well."

"Cheers, mate." The barkeeper touched his forelock, spun about, and headed to the bar where another customer waited.

Mitchell didn't intend to go to the pub right now, at least not inside it. But he'd quickly inspect the exterior and surrounding streets, then catch a hansom cab home.

Fifteen minutes later, Mitchell stood in front of the corner lot pub. The front entrance was dark wood, with large windows on either side. Above the hanging sign, the building had two stories with red brick walls. Is that where Hallahan lived and where he had housed his brothel? The rest of the street was filled with various flats and small businesses, some in better condition than others. Rising over the horizon, farther along the street, he saw the brick pipe stack of Trueman's Brewery. Mitchell inhaled. He could detect the faint odor of hops. And the underlying smell of sulfur from the yeast. He wrinkled his nose in distaste.

Mitchell returned his attention to the pub. It was a lively spot, with waitresses carrying trays of food and drink to the many tables and booths. The aroma was heavenly, an olfactory mixture of fried onions, bacon, and grilled steak. It all but eradicated the odors from the brewery. A tall man appeared from the rear, yelling instructions to the servers. Mitchell had a good look. Just as the barkeeper described, the fellow was big, as in muscular and tall, and dark Irish all the way—it had to be Hallahan.

Yet another half-brother. God above!

Mitchell turned and hailed a hansom. He would return to this pub with Drew—and soon. How he'd approach the Irishman was another question.

As he settled in the cab, his thoughts returned to Lady Addington. It would be best to wrap up her case as quickly as possible. Married or not, she appealed too much to him, and Mitchell didn't know how long he could hide it.

If he had hidden it at all.

CHAPTER THREE

MITCHELL ARRIVED AT Gloucester Square thirty minutes later. As he exited the carriage, he stopped short, for there was a flurry of activity. Workers were carrying furniture out of the bottom flat and taking it to the floors above, while others brought some from upstairs. Were he and Hornsby being evicted? It wouldn't surprise him, given the constant turmoil in his life as of late.

Drew came to greet him. "Good day, Mitchell. I was hoping the laborers would complete this move by the time you arrived. We are taking the bottom flat. It's larger anyway."

Mitchell cocked an eyebrow in question. "And the landlord is fine with this?"

Drew pushed his spectacles up his nose with the tip of his finger. "Actually, I am the landlord. This building is mine, lock, stock, and barrel, as the saying goes."

Mitchell shook his head. "I had assumed your family rented the flat for you. So they gave you the building?" Drew's father was a viscount, and his uncle was the Duke of Gransford, so Mitchell figured the family had money. He had only lived with Drew for ten days, but already, he liked him. Drew had no airs about him, no guile at all. His first impression was that Drew was intelligent and honorable. A good man to have for a friend.

Drew nodded. "For my twenty-first birthday. I had it renovated three years ago. A doctor working at a free medical clinic with only intermittent paying patients makes little income, so I turned it into flats and became a landlord. There is also a four-room rental upstairs at the rear. I hope you don't mind, but I plan to let both the upper flat and the upstairs rooms very soon. So I am rearranging some furniture and moving our belongings down here."

"As you wish. It's your house." Mitchell paid next to nothing in rent, so he had no reason to object. Not that he did. Navigating those stairs was more difficult than he cared to admit. "What happened to the older gentleman renting the flat below?"

"The elderly baronet departed this morning. He is going to live with his daughter and her family in the country. I hired men to clean this flat and switch out some furniture. The baronet also gave me his housekeeper. He paid her in full until this coming May. Mrs. Evans comes daily for a few hours to clean and prepare a meal—food we can easily reheat ourselves."

So far, he and Drew had mostly eaten in pubs, cooked fried eggs and bacon, or fried a chop. It was all either of them knew how to prepare. A housekeeper/cook was a welcome development.

Drew showed him into a large, elaborate entrance and hallway, complete with crystal chandeliers, then pointed to the front stairs. "That leads to the bedrooms. There are four, along with a water closet and a separate bathing room." They climbed the stairs to the second level. The stairs were boarded up, cutting off access to the upper levels. "As you can see, we cannot take the stairs any farther, but if someday I wish to convert this back into a single residence, I can see it done easily enough. I had the workers put a WC on each floor in case I want to make this into four flats instead of two."

"Very wise," Mitchell murmured. The entrance to the upper flat was on the right side of the residence, so Mitchell had never seen the downstairs hallway.

Drew opened the first door on the left, indicating that Mitchell should step inside. "This will be your room. Do you see the door? It leads into a smaller room you can use as a sitting room, a study, or an office area. I think it was originally a drawing room or boudoir. Who knows? A fireplace makes it much cozier than the upstairs flat. The rooms are larger, too. I am across the hall, with two rooms of much the same size. At the end, there is a full bathing room with a water closet next to it. Below this flat in the basement is the large kitchen, a wine cellar, pantries, and the like. The old servants' hall is used for storage now. And the former morning room is now the dining room, which leads into a garden area. Come, I will show you."

They descended the stairs and entered the room. It was cozier. Mitchell immediately liked it. He followed Drew into the garden.

"Not much to look at now," Drew said, looking around. "But the baronet liked to putter about, so come spring, it will be a lovely area to sit and indulge in quiet contemplation. Are you much of a gardener?"

"Me?" Mitchell scoffed. "Not at all."

"I know a little, since I'm a doctor, but my greenery skills run more to herbs than flowers. We will figure something out. See that building in the back? I am toying with the idea of converting that into another couple of rooms to rent. It hasn't been used as a carriage house in several years."

"A wise decision."

"We will also share the library, the sitting room, and the small formal parlor. I need the study for my medical research."

"That's fine by me. I will set up a small desk in the room off of mine for my work."

"I will see that the room is prepared for you. Now, I thought we would have supper at The Victoria. It is not far from here. I shall pay, as the baronet told me to keep January's rent as a thank you. So technically, I suppose dinner will be supplied by the baronet."

Drew gave final instructions to the workers, then the two men left, strolling through Gloucester Square Park until they reached Strathearn Place and the pub. There was a slight chill in the air, and Mitchell pulled his wool scarf tighter across his neck. They arrived at the corner pub, a posh place situated in a Georgian-style building. Mitchell looked forward to ordering a sirloin of beef with all the fixings.

Once settled in a corner booth, they ordered their food, pints of bitter, and a bottle of red wine.

"How did you become injured, if you don't mind me asking?" Drew asked.

"Annoyance."

"What?"

"As I mentioned before, The Rakes of St. Regent's Park asked me to join their group. I hesitated, as its members are either peerage, wealthy, or both. Why were they interested in me? Obviously, it was my connection to Damon Cranston, who heads the group. And I made friends with another member, Viscount of Tensbridge. I admit I was flattered, until I discovered they wanted to use me as a connection within the police department. At least, that is how it seemed to me. I categorically refused to assist them in their schemes."

Drew gave him a quirky smile. "Come now. I am sure that was not the only reason they asked. I know the club started out as a group of indolent young rakes drinking and bragging about their conquests with women, but in the past year and a half, they have changed their focus to charity ventures."

Mitchell took a long swallow of the bitter. "The charity initiatives were why I briefly considered joining. But assisting them with legal difficulties wasn't the only reason they asked me to join. It was friendship as well. I came to realize that soon enough. So I joined the scheme and was shot for my trouble."

"And yet, even though you initially refused to assist, you barreled into Notting Dale with policemen in tow."

"Yes. While recovering, I received a dressing down from Inspector Stanhope for the misuse of police resources. Still, by the end of the reprimand, the inspector grudgingly admitted that the police had ignored Notting Dale for far too long." Mitchell paused. "On a deeper level, I wanted to protect my friends."

"But you cannot discuss the particulars," Drew murmured.

"It is not my story to tell." No, that was Oliver Wollstonecraft, Viscount Tensbridge's story. Tensbridge's secret life as a vigilante in Notting Dale was the reason they met. Claudia Ellingford had worked for the Galway Investigative Agency. The three of them became immersed in quite the adventure, culminating in the confrontation with Danaher. Oliver and Claudia were now off on a five-month-long honeymoon to Spain and Scotland. Mitchell had missed the small wedding due to his injury, but they'd come to see him before they departed. He and Oliver had become good friends—Claudia, too.

Mitchell glanced at Drew, reflectively studying him from across the table. Drew was very different from Damon. He was much more self-contained. Though Mitchell supposed the same could be said for him, to a point. Except where the baroness was concerned.

Mitchell took another swig of his drink. "I found Hallahan."

"Well, you are good at your job," Drew said, smiling.

"It was luck, pure and simple. Hallahan has a reputation, though according to a source, he no longer runs a brothel. By all accounts, he is trying to run a more legitimate business. I walked by, and the place was packed to the rafters. I admit the food odors emitting from inside were enticing."

"Did you go in?" Drew asked as the server delivered their beefsteaks. Mitchell delayed his response until the waiter departed.

"No. I thought I'd wait until we could go together. He is huge, taller than both of us and muscular. And he has dark hair. But get this: the man I spoke to described him by saying, 'he has blue eyes like yours.' Imagine."

Drew shook his head. "That appears to be the one feature that all of the duke's progeny share."

Mitchell grunted in the affirmative as he cut into his beef.

"When will you be seeing your father next?"

"Tomorrow. I am invited to a family dinner. They came to London for shopping but are heading back to the country estate in East Sussex for Christmas in a few days."

"Are you going with them?"

"Not this year. Why do you ask?"

Mitchell shook his head. "Never mind. Your viscount father is only in town a few more days. I'll find another way."

"Go on, tell me. My father knows just about everyone worth knowing and some who are not. He runs a large progressive caucus within The House of Lords."

"I need information on the new Baron Addington. My appointment this afternoon was with Lady Addington. They are estranged, and she wishes me to follow him, to find out what he is doing with his days. But first, I need background information on him."

Drew took a forkful of roasted potatoes. "I will discover what I can." He ate the food and swallowed, then gave Mitchell a sly smile. "The baroness? The very one that nursed you back to health? The one you gazed at yearningly when she came into the room?"

Mitchell snarled in response.

"Easy… I shouldn't tease. I usually do not display such mawkish behavior. But I feel at ease around you and let down my guard. I want us to be honest with each other and, yes, be more than doctor and patient, or landlord and tenant. I want us to become friends. And if you think it possible, at some point, brothers."

"You have siblings, don't you? With the Hornsbys?" Mitchell asked gruffly.

"I do," Drew replied as he sipped his wine. "Brother Hayden, and sisters Covina and Clarrisa. But I am quite a bit older than they are."

"Just how old are you? I never asked."

"Twenty-five. I will be twenty-six at the end of this coming

March."

As young as all that? Mitchell might have guessed around thirty.

"You look shocked," Drew stated.

"I am, rather."

"And your age?"

"Thirty-two. My thirty-third birthday is this coming June."

Drew cut into his steak. "I always wanted an older brother. Now I have two."

"And probably more than we'd ever want or need," Mitchell replied sardonically. "Do not forget the four youngsters coming to live with Damon and Althea next month."

"That is right. I told Damon I would stop by in the new year to meet them."

"As to us being friends, we can do that," Mitchell said as he cut into his beef. "We will take the brother thing as it goes."

Drew gave him a warm smile and lifted his wine glass. "To The Duke's Bastards."

Mitchell picked up his goblet and gave a salute. "To us all, wherever we may be." He took a sip, then frowned. "We may be turning over stones best left unturned. The late duke was a reprobate. I attended his death scene."

"What? How?"

"It was before I transferred to the precinct I'm at now. At the time, I didn't know my connection to him. It was a suspicious death, seeing he had a rope around his neck and was tied to the bedpost. There was a woman with him. They were playing some erotic asphyxiation game when he had a heart attack."

Drew sat back in his chair, clearly shocked. "My God."

"What other horrible things are left to discover?" Mitchell questioned. "What if some of these offspring inherited his loathsome personality and immoral tendencies?" Mitchell could only hope they were not making a mistake digging up secrets best left buried.

CHAPTER FOUR

CORRINE WAS SHOCKED to find Travis waiting for her in the sitting room when she came downstairs the next morning. He immediately stood. Her husband was immaculately dressed in a black morning coat with dark gray striped trousers. Travis also wore one of those new silk neckties that had become all the rage.

"Corrine. Good morning."

So formal. So removed from it all.

"Good morning, Travis. Have you had your breakfast?" she asked in a similar tone.

"I have. I will not be staying long. I came to collect my correspondence and other incidentals. My case is waiting for me at the front entrance."

Corrine exhaled. "Please, Travis. Sit with me for a moment." She strolled to the door and closed it.

Travis looked like a trapped animal, his gaze darting about the room as if looking for a means of escape. Something was seriously wrong with her husband. Empathy took hold, and she approached him slowly.

"Can we not talk?" she soothed. Corrine took his arm, and he immediately stiffened. But she ignored his reaction and led him to the sofa. They sat upon it, and she noted he kept his distance from her. "I did not expect romance in our marriage, but I want us to be truthful with each other."

Travis exhaled. "It is not you. It's me."

"When people say that, they really mean it *is* the other person. I do apologize for insisting on children. I thought trying for an heir was prudent—as in carrying on the title. I assumed that was why you wished to be married. I also admit to a selfish motive; a child would keep me occupied. It would be someone to love and to love me in return. I presumed you wanted the same. I am sorry." Corrine spoke from the heart.

"I never sought out marriage and children," Travis stated wistfully. "When I became the heir, Gilbert repeatedly stated that my duty was to carry on the barony. He was most insistent about it. So, I thought of the ladies I'd met over the years, and you were the most kind and lovely one I could recall. And the most honest."

"Yes, I was certainly upfront about my demands," Corrine scoffed. "And I'd never sought out marriage and children either. It was not something I'd yearned for."

"I find your honesty refreshing, then and now. Your family was in dire financial straits, and of course, you wanted to assist them. I was happy to help in that regard."

Corrine turned to face him. "Is it me you find abhorrent, then? Is there another woman, perhaps? Or do you prefer—men? Or both?"

Travis shook his head. "No, my dear lady. To all your questions."

Travis clearly struggled, trying to decide what to reveal, if anything at all. Peppering him with questions would only make him run from the room like a skittish horse. So they sat silently, the logs crackling in the fireplace the only audible sound.

He reached into his pocket and handed her a roll of pound notes. "There are one hundred pounds there, give or take. It is enough for the household expenses and pin money for yourself. I must go." Travis stood, looking eager to depart.

Corrine remained seated. "Where will you go? To your old residence?"

"Yes, for a time. I need to think. But I'll be in touch soon."

Travis strolled over to the table, retrieved his hat and gloves, and then quit the room.

Confused, Corrine shook her head. None of this made any sense. Still, at least they'd been cordial and had managed to have a little honest conversation. But inside, she hurt, not only for herself but for him. With some work, perhaps they could make their marriage a success and become friends and partners. Perhaps... Sighing, Corrine made her way to the desk, placed the money inside the top drawer, and locked it, placing the key in her gown pocket.

At least they were speaking—to a point. It was a beginning.

But of what? What could he possibly have to ruminate over?

What secrets did he hold close to his heart?

MITCHELL SAT IN the hansom cab across from the Addington residence on Wimpole Street. He had followed the baron there. Mitchell reached into his waistcoat pocket, retrieved his watch, and popped open the cover to check the time. Addington has been inside with the baroness for twenty minutes. He had no sooner made that observation when the door opened, and the baron exited, holding a large leather valise. Had he been picking up personal items? The man appeared troubled. Had he argued with Lady Addington?

The baron climbed into a waiting carriage, a fancy two-wheel brougham that looked to be a recent purchase. It had come to pick him up from Carol Street, which meant the carriage and horses were kept at a nearby livery. The property wasn't large enough to support a barn for the horses.

A loud bang caught Mitchell's attention. It came from an Arnold motor car, spewing black smoke as it rumbled by. More automobiles were cropping up monthly, along with just as many motor car manufacturing companies. At least half a dozen of them that had set up shop in '96 were out of business already. Some saw these 'horseless carriages' as a fad. Mitchell did not. Like the telephone, he believed they were here to stay.

Something caught his eye in the direction of the motor car—a man wearing a shin-length long cloak with a hood obscuring his face. The garment looked to be something a medieval monk would wear. Because it was not in fashion, the man stood out. Mitchell's internal detective alarm clanged incessantly. The man—at least he assumed it was a man, considering the height and build—kept casting surreptitious looks toward the baron's house, then seemed to watch as the baron climbed into his carriage.

Once Addington's coach pulled onto the street, the hooded man waved down an approaching hansom cab. Mitchell banged on the roof with his cane.

The hatch slid open. "Yes, sir?"

"Follow the brougham with the two matched grays. But wait a moment. Allow that hansom to go first."

"Yes, sir." The hatch slid shut. Mitchell watched the hooded man climb into the cab in front of him. His inner warning alarm increased in volume when he saw the man's face peeking from under the hood. He wore a mask. All Mitchell could see were two dark eyes darting about suspiciously.

They were immediately on the move, but before they approached Carol Street, the hansom turned off onto a side street. Perhaps it was a coincidence that the man in the cloak headed the same way. But Mitchell didn't believe in coincidences. Addington's carriage stopped before his residence, and the baron hurried into his home.

The hatch slid open. "Anywhere else, sir?"

"Yes, travel along the next few streets. I want to see where that other hansom went."

They did, but there was no sign of the cab or the cloaked man. *Blast it.* Using his cane, he banged on the roof. When the trap door opened, he said, "Return me to Wimpole Street."

Once he arrived at the baroness's residence, Mitchell paid the driver, then gave the door knocker several raps. The butler opened the door.

"Thomason, correct? I need to see Lady Addington at once."

"I will see if she is available, Mr. Simpson," the butler said with a sniff.

"It is all right, Thomason. Show Sergeant Simpson inside," a feminine voice called out.

The butler stood back and opened the door.

Once inside, his breath caught in his throat at the sight of Corrine, resplendent in yet another glorious tea gown. This frock was a shimmering gold shade with embroidered pink roses down the left side and around the high neckline.

It was not very wise to think of her by her first name, but no matter how inappropriate, he could not help doing it, all the same. But what caught his attention was that she clutched a lace handkerchief and dabbed at her eyes. Corrine had been crying. He was at her side instantly—at least, as swiftly as his injured leg could take him.

"My lady, you are distressed," he said softly.

"You followed him here."

"I did."

Corrine looked at the butler. "We are not to be disturbed."

"Yes, my lady."

Mitchell offered his arm, and they headed to the sitting room. Just that brief contact of her hand gently resting on his arm sent bolts of desire through him. He closed the door behind them, then sat in the wing chair opposite the baroness, who still dabbed at her eyes.

"He was here twenty minutes," Mitchell stated.

Corrine sniffled. "Yes. He came to collect his correspondence and more clothes, I imagine. I should not be upset. We did not argue. I feel sad about our situation. He denied it was someone else or that he preferred men. He also said it was him, not me, whatever that means. Travis said he needed more time to think.

I'm not sure about that aspect, either." She tucked her handkerchief under the sleeve of her gown. "He told me he felt pressure from the late baron to marry and carry on the name and title, but for whatever reason, he cannot go through with it, even though he says I am the kindest woman he has ever known. What a muddle this is. And I am prattling again."

Mitchell found he was growing rather fond of her chattering. "The baron returned to his home. I will head there and pick up the surveillance, my lady. I also have feelers among my peerage acquaintances regarding any information about your husband."

"I know it is none of my business, but I am curious—"

"As to how I have aristocratic ties?" He smiled to show he wasn't offended by her question. "It's a recent development. The Duke of Chellenham is my half-brother. We share a horrid father. I only found out about our blood connection recently. Through him, I have met the men in his social group and even made friends with one recently—Viscount Tensbridge."

To her credit, Corrine did not seem shocked by his pronouncement. Still, he was surprised that he'd felt comfortable sharing such a personal aspect of his life. They conversed so easily that he knew he could trust her with such intimate information.

"That explains why you were caught up in Tensbridge's and Claudia Ellingford's mysterious adventure. And how you were injured." She paused, and her look softened. "It must have been a complete shock to find out the late duke is your father."

"It was, and still is, my lady." Mitchell hesitated. "Here is a strange coincidence. I was called to Queen Anne's Gate a few months ago to attend to the death of a peer to see if it was suspicious. It wasn't. However, less than two weeks later, I found out that the peer in question, the Duke of Chellenham, was my biological father."

Corrine's hand flew to her mouth in shock. "Good lord! You attended the death scene? That is astonishing, indeed. Did the new duke, Damon Cranston, know you were his half-brother at the time?"

"Damon had just been given a list by his mother of her husband's illegitimate children, at least those she knew of. When I introduced myself at the scene, he stated he was completely floored. He approached me with the information shortly after that." Mitchell paused, for speaking of this was still difficult. "I will never think of the late Duke of Chellenham as my father. I had a decent and kind father. The Simpsons were an older couple; my father was a retired policeman. They gave me a good home, a decent education, and more love than I ever needed."

Good God, yet another personal revelation.

Corrine's eyes shimmered with emotion. "How gratifying. If only all orphans could find loving, caring homes. I cannot begin to describe the misery I witnessed nursing at a workhouse infirmary. It certainly put my family's financial woes in perspective."

"Experiencing and witnessing poverty and misery over the long term can take its toll," Mitchell offered sympathetically.

"Yes, it can do that. You have seen your share as a policeman. But witnessing it is not as devastating as living it."

Their gazes locked. They shared a profound philosophical understanding of what they had seen while acting in their professions, knowing it caused its own trauma. Although, as Corrine said, it was not nearly as difficult as it was for the people experiencing it.

But understanding was not the only thing passing between them. Their mutual attraction crackled with energy. All he wanted to do was pull Corrine into his arms, hold her—and never let go.

Mitchell grabbed his cane and stood abruptly. "I must return to Carol Street. I will let you know if I find anything important."

"Thank you—Mitchell."

Hearing his name on her lips again made his heart ache with yearning. Turning away, he closed his eyes briefly before exiting the room.

These meetings alone were *not* a good idea.

Corrine was married. Out of reach. Not for him. And he would do well to remember it.

CHAPTER FIVE

MITCHELL RETURNED TO his flat at seven o'clock that night. Addington had not left his house, and since he couldn't watch the baron twenty-four hours a day, he decided to pick up the surveillance tomorrow afternoon. After unlocking the door, Mitchell entered the front hall and started when he found an older lady scrubbing the tiled floor.

"Mind where you step!" she called out.

"Mrs. Evans?"

"Aye, that's me. Sergeant Simpson, I presume. Walk close to the stairs, as I haven't done that part of the floor yet. You'll find the doctor in his study. I just took him a tea tray. You'll be hungry, I'll be bound. I've got a roast chicken in the oven as well."

The woman spoke so rapidly that Mitchell could hardly understand what she said. "Thank you."

A few minutes later, he found Drew in his study. The room was already set up, with his diplomas on the wall and various medical books neatly displayed on the shelves.

"Good evening, Mitchell. I imagine you met Mrs. Evans." Drew smiled.

Mitchell removed his hat and coat and flung them to the leather sofa. "Irish? Or Welsh?"

"Oh, Irish all the way. She said, 'I may have a Welsh last name, but my family has been in Ireland for donkey's years.' She is quite the worker. Changed our bed sheets and cleaned the kitchen. She will be departing when she finishes the floor."

Mitchell poured himself a cup of tea, grabbed a raisin biscuit, then sat on the sofa. "Can I get your professional opinion on something? What do you call a man who isn't having an affair, yet refuses to have intimate relations with his new wife?"

"A homosexual, perhaps?"

"I have heard that term when performing my police duties. It's relatively new," Mitchell replied. "But it doesn't apply to the man in question—so he says."

"There are other terms for the classification of sexual preferences. Ready for a history lesson?"

Mitchell sipped his tea. "Go ahead."

"In '69, a Hungarian doctor, Karl Maria Kertbeny, wrote a pamphlet deriding a German sodomy law. In his writing, he classified three types of orientation: heterosexual, homosexual, and monosexual, meaning the person is only interested in self-gratification. Two years ago, I read a paper by a German physiologist where he crafted a new orientation: he referred to people without any sexual desire at all as anesthesia sexual. Some doctors have shortened that to a-sexual."

Could that be it? Did Addington detest physical contact and harbor no desire toward anyone? "So it's a rare sickness, then?"

Drew shook his head. "Some medical quacks think anyone's sexual preferences beyond heterosexual is a mental illness. I do not subscribe to such narrow thinking, however. I also am not sure how rare a-sexualism is. Sex, in general, is not considered polite conversation, even within intimate relationships. So, because no one discusses it, studying it is problematic. Does this have to do with the baron you are following?"

"You will keep this confidence?"

"Of course."

Mitchell popped the biscuit in his mouth, chewed, then swallowed. "Yes, it's Addington. He told his wife he specifically married to continue the line. But on their wedding night, he couldn't—and hasn't. The baroness thinks he is having an affair, and so, is contemplating divorce."

"Divorce cases are public. How mortifying for all concerned if a-sexualism is the reason for severing the marriage. It will make all the papers. Honestly, Mitchell, you cannot mention this to Lady Addington. First, this is just speculation on my part, nothing but mere conjecture. Second, this is a private and personal matter between a husband and wife."

Mitchell raised an eyebrow. "So I am to allow the lady to believe her husband finds her abhorrent?"

Drew nodded. "You were hired to follow Baron Addington and report to the baroness. That is all. Professionally speaking, that should be the sum total of your actions. Unless your feelings run far deeper than you are letting on."

Mitchell frowned. Drew Hornsby, though maddingly annoying at times, was correct. Mitchell had no business inserting himself into a personal situation that was none of his business. He knew this. And yes, damn it all, his feelings ran deeper than was proper. He remained silent, sipping his tea and speculating whether he'd made a momentous mistake taking this case.

"By the by, I spoke to my father this morning," Drew said, breaking the silence. "Alas, he has nothing scandalous to offer regarding Addington. The baron diligently attended the House of Lords before the recess and expressed an interest in joining my father's progressive caucus."

So, the baron conscientiously performed his duties and even showed eagerness to bring about reforms. Nothing scandalous there, indeed. It proved he was a decent sort, at least as far as society was concerned.

Mrs. Evans strode into the room. She looked no more than one or two inches over five feet. "The doctor and the detective! Everything is just grand! The chicken is in the icebox, along with the tats and carrots. Pick at it as you will. I'll pop around the shops on the morrow to put in a grocery order; then I'll make a nice apple tart. Make me a list of your preferences so I'll know what to cook. That's it, gents. I'm off." With a wave, she was gone.

"Did you make out what she said?" Mitchell asked.

"She speaks fast, to be certain. Chicken and vegetables are in the icebox. She will be getting groceries tomorrow, and we are to make a list of our food preferences. Sorry, I couldn't make out the rest."

Mitchell chuckled. "I heard apple tart tomorrow."

"Back to your case. It is not for me to tell you what to do. I do apologize. I was offering advice as a friend."

Mitchell raised his teacup. "Cheers. As a friend, I will take that advice."

And he should wrap up this case as soon as possible. Pining for a married woman would bring nothing but misery and heartache.

JEDIDIAH DANAHER WAS alive.

Although, alive was a relative term. He walked about and breathed in and out. But since he'd been caught in the cellar when his burning pub had collapsed on him, he should be an unidentifiable blackened corpse that had been carelessly tossed into a pauper's grave.

By the luck of Hades, he had escaped his fate. Peter Tassel, a homeless drunk who often swept up in Jedi's Black Moon pub for the price of a pint of port and permission to sleep occasionally in the cellar, had been in the wrong place at the wrong time. And that had been convenient—for Jedi.

Maybe his plan to kidnap a viscount's brother for ransom had been ill-fated, although it worked many times before. But that bloody vigilante showed up, and then, that bloody copper Simpson, a thorn in his side, had arrived and mucked things up good and proper. Jedi was still not completely convinced Simpson was not the vigilante, even though the copper stood alongside the masked bugger. It could have been an elaborate ruse to confuse him, or maybe Jedi was seeing conspiracies where there were none.

Regardless of the reasons, Jedi had managed to escape his fate. He wasn't the king of Notting Dale for nothing. He'd built a tunnel from the pub cellar into the condemned building next door. As soon as he fell through the burning flooring into that cellar, he rolled around on the dirt to smother the fire engulfing his arm, then jumped to his feet and trundled the sleeping drunk directly into the pile of fiery wood, where Homeless Pete became immediately engulfed in a wall of fire. The man had probably been drenched in alcohol. Tassel had screamed briefly, but it was all over in an instant. Poor bugger, but as Jedi reasoned, "Better him than me."

Since that had transpired a month and a half ago, Jedi had been scuttling about the dark alleys and dank crevices of the Notting Dale rookery. To the world, he was dead, and Jedidiah Danaher wanted to keep it that way. Escaping the fire was one thing, but the way he'd eluded the police in the aftermath had been the devil's own luck. Jedi had thought his goose was cooked when he found himself trapped in the tunnel between the two buildings. The hinges on the door leading into the condemned building had been rusted shut, and he hadn't dared kick at it with coppers and firefighting blokes directly overhead and out in the streets.

Hours after the fire was extinguished, he'd heard the men jump into the Black Moon Pub cellar. Jedi had held his breath, for they'd have found the tunnel door if they'd looked close enough. But because they'd stumbled across Tassel's charred corpse, the coppers had immediately assumed it was him and hadn't bothered to inspect the cellar further.

Jedi took a bite of the meat pie he had bought from a street vendor outside his rented room. Being a rookery boss, the king of a slum full of tenements, he had planned for any scenario. He'd had a small stash of cash in a tin box hidden behind a loose brick in one of the buildings on Bangor Street, and with those funds, he'd been able to rent a room near Notting Dale on Talbot Road, buy three different hooded cloaks, and kept himself fed while he planned his next move. He glanced about the room. It was comfortable enough, and if he lived frugally, the money could last a good while...but not indefinitely. That was the reason he'd sought out his baron father. He had to plan for the future. With money, he could leave England, change his name, and start a new life. Or perhaps he should try to take another foothold in Notting Dale or move on to greener pastures as he had done in the past. He'd had to start over a few times in his forty-plus years of living. During those rare low ebbs, he'd had to swallow his pride and seek out his baron father for an infusion of money. Baron Addington had always given in—if only to be rid of him. Jedidiah knew the baron would rather forget Jedidiah existed. What upright low-level peer wanted an illegitimate son lingering about?

When Jedi knocked on the baron's door earlier, the last thing he expected to hear was the miserable cur was dead. He felt nothing upon hearing the news. Shocked, perhaps, and irritated since the man cocked up his toes before Jedi got everything he was owed from the baron. But those fleeting emotions dissipated swiftly enough.

Because as far as Jedi was concerned, he was *still* owed.

A new baron, eh?

And with a fancy piece for a wife. When the woman had approached the door, he'd thought his decrepit so-called father had married again. But no—a distant cousin was now the baron. Jedi must have missed the death announcement in the papers. But this meant that the distant cousin was also a cousin to Jedi. A blood relation was now in charge of the purse strings—a relation who kept separate lodgings.

Interesting, that.

Jedi followed the new baron from Wimpole Street to Camden Town. Because Jedi had the distinct feeling he was being followed, he had the hansom cab driver pull off to a side street, but he knew the general vicinity of where Addington lived. He would discover the address soon enough.

Meanwhile, he would lay low, plan and scheme, and when the time was right, he would let the new baron know that the previous baron's by-blow was still alive.

As for retribution for past events?

Finding out the copper Simpson was *not* the annoying masked vigilante who prowled Notting Dale's streets had been a shock. Last he heard, the detective was off on sick leave, maybe never to return. From what he heard on the streets, the vigilante hadn't been about lately either. So, as far as Jedi was concerned, that was old news that belonged firmly in the past. He did not have the time or inclination to settle old scores. Why bother? It was a lesson Jedi had learned early on. Life was too precarious and short to expend valuable time, resources, and emotions in satisfying a perceived hurt or insult. He had new and exciting fish to fry. Besides, money was more important than revenge, at least in Jedi's book—another hard-earned truth.

And Jedi would make certain he received his share.

CHAPTER SIX

"ARE YOU SURE you wish to do this?" Mitchell asked Drew.

They stood at the corner of Brick Lane and Chicksand Street. The hanging metal sign above showed a rooster crowing at the morning sun. Its hinges creaked in the breeze. "Now that we are here, I'm not certain. But as you mentioned, perhaps it is best to pull the bandage off the wound quickly. As a doctor, I say that is sound advice."

"Then, after you." Mitchell held out his arm, indicating Drew should go first.

They crossed the threshold into an active environment. The restaurant had booths along the side walls, with wooden tables and chairs making up the rest of the floor space. The bar area was located along the back wall, with multiple shelves filled with bottles, glasses, mugs, and goblets of every size and shape. The bar had four taps, with various types of beer. There was no fireplace, but numerous gas lights hissed overhead, throwing a subdued illumination over the eating area but bright enough to make out what you were eating.

They arrived at two in the afternoon when it would not be as busy, but there were still more customers than Mitchell thought there would be. The Crowing Cock had the appearance of a restaurant more than a pub, but that was probably what the Hallahan bloke was going for. The place looked spotless, and the waitresses wore matching uniforms that resembled what maids would wear in a wealthy man's house—all black with white frilly aprons and caps.

"There is a booth in the back. It will give us some privacy," Drew said.

They made their way there and slid in across the dark green leather bench seats. The high wooden dividers between some booths offered a modicum of privacy. Mitchell rested his cane, hat, and gloves on the seat beside him.

An attractive waitress immediately came to the table and gave them a winning smile. "Good afternoon, gents. The full luncheon menu is unavailable now, but we have afternoon offerings. The special today is beefsteak and onions with colcannon and roasted carrots. This afternoon, we also have a variation of a full breakfast consisting of sausage, fried eggs and potatoes, grilled mushrooms, and black pudding. There is also our famous Irish version of cock-a-leekie soup served with soda bread."

"Varied and delicious choices," Drew stated. "What is colcannon?"

"Mashed potatoes with leeks and cabbage, sir," the waitress replied.

"And the Irish version of the soup?" Mitchell asked.

"We do not use prunes like the Scots, sir, but common vegetables like turnips and potatoes."

"Well, we might as well have something hearty while here," Drew said. "I will have the beefsteak and a pint of Guinness."

"I will have the same," Mitchell declared. "We would also like a word with your chef. Is Liam Hallahan here? Can he spare us a few moments?"

The waitress, momentarily taken aback, smoothed her features into a neutral look. "I'll ask him, but he is busy in the kitchen."

"Tell him it is personal," Drew said kindly. "And he can see us at his convenience, of course. There is no need for urgency."

The waitress nodded, then quickly went to bring their pints of stout. A big Irishman came through the door as Mitchell took his first sip. He leaned down to listen as the waitress whispered in his ear, motioning toward their booth.

"He's out of the kitchen," Mitchell murmured, "And the waitress is filling him in on our request."

"How does he look?" Drew asked. His seat was facing the opposite direction.

"He looks annoyed and is heading this way."

"What can I do for you, gentlemen?"

Hallahan's voice was deep, and his words clipped, but they were not unfriendly. Mitchell didn't hear much of an Irish accent, either. The man was easily three or four inches over six feet and broad of shoulder. He wore black trousers and a white shirt, and his sleeves were rolled up to the elbow, showing muscular forearms. Mitchell glanced at Drew.

Drew turned to the man. "I am Doctor Drew Hornsby, and this is Detective Sergeant Mitchell Simpson. I believe we have a father in common."

That was candid and to the point, and Hallahan's eyes widened briefly—the same blue eyes they possessed.

The tall man recovered swiftly enough. "So?"

The tone was not so friendly now.

"You know who we are talking about, don't you?" Mitchell stated. He wasn't a detective for nothing. He had seen the brief shadow cross Hallahan's eyes at the mention of their 'father.'

"I met him once, and I kicked his aristo arse out of my place. I'll do the same to you two if you don't get to the bloody point," Hallahan growled in a low voice.

Drew moved over on the large bench seat. "Please, Mr. Hallahan, sit with us a moment. We have no notorious intent. We merely wish to speak with you."

Hallahan grunted as he visually scanned the restaurant. "I only have your meals to cook; everyone else is served. I can talk to you until more customers come in. Fair play?"

"That is more than satisfactory," Drew replied.

The chef stomped away, clearly agitated.

"We stirred up something there," Mitchell said as he sipped the stout.

"It is obvious the late duke sought him out at some point, and it did not go well. Either that or he is generally an unpleasant sort. Many talented chefs are, or so I hear."

"Possibly. We will soon discover if he is talented or not. Hallahan will surely kick us to the cobbles as soon as we eat and pay for the meals. What do we want from this bloke, anyway?" Mitchell asked, still keeping his voice low.

"We started this to see if any of our relations needed assistance. Observing this restaurant, I would say Hallahan is doing well enough. Look at the businessmen sitting at the table near the window and at the family in the booth opposite. Decidedly middle-class or above. This is not exactly a middle-class area. If he wants nothing to do with us, I say we move on to the next name on the list."

Mitchell nodded. "You may have the right of it. We'll see what he has to say."

Ten minutes later, the waitress brought them two large platters heaped with food, along with a wicker basket filled with Irish soda bread and small dishes of whipped butter. Hallahan emerged from the kitchen, whispered something to a different waitress, and then stomped over to their table, sliding beside Drew.

"Go on. Speak. I'm a busy man."

Mitchell sliced into the beefsteak. It was like cutting through butter. He speared a piece of the tender meat on his fork, twirled it through the creamy potatoes, and ate it. After he swallowed, he looked up at Hallahan. "*That* is delicious. The best beefsteak I have had in a long while." He spoke the truth. The meat was far tastier than the one he had two days ago at a pub in Camden Town.

Hallahan grunted and nodded, obviously pleased. "What do you care about the late duke? Aye, I read about his death in the paper a few months back. Why seek me out? And how do you even know about me?"

Drew reached into his coat side pocket and pulled out the record of names. "You are on this list that the dowager duchess recently gave her son. In his investigations, the new duke, Damon Cranston, discovered a tangled web of a conspiracy. Beyond this list is a ledger with names spanning over three decades. I recently learned of my connection from my adopted father when the old duke passed. Mitchell found out shortly before that, when the new duke sought him out."

Hallahan took the list offered and scanned it. "I don't see the name Simpson here."

"I recently took my adopted family's name. I am on there as Mitchell Evercreech."

"All right. So, I am on a list. What do you want from me? My life is demanding enough. I don't need complications mucking things up," Hallahan said brusquely.

One of the servers came over. "We have customers, Liam."

"I've got a business to run." He stood abruptly. "At seven, this place turns into a pub with card games at the tables. That is when I knock off, and my night manager takes over. Be here thirty minutes past seven, ask for Fiona, and she will show you to my quarters. I live upstairs. The meals are on the house, but leave a donation on the table. I feed the poor of the neighborhood in the mornings." Hallahan turned and strode toward the rear of the restaurant.

"Well, I am intrigued already," Drew whispered. "And this food is outstanding."

"Then we will return early this evening." Mitchell buttered a piece of bread and bit into it. "This bread is delicious as well. I can see why this restaurant is popular." He glanced up at the entrance as more customers came through the door, a young family of four and a couple of men wearing suits. Outstanding, indeed. Wistfully, Mitchell imagined bringing Corrine here. She would undoubtedly like it as well. Did he dare ask her?

Get over it, man.

Mitchell turned his attention to the food and the night ahead. After meeting with Hallahan, he should head to Camden Town and check in on the baron. Hopefully, that would remove all thoughts of the lovely baroness from his mind.

THE CROWING COCK had been transformed from a restaurant into a pub. The place was packed; all the tables were taken up with men and a few women of all classes playing cards. He recognized the waitress that had served him and Drew that afternoon. Only tonight, her uniform was that of a barmaid's, complete with a flowing skirt and a tight bodice, showing ample cleavage.

She strode toward them, carrying an empty tray. "You're back. Here to see Liam?"

"Yes," Mitchell replied. "We are to ask for Fiona."

The waitress stuck her thumb and index finger in her mouth and gave a shrill whistle. A woman at the rear of the pub looked up, then came before them.

"Thank you, Hannah. The doctor and the detective?"

"We are," Drew answered.

"Then come this way, through the back."

Smoke filled the air, along with loud laughter and animated conversation. The beer flowed, and from what Mitchell could see, a lot of money sat on the various gaming tables.

Once they stepped outside, Mitchell said, "Hosting a gaming hall in the evening appears profitable."

"It is," Fiona replied. "It helps to fund the rest." She pointed to wrought iron stairs. "Up there and through the door." She glanced at Mitchell's cane. "Can you manage? We have a man on the premises who can assist you."

"I can manage, thank you."

"Fair play. Once you are through the main entrance, head straight down the hall and knock on the door directly before you. Good evening." Fiona gave them a pretty smile and disappeared through the rear of the building.

As they slowly climbed the stairs, Drew stood alongside

Mitchell, ready to offer aid. By the time they reached the top, Hallahan stood at the entrance.

"You're prompt, I'll give you that. Come in." Hallahan opened the door to his flat. The coziness of it immediately struck Mitchell. Older and possibly used furniture, but high quality, filled the room. Dark wood walls and gold and green accents gave the place a masculine appearance. However, the sound from downstairs was incessant, a low drone of muffled voices and laughter. "Sit there." Hallahan pointed to the sofa. "There's mugs of tea and bowls of flummery. It is basically milk and bread in the Irish workhouses, but I have added oats, honey, blackberries, plums, cream, and a dash of Irish whiskey."

"This is very hospitable of you," Drew exclaimed as he sat. Hallahan sat across from him in an overstuffed chair, large enough to comfortably support his frame.

"My mother taught me some manners," Hallahan scoffed.

"Was it your mother who told you of the duke?" Mitchell asked as he sipped his tea.

"Always the detective, eh? She did, but I never believed her. We were barely surviving, hardly a crust to eat, yet she goes on and on about a duke? She died when I was twelve years of age, and I was left an orphan alone on the streets. Is that what you wanted to know?"

There was an edge to his voice that lingered, regardless of the subject matter. A barely contained rage, not at them specifically, but no doubt at life itself. Or at least, when speaking of his past life. Mitchell placed his mug on the table and picked up the crockery bowl of flummery. It smelled enticing, and he took a heaping spoonful. He audibly groaned at the tastiness of it. "You are very talented. This is amazing."

The corner of Hallahan's lips twitched—an almost smile.

"We do not wish to furrow about your past," Drew offered, his voice soft with empathy. "Far from it. We are here to offer an invitation. We are forming a group to assist those associated with the duke through a common bloodline. But not specifically that. I work at free medical clinics in between seeing a few paying patients. We can band together to help those in our vicinity. For example, those less fortunate who come here to be fed every morning?"

Hallahan arched an eyebrow. "Aye. What of it?"

"I can come once a week and offer free medical care. I would guess most people do not know about free medical clinics. I can refer those needing more serious attention. Another example? The new Duke of Chellenham's group sends leftover food to soup kitchens. What if I divert some of the food here?"

Drew had Hallahan's undivided attention now.

"And what would I do with it, exactly?"

"Well, you are the chef. I suppose you could—repurpose it. Repurpose is not really a word. What I mean is sell it to your customers and use that profit to fund your free meals or any other charity plan you may have. Or give it away to the hungry."

Mitchell was dually impressed with Drew's suggestions.

Hallahan took his mug of tea, sat back, and regarded them closely. "You say there are more names beyond what you showed me."

Drew took a spoonful of the fruity dessert. "Mitchell is correct. This is very tasty, like a comforting blanket of warmth. To answer your question, yes. There are dozens upon dozens. The youngest that we know of is five years of age. She and three others are moving in with Damon Cranston, the new Duke of Chellenham, and his bride, the first of next month."

Hallahan arched his eyebrow again. "A ready-made family. Here's the thing: I'm not looking for one. I got this far on my own, more or less. The closest thing I have to family are the ladies downstairs. Some of them worked in the brothel until I closed it. Now, they are waitresses, managers, and more. I look out for them. They look out for me. That is the definition of a family in my eyes."

"You are correct," Mitchell murmured. "We are not here to recruit you as a brother but as someone with a common purpose:

to rise above Edward Cranston's despicable legacy. To assist those less fortunate, whether in our immediate sphere or beyond. And especially those Edward Cranston left to flounder: his own children."

Hallahan was giving it some thought. Mitchell could almost hear the wheels turning in the Irishman's mind.

"All right. I will join your group for now. You can ask your nob friends to make a donation as well, to buy vegetables and meat for the stew I serve. Hornsby, come here in five days, at ten in the morning, and we will see how it goes. Also, I can reuse, or as you call it, repurpose the toff food and sell it. I would welcome that, too."

Drew placed his empty bowl on the table. "I will come at ten." Drew reached into his coat pocket and pulled out a folded paper. "Our address."

Hallahan read it, then snorted. "Gloucester Square? Pardon me all to hell."

Drew shrugged, then stood. So did Mitchell. "My father is a viscount, my uncle, a duke."

"And yet you labor in a free medical clinic?" Hallahan questioned.

"Like you, I do my part." Drew held out his hand. "Welcome to The Duke's Bastards."

Hallahan tucked the slip of paper in his trousers pocket, took Drew's hand, and shook it. "The Duke's Bastards. An appropriate name."

After shaking Mitchell's hand, Hallahan turned to go.

It was an interesting beginning to their group, Mitchell thought. What would become of it all remained to be seen.

Tomorrow, he'd have to turn his attention to his Addington case. How inappropriate that he physically ached to see Corrine again.

Oh, this is not good at all.

Chapter Seven

Corrine paced back and forth in the sitting room, impatient, bored, and mildly irritated—not a healthy combination. But five days had passed, and there had not been a word from Travis or Mitchell. What was going on? Had Mitchell discovered any information?

The cook/housekeeper, Mrs. Morris, had already questioned her about Christmas, the menu, and who might attend, such as her family—if anyone. But Christmas was the last thing on her mind. She definitely did not feel like celebrating anything. Especially because she knew that Travis's absence had been noted—and discussed—by the staff. What to do?

There was a small country estate outside of London belonging to the Addington barony. Still, Travis had never suggested going there for the winter, although many in the aristocracy spent the colder months away from London. Nor was she aware of where it was located. Somewhere west of the city? Aldershot? Or was it in Alton? It started with an A. She was sure of it.

Corrine gazed out the window. Her family also owned a small country estate but had started renting it out years ago for the income. Even that monthly stipend hadn't been enough to keep her family's head above water. Now they had money, or rather, she did. Corrine had Travis authorize a trust account in her name, and only she could draw on it. She paid her father and brother a generous stipend every month. To her brother Jeffery's credit, he remained working at the bank. Their lives were finally stable—at least for now.

If only her life felt as steadfast. So much remained unsettled, including her marriage. Corrine was not one for sitting still. And in that moment, she decided to do something about it. Her nurse uniforms were stored in a trunk with other garments she had not unpacked yet. She could use one of those as a disguise and do a little investigating independently.

Corrine rushed upstairs to the empty room next to hers. Upon opening the trunk, she rifled through the neatly packed clothes and located her most recent uniform and cloak. The fact that she hadn't even finished unpacking yet spoke of her continued uncertainty. The tiny lace cap would not do, so she located the long veil that most nurses no longer wore. If she pulled the veil forward, it would hide most of her hair and partially conceal her face.

Grabbing the garments, she hurried into her bedroom and swiftly changed. As she emerged from her room and descended the stairs, Corrine looked about for the footman. Frustrated, she entered the sitting room and pressed the buzzer twice.

"There you are, Jonathan. Please hail me a hansom cab."

The footman was startled at her attire but soon showed a neutral expression. "At once, my lady."

As Corrine climbed into the cab, she had no earthly idea of what to do next.

The roof hatch opened. "Where to, miss?"

"Carol Street, Camden Town." She wanted to see Travis's residence for herself.

As the cab lurched forward, Corrine started having second thoughts. A nurse would stand out in a crowd. *Too late now.*

Clasping her nurse's bag tightly, she watched the bustling city pass by. What did she hope to find out? How impulsive of her to do this. Still, there was no use wringing her hands over it.

Once she arrived on Travis's street, Corrine paid the driver, pulled the veil over her face, and then leisurely strolled along the walkway. Travis's house was located at the opposite end. Walking up and down the lane more than once would draw attention. Shaking her head, Corrine lamented that she did not think this through at all.

The street consisted of tightly packed rowhouses. There wasn't much of a vantage point to do a surveillance since there were no alleys, shops, or a park. Corrine had never been here before. The houses were modest and middle-class. What did Travis do before becoming the baron? To her eternal shame, Corrine never bothered to ask him about his occupation or past—another negative mark to add to her regrets.

She spotted a vendor selling gingerbread, crumpets, and raisin cake from his wooden cart. Everything looked and smelled delicious. As she passed, Corrine glanced at the goods, finding fresh bread and ginger biscuits. It was a good thing she'd brought a few shillings with her. She would buy some items on her way back.

Travis's home finally came into view. She slowed her gait and had a peek. The draperies were open, and Corrine saw Travis sitting across from another man through the window. They were deep in conversation. Then the man handed Travis a sheath of papers, and he sat back in his chair to read them.

Good lord, was he meeting with a solicitor to begin divorce proceedings? She stopped and took a deep breath. Of course her fevered mind would race to that conclusion, but she knew it wasn't likely. Corrine pretended to look up and down the street while snatching glances through the large window. There was more discussion, and the other man took notes. Standing before the costermonger's cart, she pointed at the ginger biscuits. "How much?"

"Two for a penny, miss. One penny for a crumpet or slice of cake. Four pennies for the bread."

"I will have twelve biscuits and a loaf of bread."

"Right away, miss." The costermonger was busy wrapping her goods in brown paper when someone approached her from behind and clasped her elbow.

Corrine gasped in response.

"What are you doing here, Corrine?" a male voice whispered in her ear.

Every nerve ending came alive at his touch and nearness. *He called me by my name.* Only one man caused such emotional turbulence within her.

"Good day, Mitchell," she murmured in reply.

MITCHELL COULD NOT believe it. He had been sitting in a carriage across the street, observing the comings and goings at the baron's residence, when he spotted a nurse perambulating on the walkway. Although the woman tried to act inconspicuously, her movements sparked Mitchell's suspicion. The more he watched her, the more it dawned on him that the woman was Corrine. Especially when every nerve-ending sparked to life. The sway of her hips and the confident way she strolled along the walkway, her head held high, also aided his conclusion. Now, he still held her arm at the elbow, and heat licked through his blood at the contact.

"Here, let the nurse go," the costermonger snapped. He pulled a whistle out from around his neck. "Or I'll call for the coppers."

Mitchell released Corrine's arm, reached in his pocket, and brought forth his ID card. He flipped the leather wallet open. "I am the police." He shouldn't be flashing his division card about while on medical leave, but right now, it was necessary.

After tucking his card in his coat, he again took Corrine's arm.

"Can I at least wait for my purchase?" Corrine asked.

"Of course," he replied.

The tradesman handed her the brown paper-wrapped parcel, and Corrine paid him.

The transaction was completed, and Mitchell steered her toward the carriage.

"Is this yours, Sergeant?"

"No. Doctor Hornsby's family returned to their country home for Christmas, leaving this carriage behind for Doctor Drew's use. He allowed me to borrow it today. Inside, my lady." Mitchell opened the coach door and assisted Corrine inside. Then, with great difficulty, he climbed in after her, sitting on the bench opposite.

Corrine pulled the veil from her face. "How did you know it was me?"

Because every fiber of my body and soul is attuned to your every movement. "A lucky guess. Why are you here?"

Corrine slammed her case on the bench next to her packaged baked goods. "Because I have not heard from you!" she snapped irritably. Then she exhaled. "I apologize. I should not vent my frustrations on you. I had to see for myself what was going on."

"I have not been by to see you because there has been nothing to report—until today. There is no need to apologize."

"Yes, there is. I am afraid I have a quick temper, but it dissipates swiftly enough. The report. Does it concern the man visiting with Travis?"

"It does. His name is Mr. Stanley Dobson, and he is a solicitor and partner with Dobson, Weiss, and Handleman," Mitchell replied.

"Oh, I see," Corrine replied softly. "So Travis *is* planning to divorce me."

"No, my lady. I do not believe so. Dobson specializes in estate planning, inheritance, and wills. He came to Addington's yesterday afternoon, and I followed him back to his office not far from here. I then went inside and questioned who in the firm handles divorce cases. The lady receptionist gave me all the particulars of which partner does what legal activity. Dobson is strictly the kind of solicitor I mentioned."

Corrine frowned. "Wills and inheritance. To what end?"

"Probably, Addington has not had a chance to sort out his will since becoming the baron. Is there someone to inherit the title if anything should happen to him, my lady?"

"I would prefer you call me Corrine, as you did earlier. At least when we are alone."

"It's not proper," Mitchell mumbled. "You hired me. You are a baron's wife." As he kept reminding himself—to no avail.

"Nevertheless, I do request it."

Why argue? "Very well—Corrine. My question?"

"And it's an excellent inquiry. I have no earthly idea. My husband and I rarely discussed anything of consequence, especially concerning the past and the future. I will bring it up casually next we speak. If we ever speak again." Corrine glanced out the window. "Mr. Dobson is leaving. Shall we follow him?"

Mitchell's eyebrow cocked. "We?"

"I want to assist with this case. Please allow me to help when I can. I am going mad sitting alone in the parlor, imagining all sorts of things. Please, Mitchell."

Her suggestion was tempting. Spending time with the beautiful baroness? He should shut this down before it went any further. Wasn't this how many of his acquaintances began intimate relationships? By having someone assist with an investigative case? But none of the couples in question had been married at the time. That was a barrier Mitchell would never cross, no matter how enticing the lady. He hadn't known Corrine for long, but had the distinct impression that she would never break her marital vows. Not that he would ever propose they do so.

"It is rather dull doings conducting a surveillance, and two people are not usually needed in such a circumstance. There's no need to follow Dobson, for I would guess he is returning to his office." Her lovely face showed acute disappointment. "However, if I should require assistance, you will be the first person I contact."

Her smile lit up the carriage's interior, basking him in soothing warmth.

"You may consider this forward of me," Mitchell continued. "If you are going mad sitting in the parlor, I have a place where you can put your nursing talents to use at least once a week."

"Do tell."

"Remember I told you about the late Duke of Chellenham?"

"Yes, I do. You are his biological son."

"I am not alone. You see, the late duke was an egotistical, despicable creature who believed his bloodline was superior to any other. Damon found numerous books on eugenics in his study."

Corrine shook her head. "I have heard of it. It is a belief and practice to improve the so-called quality of the human population by excluding those deemed unworthy. It's entirely repugnant. The late duke believed in this preposterous theory?"

"He did, to an extent. Damon said his father aimed to produce beautiful children but wasn't overly concerned with the intellectual aspect. He set up a home for foundlings, brought in some like-minded peers and business acquaintances, and set up a profitable pyramid scheme to sell children and babies, some of them, his own."

Corrine's hand fled to her mouth in shock. "My God. Don't tell me—"

"Yes. I was sold to the Simpsons, all but wiping out their savings. It worked out well enough for me. And for Drew Hornsby."

"The doctor is your half-brother. When did you discover this?" Corrine asked with a shocked tone.

"Shortly after Drew did, while he treated my injury. There are possibly hundreds of us. Drew suggested we form a group to locate and offer assistance to those siblings we know of. We have an initial list that Damon's mother had in her possession, plus there are ledgers of names beyond that. Decades' worth. I cheekily suggested we call ourselves 'The Duke's Bastards.' The name stuck."

"What do you want me to do?"

"Drew and I contacted the next name on the list. The man's name is Liam Hallahan, and he owns a restaurant and pub in Spitalfields. In the morning, before his place opens, he feeds the poor of the neighborhood. Drew offered medical care. He is there now. Why don't we join him, and perhaps you can assist? After all, you're wearing your nurse's uniform. Or am I stepping over the bounds?"

Mitchell couldn't believe he had discharged all this information on Corrine, but he felt comfortable and at ease in her presence. He knew he could trust her, even after such a short acquaintance.

"Yes," Corrine replied softly. "Let us go there right now." She leaned forward and squeezed his hand. "I am glad you told me. I will keep your confidence."

He felt her reassuring touch through their gloves. He lingered momentarily, basking in the connection, then slowly pulled his hand away. Then he knocked on the roof.

"Yes, Sergeant?"

"Forty Brick Lane, Spitalfields."

"Right away, sir."

The carriage jerked forward, and they locked gazes. Corrine gave him an empathic look. "Your life has had its upheavals these past months. I commend you for pushing onward. I should do the same, starting by admitting my mistake of marrying Travis Addington."

"Allow me to continue with the case for a while longer before you do anything. Call it my detective intuition, but I believe there is more going on here than we know."

"Very well, Mitchell."

As they headed to the East End, a hope bloomed within him—the outlandish possibility that if she detangled herself from her ill-fated marriage, he and Corrine could become—more. The thought was fanciful at his core and not like him at all. But then, no other woman had ever caught his notice like this. Mitchell was swimming in uncharted waters.

CHAPTER EIGHT

THE CARRIAGE PULLED up in front of an establishment situated on a corner lot. Corrine stared out the window at the busy street, then at the sign over the door.

"The Crowing Cock?" she questioned, a smile tugging at the corner of her mouth.

"It's not what you think," Mitchell replied. "Although, as Hallahan also ran a brothel upstairs until six months ago, it fit once. I hope I am not being too bawdy in front of a lady?"

Corrine chuckled. "I was a nurse for ten years, so I have heard and seen all sorts."

"Drew told me the name comes from cock ale, a nourishing elixir from the early 1700s. It consisted of ale mixed with minced, boiled game cock and spices. It supposedly helped the blood and humors, invigorating the lungs and the like. It is why many older pubs have the word 'cock' in them."

"How fascinating," Corrine exclaimed. "I did not know that."

"Drew is certainly full of intriguing statistics. Come, let us head to the rear of the building." Mitchell took his cane and knocked on the window. It slid open. "Wright, stay put. We won't be long."

"Yes, Sergeant."

Corrine slipped the paper bag of ginger biscuits into her case, then she took Mitchell's hand as he assisted her from the carriage. The street teemed with activity, with many wagons, carriages, a horse-driven omnibus, and a couple of automobiles filling the street. All manner of people strolled along the walkways, occasionally stopping to gaze in a shop window or at the various goods from the many sellers' wagons.

Mitchell offered his arm, and Corrine took it as they headed toward the alley leading to the rear courtyard. Corrine gasped aloud when she saw the line of people. There had to have been fifty people there, at least, all holding wooden bowls and spoons in their hands. At the front of the line stood two women ladling soup from two large stock pots.

They worked their way through the crowd until they reached a small area behind a wooden partition.

"Doctor Hornsby. I bring you some assistance," Mitchell announced. "Nurse Corrine."

Doctor Drew stood. "I certainly welcome it. Over here, nurse. Assist with the children, if you please."

Corrine could see that the doctor was overwhelmed. There had to have been forty more men, women, and children lined up to see him. Corrine laid her bag on the table and removed her veil. She sat in the chair next to the doctor. Thank goodness it wasn't cold this morning, but it was chilly enough. Many people shivered, and it made Corrine's heart ache with empathy.

"There on that paper are the names and locations of the Hornsby-Wollstonecraft free medical clinics," the doctor murmured. "Refer those needing more immediate and serious care than we can provide."

"Yes, doctor."

The next hour and a half passed in a blur. Most people suffered from poor nutrition, hygiene, and various minor ailments, but a few severe cases were referred to the clinics. One woman had visible tumors on her neck. At a glance, Corrine knew the poor lady was not long for this world. So did Doctor Drew. All he could do was give her was willow bark and a packet of hard-to-acquire aspirin powder to assist with the worst of the pain.

Corrine broke the ginger biscuits into pieces and handed

them out to the children. Her heart ached to see some without shoes, in December, no less. She watched as Doctor Drew handed out old newspapers and strings to act as temporary footwear.

By half past noon, the courtyard stood empty.

"Lady Addington, I thank you for your assistance," Doctor Drew said as he stuffed his stethoscope in his bag.

"Sergeant Simpson says you will be doing this once a week?"

"Yes."

"I would like to assist you. If you will allow it."

"I welcome it. Your nurse uniform caused more women to stand in the queue, which is already a positive benefit. Some women find it difficult to speak frankly with a male doctor. Be here at ten o'clock next Thursday, my lady, and we will do it all again."

"I believe I can find some used children's shoes. I will try to locate woolen mittens as well."

"Thank you. It would be a help."

Mitchell came toward them, a tall man with coal-black hair by his side. Seeing them so close together, Corrine could recognize the resemblance. Then she glanced at Doctor Drew. Yes, it was apparent they shared the same loathsome father. It was as if a portrait artist had painted slight modifications in their countenances. They all had the same square jaw and sky-blue eyes, but their noses were dissimilar, though only slightly. The same went for the shape of their mouths. But they were all handsome men…which was precisely what that dreadful duke had set out to do.

"Baroness Addington, this is the proprietor of The Crowing Cock, Mr. Liam Hallahan."

Corrine held out her hand. "A pleasure to meet you, Mr. Hallahan. I commend you for feeding the unfortunates of the neighborhood."

"My lady," Mr. Hallahan replied gruffly. He took her gloved hand, shook it quickly, and released it. "I've luncheon ready for the three of you."

Doctor Hornsby grabbed his case. "Thank you, Hallahan, but I am due at the clinic immediately."

"I figured as much." Mr. Hallahan gave a low, shrill whistle, and a waitress brought forth a paper bag. She handed it to the doctor. "Sandwiches on whole wheat bread with ham, shredded cheese, lettuce, and ground walnuts."

"A wholesome meal. Thank you," Doctor Hornsby said softly. He looked genuinely touched by the gesture. He opened the bag and peered inside. "Biscuits and loaf cake as well."

"I received the first lot of food today from your nob friends. That's some of it. Come this way, Simpson, Baroness. Your table awaits."

They followed Mr. Hallahan inside and through the kitchen. There were young lads of about thirteen chopping vegetables or washing dishes while two women operated the three gas stoves. The enticing odors of frying onions and beef made Corrine's mouth water.

Mr. Hallahan led them to a private booth. There was a teapot and two mugs on the table. "Luncheon today is a beef pie with toasted cheese. I'll have the waitress bring it directly." He was gone before Corrine could thank him.

"What an interesting man, and so is his restaurant. Mr. Hallahan acts gruff, but I am guessing there is a complicated man beneath the surface. One who assists his fellow man. What did he mean about the food delivery?" Corrine poured the tea, remembering Mitchell preferred milk. She used the pitcher on the table, added the milk, and handed him the mug.

"The suggestion was one of our enticements to get him to join our informal group. My aristocratic acquaintances send leftover food to various charities. Drew and I asked them to divert some to Hallahan. He can resell it to raise money for his venture or give it to hungry people."

"I think that is inspired. Thank you for bringing me here. Doctor Drew says I can assist him every Thursday. In the meantime, I have a week to locate children's shoes and mittens. Unfortunately, I know of places where I can gather them—hospitals and workhouses."

"That is a depressing thought," Mitchell observed as he sipped his tea.

"Too many children die. Some are alone. Most clothes and belongings are burned because of fleas and the like, but some are not. I know who to contact. You have given me a purpose, indeed." Corrine hesitated. She wanted to say so much more, but how to go about it? "Mitchell?"

"Hmm?"

"You interest me. I genuinely like you. I also am attracted to you. Am I being too candid? Tell me the truth, am I being too forward for you?"

MITCHELL NEARLY SPEWED the mouthful of tea he had just taken. As it was, he started coughing. He took another swallow of tea to clear his airway.

Candid? Too forward?

Hell, yes, she was too forward, but he liked it. A great deal. Should he be honest as well? What purpose would it serve? Then again, why deny the mutual interest? Corrine already felt rejection from her husband's thoughtless rebuff. He'd be damned if he would do the same. Mitchell wouldn't hurt this lovely lady for the world.

"Forward? Perhaps—or perhaps not. You're only saying what we are, no doubt, both thinking. And feeling." He paused. "But whatever we are discerning or dreaming of, we cannot act on it."

Corrine gave him a sad sort of smile. "No, at this particular time, we cannot. I am a practical woman in all things. I speak my mind. And I keep my promises."

"And vows," Mitchell added.

"Most especially vows."

The waitress picked the right moment to bring the food, for Mitchell's heart banged like a soldier's drum. He had never before given voice to his emotions like this. Would it make their future interactions awkward? That was the last thing he wanted to do.

"Oh, my. Look at this meat pie. Baked to perfection," Corrine enthused. She glanced up at the waitress. "Is it made with a hot water crust?"

"Yes, ma'am. Strong enough to keep in the meat and veg, but buttery and flaky within. Or so Liam says. Enjoy your meals." The waitress smiled, then moved toward nearby tables.

"And this cheese sandwich looks delicious," Corrine continued. "It is grilled and golden brown." She bit into it, and the look of ecstasy on her face aroused him to the point of pain. Corrine swallowed, then met his gaze. "You are not eating. Is something the matter? Is my candor going to cause a chasm to grow between us, for that is not what I want."

"It's not what I want, either. We are adults. We can set aside what we discussed—for now." Taking his knife, Mitchell sliced into the meat pie, and a thick gravy, along with cuts of beef and bits of vegetables, spilled out.

"I feel at ease talking with you. I have from the first. I consider us friends. Does that sound peculiar? Men and women—friends?" She took another bite of her sandwich. Mitchell picked up his and did the same. *Delicious.*

"It's possible. And I always believed a couple had to like each other before progressing to the next step. Not that I know much about it." He should not have said that—any of it—but it was too late to call the words back. It sounded as if he were intimating that they could be a couple in the future. As much as he yearned for it, he never should have voiced his innermost thoughts.

Corrine frowned and placed her sandwich on the plate. Then she daintily dabbed at her luscious mouth with the corner of the paper napkin. Blast his unruly physical reaction to her every movement—and his ill-advised statement about couples.

"I skipped all those stages with Travis. I should have taken the time to get to know him better before agreeing to the marriage, but I could not afford to. I acted selfishly." She shook her head and put her sandwich down. "And now, I fear I have lost my appetite."

The sadness and regret in her voice touched Mitchell's heart. He reached across the table and took her hand, reassuringly squeezing it.

"Don't admonish yourself. Addington came to *you*. It's not as if you pursued him for financial gain. He made a business proposal, and your family's survival was at stake." Mitchell glanced at the table across from them. The family of five was staring at them, and the woman, in particular, looked shocked. God forbid anyone show any public display of emotion or empathy. He withdrew his hand. "Come now, eat your meal. This delightful food should not go to waste," he coaxed gently.

"You're correct. Thank you, Mitchell. You *are* a good friend."

Oh, how he wanted to be so much more. Keeping their interactions friendly, and nothing else, would prove to be a challenge, but he would do it, for he respected Corrine too much to do otherwise. If he were a different sort of man, he could subtly encourage her to divorce Addington while slowly and seductively urging her to come to his bed.

But he wasn't that man.

The Simpsons had brought him up better than that. For all Corrine's strength and confidence, underneath it was a vulnerability he would never take advantage of. The decision to divorce Addington must come from her and her alone.

He glanced up at Corrine, who was busily cutting into the beef pie.

"I'm here for you," Mitchell said, his voice husky with a rare show of emotion. "To assist you in any way. As an investigator and as a friend."

Corrine met his intense stare, and her eyes shimmered. "Thank you."

And he meant every word.

CHAPTER NINE

MITCHELL ESCORTED CORRINE to her residence. After assisting her from the carriage, he passed her the wrapped loaf of bread.

"I will come around in about three days. Hopefully, I will have further information regarding the baron," Mitchell said.

"Thank you. I enjoyed our luncheon. And thank you for suggesting I assist Doctor Hornsby. Next time I see him, I shall ask if he could use my help at one of the free clinics one day a week as well."

"I'm sure he would appreciate that. Goodbye, Corrine."

Turning the key in the lock, she entered the front hall, where Thomason stood at attention. "You have a guest, my lady. The Honorable Jeffery Edgeworth. He awaits you in the sitting room. I was about to bring him sandwiches and tea. Shall I bring dishes and utensils for you as well?"

"Just a cup, thank you, Thomason."

Removing the veil, she stepped across the threshold of the sitting room. "Jeffery? What brings you here?"

Her younger brother stood and faced her. "To see if you are still living," he replied sardonically. "Father and I haven't seen you in weeks. Why are you wearing your nurse's uniform?"

"I am assisting a doctor to treat those in need in the East End. Spitalfields, to be exact."

"I am rather surprised to hear it. I would have thought you

had had enough of nursing the indigent." Jeffery looked about the room. "What is going on, and where is Addington? At his office?"

Corrine winced inwardly. Her brother knew of an office, and she did not? She removed her cloak, tossed it on the sofa, and sat beside it. "Why do you ask about Travis? Do you want to speak to him?"

Jeffery shrugged. "No. I just thought he'd be here."

"Please sit, Jeffery. And what office are you talking about?"

Her brother sat in the wing chair facing her. "I have no idea where his office is located. I simply assumed he has one, since he is a consulting engineer for the London and South Western Railway. At least, that is what he told Father when he came to ask permission to offer for you. Though why he asked seemed odd—you were well past the age of consent."

Corrine blinked rapidly. "Maybe because Travis is an honorable gentleman? But really—Travis came to see Father? When?"

"Sister, you've gone as white as a sheet. Are you telling me you knew none of this, including his occupation?"

The footman entered with the tray and placed it between them.

"That will be all, Jonathan. Close the door behind you, if you please," Corrine murmured tonelessly. The footman departed, and Jeffery immediately piled his plate high with sandwiches.

Corrine poured the tea, her hand shaking. "Now, as for Travis, he is at his previous residence in Camden Town. In fact, the baron has been there for some weeks. We are—separated. And no, I knew nothing of him coming to see Father or that he had any occupation at all."

"What have you done to chase him away?" her brother asked between chewing his ham sandwiches.

Corrine slammed the china teapot on the tray, the cover rattling precariously. "Of course, if there is any disharmony in a marriage, it must be the woman's fault. *He* is the one who left, and I will not be discussing what happened with anyone, including you. It is my private business. Travis is a veritable stranger. I married him to save our family from financial collapse. You have no idea how close we were to complete ruin."

Jeffery reached for the cup of tea she poured. "I've no idea because you have never said. Ever."

"You have just turned twenty-three and have only been employed at the bank for over a year. I didn't tell you earlier because you were too young to be of any assistance. And our viscount father?" Corrine exhaled. "He was oblivious. Trying to make him understand we had no money was a daily chore, but he continued to open accounts and purchase items on credit. He is a viscount. What company or retail store would refuse him? I'd no sooner pay off one debt than I'd discover another. And God forbid he buy useful items like food, medicine, or clothing. Father purchased paintings, bottles of French brandy, expensive suits, and—" Corrine shook her head. "I should not be speaking ill of Father. He tried, in his insensible way."

Jeffery frowned. "I had no idea. I am sorry, Corri."

Corrine raised a dubious eyebrow. "No idea? Hadn't you noticed the servants leaving and not being replaced over the years? Items disappearing because I had to sell them? Why I labored as a nurse all those years while you and Father waltzed through life without a care in the world?" It was challenging to keep the annoyance from her voice.

"Our hardship was not discussed in the open, so how would I know? But that is no excuse. I should have taken more of an interest. I was ignorant of our dire situation because our father spoiled me rotten. I know that now. You paid for my university, didn't you?"

Yes, Jeffery had been pampered as the only son and heir would be, but more so after their mother died. "I did. It certainly wasn't our father. I sold the train painting by Joseph Turner for a few hundred pounds. That paid for most of it."

Jeffery shook his head. "I wondered where it went but didn't care enough to ask. How bad was—or are—our finances?"

Corrine took a fortifying gulp of tepid tea. "In '69, the Debtors Act limited the ability of the courts to throw people in debtors' prison. But the courts can still do it if they deem a person has the means to pay but doesn't, or if the person defaults. Believe me, I researched this. I had to. When Travis approached me, we were about to default, which meant Father—and us as well—could have been incarcerated for up to six weeks. Or longer. We would have lost our hard-won positions. Shame would cover this family, one we would never recover from—financially or socially. I made a snap decision, and I'm not sorry I did so."

Her brother's mouth dropped open briefly in shock. "My God, Corri. Why didn't you tell me? I could have helped."

"No," Corrine replied sadly. "There was nothing to be done. What little money I managed to save, I hid away. When Father found it, he bought stock in a failed automobile company last year. That put us behind again, and I could never catch up. I was just so weary of it all. I also needed to get away from Father before I did or said something I would regret. Travis Addington offered me a lifeline. I took it."

Jeffery shook his head sadly. "You sold yourself. For us. I will never forgive myself for being such a feckless lad. I went to our father and asked for new clothes, books, and the like because I thought we had a little money. I mean, I knew we weren't wealthy, or why else would you be working? But he led me to believe we were at least comfortable. I had no inkling the finances all rested with you. Dash it all, I *am* sorry."

Corrine sipped her tea. "I paid all the outstanding bills once I received my marriage settlement. At least, the ones I was aware of. I told Father not to open any more accounts and buy frivolous items." Corrine placed her cup on the table and strode to the desk. Opening the drawer, she grabbed a fistful of invoices. "I pay a stipend to both of you every month. These are Father's recent bills. He sent them to me yesterday with a note claiming he has no money to pay them." Her voice raised in distress with each sentence. "Granted, they are not large bills, but bills nonetheless.

Father has not heeded my directions at all."

Jeffery shot to his feet and rushed to her side. "Give them to me," he said gently, taking the papers from her. "I will deal with Father. I will personally go around to these places and close his accounts, then demand they do not give credit to him any longer. I will take over the finances of the viscountcy. You have my word. I will take firm control of this." Jeffery gathered up the invoices. "Going forward, I will ensure Father lives within the means you have generously provided."

Corrine threw her arms around her brother's neck. It was such a relief to unburden it all, and she was thankful he would take over dealing with their father.

Jeffery held her close and patted her back. "There, dear sister. All will be well. Come and sit and have more tea. It's surprising how comforting tea can be." He assisted her to the sofa and then sat across from her, placing the pile of outstanding bills in front of him. Her brother had grown into a fine man, tall and handsome, with light brown hair and eyes. He had some threads of auburn in his hair, but she had more.

"Now, what will you do about Addington?" Jeffery asked.

"I'm not certain. Try and salvage this unfortunate start, perhaps? See if the rift can be repaired. Or do I obtain a divorce?"

Jeffery grabbed a sandwich wedge from the plate. "And is the crippled man who escorted you home the reason you are contemplating divorce?" her brother asked quietly.

Corrine glared at her brother. "You watched through the window."

"Yes. Your parting appeared—intimate."

"First, I cannot abide that word—crippled. I never liked it. The man is Detective Sergeant Mitchell Simpson, and he was heroically injured in the line of duty. He is on medical leave while he recovers the use of his leg. I met him through mutual acquaintances. And if you mean we acted friendly, I suppose it was intimate. I consider Mitchell a friend. That is all."

"No need to become annoyed. I'm merely worried for you.

The word you dislike has been around since the 10th century. See? My train painting education was good for something."

A smile tugged at the corner of Corrine's mouth. She never could stay annoyed at Jeffery for long. "Nevertheless. Apart from that, it is none of your concern who I'm friends with or how I spend my time."

"Forgive me for prodding in your life, but I've missed you these past months. I was and am concerned. I do not want gossip hounding your every step. Especially when it becomes known that Addington is living elsewhere. You know how the tattle spreads and how vicious it can be." Jeffery stood, then gathered up the pile of invoices. "I meant what I said, Corri. I will take on this responsibility for Father. Will you come and see us soon?"

Corrine placed her cup on the saucer and stood. "No. I cannot. Not for a while. If I come face-to-face with our father, I will lose my temper. I love him; he is my father, after all. But it's best I stay away from him for now."

Jeffery strode toward her and then affectionately kissed her cheek. "I understand. But let us keep in touch."

"How about we meet for luncheon? I know just the restaurant. I will send the particulars to you at the bank. Is that all right?"

"More than all right. Goodbye, Corri. Be well."

Corrine walked him to the sitting room entrance and watched as Thomason escorted her brother to the front door.

"Shall I take the tray away, my lady?"

"No, thank you."

"You have some correspondence, my lady. I placed it on the desk."

"Thank you, Thomason." Corrine closed the door and then strolled toward the desk. She sat and, taking the letter opener, slid it under the seal. The note was from Althea Galway-Cranston, the newly married duchess and co-owner of the Galway Investigative Agency.

Good day Corrine,

We have an assignment for you! Our client, The Duke of Barnsdale, is convinced his much younger wife is having an affair. The Duchess will be attending an afternoon tea charity fundraiser at the home of the Duchess of Gransford. I contacted Doctor Drew Hornsby since the Duchess of Gransford is his aunt, and he checked with the guest list. You were already sent an invitation. Let us know if you can attend. We ask that you observe and gather any information as subtly as possible.

Wait. The Duchess of Barnsdale? Selena Seaton? Corrine had read of the marriage in the paper. How long ago? Eight years or more? Corrine had attended Miss Langston's Finishing School for Girls with Selena. They had been close. However, when Corrine's mother died, Corrine had no choice but to leave school and had lost all contact with her friends.

Corrine opened the desk drawer on her left and pulled out a handful of unopened correspondence. Since the upheaval with Travis, she had not bothered to read any of these invitations, let alone reply to them. She rifled through the pile until she located the one in question. After opening it, she quickly read it. The tea would take place five days from today.

Pulling out a pen and stationery and uncapping the ink bottle, she hastily scribbled a reply to the tea invitation, saying she would be pleased to attend. Then she wrote one to Althea, letting her know that she'd accepted the invitation to the tea and would discover what she could.

It had been several weeks since Corrine had attended a social function, not since the tea party at the Duchess of Watford's residence. Other than her brother, she hadn't had any callers either. That had to change.

Wait. She'd forgotten about the strange man in the cloak looking for Travis. Corrine placed her hand on her forehead. She had been so upset over her conversation with Travis that all thoughts of that man had left her mind. So much for her investigative skills—or lack thereof. The next time she saw Mitchell, she would inform him of the short but bizarre happenstance. In the meantime, the prospect of an investigative assignment filled her with excitement. It was time she started moving on with her life.

AFTER SEVERAL DAYS of lurking about Camden Town, Jedidiah Danaher was no further ahead in discovering where Addington lived. Although he preferred to keep the world at large believing his demise, he'd have to come out of the shadows to discover more about the new baron and the barony itself. And he'd need help.

Jedi had just the person in mind: William Buckingham, the Earl of Darrington. Billy Buck, as those in Jedi's criminal circle called the sly earl, had his fingers in numerous illegal schemes. He and Jedi had done business together many times, and as recently as five months ago. Besides smuggling in hard-to-get cheap French wine, he also ran a profitable thieving ring. These unlawful acts funded his aristocratic lifestyle and that of his pampered arse of a son, Troy Buckingham, Viscount Shinwell.

Having full knowledge of Darrington's vices and predilections, Jedi waited outside the *La Fleur Blanche*, called such after the famous Paris brothel of the same name. It was nowhere near as lavishly decorated as the one in Paris, but all the workers came from France. Its location in Hampstead was close to a posh flat Darrington rented, where he coordinated his illegitimate business and no doubt entertained his hired ladies. Standing in the alley, Jedi watched the comings and goings.

Darrington's corpulent form was not easy to miss. There the man stood, puffing on a cigar, looking satiated and arrogant. He was looking around for a hansom cab when Jedi grabbed his arm. "Come with me, Billy Buck. We have much to discuss."

Darrington's eyes darted about, as if to make sure no one heard the name. Once in the alley's shadows, Jedi pulled the hood down and faced the earl.

"You! Miserable wretch, you are supposed to be dead, burnt to a cinder! By Jove, you have the luck of the very devil."

"Maybe it is the devil's luck. But no one is to know I'm alive. Not yet. You follow? Speak of it to anyone, and I will tear those ample guts from your body and place them around your corpse for the rats to feast on."

Darrington clutched his walking stick and tapped Jedi none-to-gently on the chest. "Stop with the threats, for they are useless against me. We've done business for years. Why would I jeopardize that? Speak sense. You're reclaiming your foothold in Notting Dale, are you not? I have several items to shift, and you have always been the best man for the job."

"Eventually. But I've other business to attend to first. I need you to find out some information for me."

"Hmm. Like what?"

"I want to know everything there is to know about the new Baron Addington. I also want a history of the barony, financial and otherwise, and anything you can tell me about the previous baron as well."

The earl scoffed. "You aren't asking for much. That will take some doing. How do I get word to you?"

"You don't," Jedi snapped.

"Very well. Come to my apartment here in Hampstead in ten days. You've been there before. Come under the cover of night, mind. Let us say, nine of the clock. Now, let me pass."

Jedi stepped aside, and Darrington stopped in front of him. "I advise you not to stay dead for long, or I will take my business to Lucian Sharpe in what is left of the Devil's Acre." Darrington gave him a smug smile. "They will be clearing out the remaining nest of vipers within the next year. Same with your rookery in Notting Dale. Clearances are coming. There soon will be no place left for you scurvy lot to do business. Shame, that." Darrington laughed as he exited the alley.

Lucian Sharpe.

He was younger than Jedi but just as ruthless. They were rivals but stayed out of each other's business and territory. But if things became more difficult… Well, he'd deal with that when the time came.

First things first. To find out about the barony.

And collect what he was owed. By whatever means necessary.

CHAPTER TEN

MITCHELL ARRIVED PROMPTLY at three o'clock Saturday afternoon and was shown into the sitting room. As always, Corrine, looking exquisite, greeted him warmly.

After they sat, Corrine prepared his tea and handed him the cup and saucer. Good God, he could easily get used to this, sitting in the parlor, conversing and drinking tea with her. Mitchell briefly closed his eyes, imagining Corrine waiting for him after his shift, eager to share how they passed their day while anticipating how they would pass their night. In bed. But the image dissipated, for it was only a dream. His eyes popped open as reality crashed in all around him—the stark truth of her married state.

"Mitchell?"

"I do apologize. Did you say something?"

"Yes. I asked what is in the paper bag you brought?"

Flushing furiously, he handed it to her. Instead of bringing flowers as any courting swain may do, Mitchell had brought her baked goods. "Ginger biscuits from the seller on Carol Street. I saw how you broke your biscuits into pieces and gave them to the children. So I thought you might like some for yourself."

Corrine opened the bag, then looked up and caught his gaze. "How thoughtful. Thank you." She reached in and grabbed one. Taking a bite, she chewed and swallowed. Even watching her eat had his insides tumbling with desire. "These are lovely. They melt in the mouth. Here, have one with your tea." Corrine held the bag toward him.

Leaning forward, he took one and bit into it. "That is a quality biscuit. It's way above what you usually find in a street cart."

"You should tell Mr. Hallahan. Maybe he can offer the seller some business. I take it Mr. Hallahan is more of a cook than a baker."

"I get that impression. I'll do as you suggest. Now, to business."

Corrine held up her hand. "Before you give your report, I wish to tell you of an odd encounter. I apologize for not telling you of this sooner, but it flew out of my head with everything going on. It took place the first day you came here. About fifteen minutes after you departed, Thomason told me that a man insisted on seeing the baron. When I opened the door, there stood a stranger wearing a long, hooded cloak—"

This time, Mitchell could not keep the spray of tea from leaving his mouth. Thankfully, it only landed on the front of his wool coat. How mortifying.

Corrine jumped to her feet and hurried to his side. Holding a handkerchief, she brushed at his coat. He gently clasped her hand. Again, heat rolled through him at the touch of her silky skin. "I'm fine, thank you. Please take your seat."

She handed him the cloth and sat, a look of concern on her face.

"Tell me everything." Mitchell scrubbed the tea from his coat and placed the damp cloth on the table. "Tell me of the conversation, what he looked like. Because on the day I followed the baron here, a man in a hooded cloak lurked about the street."

Corrine gasped, her hand flying to her mouth in shock.

"As soon as Addington emerged from the residence, the hooded man waved down a hansom cab," Mitchell continued. "I told my cab driver to follow the baron's carriage, and for a while, the hooded man traveled in the same direction. However, the cab pulled off several streets before Addington's house. I assumed it was a coincidence. I even tried to find the man and the cab, but was unsuccessful."

Corrine's eyes widened. "Could this be something?"

"Perhaps, or it could be coincidence. What color was the cloak?"

Corrine sipped her tea thoughtfully. "Dark brown. He had the hood pulled over most of his face and kept his head down. He said, 'I need to talk to the baron. Now.' I informed him the baron was unavailable, but he could leave his name and address with the butler, and I assured him that the baron would get back to him."

"What about his voice?" Mitchell asked.

"Deep. Gravelly. Now that I think of it, the man could have disguised it, as the tone sounded unnatural. All I know is that I felt uneasy. Not fear as such, but a warning not to reveal too much information."

Mitchell's admiration for Corrine increased. "Very wise. What happened next?"

"He barked, 'And who are you, then?' and I replied I was the baroness. He laughed and said, 'That old goat remarried? Trying for another heir, is he? He has more gumption in him than I thought.' Then I realized he spoke of the late baron, Gilbert Addington. I informed him the old baron had passed, and my husband, a distant cousin, was now baron."

Mitchell's mind raced. Who could this stranger be? Perhaps he'd hung about the baron's residence to see if what Corrine had told him was true. Or maybe there was something more to this. "What did he say to that revelation?"

"His head snapped upward briefly as if surprised by the news. I thought I saw scarring on the left side of his face, but I cannot be sure. Then he said, 'I'll seek out the new baron. I'll be back soon. Tell him to expect me anytime.' Meanwhile, I haven't seen Travis to inform him about any of this."

Mitchell placed his cup on the saucer. "And have you seen this stranger since?"

"No. Not at all. As I said, I placed the brief meeting from my mind. Should I be worried?"

Mitchell frowned. "When I saw the hooded man, his cloak was black and he wore a mask, which made me suspicious. That was why I'd tried to find him. But the man could own more than one cloak."

Corrine sat forward, her eyes sparkling. "A long, hooded cloak is not what men generally wear, regardless of class. This man purposely tried to conceal his identity. But why? The fact he asked for the old baron leads me to believe he knew him well enough, or why else comment that Gilbert was trying for another heir? It means he was well aware of Gilbert's son's untimely death. I asked Thomason if he recognized the stranger, as the butler had been with Gilbert for years. But he claimed he could not see his face, nor did he recognize the voice."

Mitchell smiled. "You are clever and resourceful. I can see why the Galway Agency hired you."

Corrine blushed. "Well, I am not exactly hired, just an occasional operative. I wanted more of a challenge in my life now that I was no longer nursing, and the Galway sisters happily agreed to my suggestion."

"Regardless, this was well done. You're thinking like a detective. And your observations are well thought out. The man acted surprised by the news of Gilbert's death, which could mean he was not in close contact with the old baron. Perhaps several years had passed between visits."

Corrine passed him the sandwich plate, and he took three wedges. "We should question Thomason. Immediately. From what I could ascertain about the old baron, he became a recluse after his son's death and his wife's passing shortly thereafter. He rarely left this house." Corrine stood. "Shall I ring for him?"

"Yes. Allow me to start with the questioning, but jump in any time you wish. Is the butler aware of the reason I'm here? How many servants do you have?"

"No, I do not believe he knows unless he's had his ear to the door. Regarding servants, Gilbert did not have many, and Travis has not mentioned anything about hiring more. Only Thomason lives in. He has rooms in the downstairs area. There is a housekeeper/cook, a footman, and a maid-of-all-work. They generally arrive at seven every morning and are gone by six each night."

"You do not have a lady's maid?"

Corrine chuckled. "I have never had one. I always looked after myself, and I will continue to do so."

"Go ahead and ring for the butler."

CORRINE NODDED, THEN pressed the buzzer, and immediately sat beside Mitchell on the sofa. "One press is for the butler," she whispered. "Two presses are for the footman, and so on." She picked up her teacup and sipped, watching the door.

Thomason, a man in his mid-fifties, or so Corrine surmised, was not the friendliest of servants. But butlers were known to keep themselves removed from emotion, at least in her experience. She'd had to fire the Rothley family butler four months after her mother passed. Corrine remembered the man was aghast that a fifteen-year-old girl had given him his walking papers. The butler hadn't acted removed from it at all that particular day. In fact, Johnson had insisted on seeing the viscount, and her father had tried to talk her around, but she'd stood her ground. Shortly after firing Johnson, she had to release two maids and the housekeeper. By the time Corrine had accepted Travis's marriage proposal, they only had one part-time maid. That was Jeffery's responsibility now.

Thomason entered the room. "You rang, my lady?"

"Yes. Detective Sergeant Simpson has a few questions for you. Please, take a seat." Corrine waved her arm toward the empty wing chair.

The butler hesitated, for servants of any rank would never sit anywhere in the family's living area. Looking discomfited, he sat in the leather chair.

"Good afternoon, Thomason," Mitchell said.

"Good afternoon, Sergeant."

"Lady Corrine has acquired my services because she is concerned for her husband's safety. Do you recall the man in the cloak who came to the door last week?" Mitchell asked.

"Yes, I do, sir."

"What can you tell me about him? Has he been here before? Especially when Gilbert Addington was still the baron?"

The butler's bushy brows furrowed as if deep in thought. "I told her ladyship I did not recognize him or his voice. And I hadn't. But something is nagging me about it right here." Johnson placed his fist against his midsection. "After Master Hayes's accidental drowning, this house was never the same. The baroness took to her room, and there she died. The baron walked these halls as if he were a living ghost. Visitors were rare, though I recall a man coming here about ten years ago, demanding to see the baron."

Corrine's ears perked up at that information. "Can you describe him at all?"

Thomason shook his head. "I am sorry to say I barely gave him a glance. Although I remember he had black hair and scarring on the left side of his face. A rather horrible scar."

Mitchell and Corrine exchanged astonished looks. Could it be the same man? It had to be!

"What happened next?" Mitchell asked.

"I went downstairs to polish the silver after the baron came to the door. I heard nothing of the conversation. I do not believe the baron asked him in, for their interaction was of a brief duration." The butler scratched his chin. "But that night, I heard the baron walking across the floor. He had a certain gait that I had come to know. Then, moments later, I heard him walk back from where he had come. Then the door slammed. I never saw the man again, and the baron never discussed it. He remained in his study the rest of the day and refused a tea tray when I brought it. He said he wished to be left alone. He looked—sad. Quite miserable."

"Gilbert's son's accidental drowning was indeed tragic. Do you know anything more about it?" Corrine asked.

"I do not know much, my lady. You could ask the Duke of Allenby or the new Duke of Chellenham. They were both there, along with other friends. The boys were fifteen or sixteen years of age. I heard that there was an inquiry, which ruled it accidental."

Again, Corrine exchanged shocked looks with Mitchell. Allenby? Chellenham? The dukes married to the Galway sisters? "If you see this cloaked man again, please let her ladyship know or send word to me here." Mitchell passed him a small card. "I'm taking on investigative cases while I recover. The address is there on the card."

"I will, Sergeant."

"Thank you, Thomason. You were most helpful," Corrine said, smiling.

Taking that as a dismissal, the butler rose from the chair, bowed, and then quit the room, closing the door behind him.

Corrine waited a few moments, then whispered, "Could it be the same man? That seems impossible."

"Impossible? No, but not probable. Still, I have learned in my police work that there is always a slim chance that something is connected. That could be the case here."

Corrine tapped her finger against her chin. "Once the hooded man found out the old baron was dead, why would he skulk about the property? To see if I was telling the truth about Travis not being here?"

"Yes. I had that thought myself earlier," Mitchell replied.

"I will be attending an afternoon tea party at the Duchess of Gransford's residence the day after tomorrow. She is Doctor Drew Hornsby's aunt. I have been given an assignment by Althea Galway to gather information on someone. Perhaps I can also gather information on the old baron."

Mitchell gave her a warm smile, the first she had seen from

him. How it enhanced his rugged good looks. "Good for you. Then why don't we meet in three days at my small office in Gloucester Square? Let's say at two in the afternoon?"

"Your place?"

Mitchell's smile disappeared. "It's not what you think. I mean, we can meet elsewhere, if you wish."

For all their talk of being friends, there would always be this underlying—tension, for lack of a better word. To Corrine, it proved the attraction was mutual, but it complicated everything.

"I never thought that. I was merely surprised. We can meet at your office. What is the actual address?" She smiled to show she meant what she said.

"Forty-eight Gloucester Square. We are on the bottom two floors." He stood and then gathered his hat and cane. "I will see you then."

Corrine stood as well and came to stand before him. For the life of her, she could not stop herself from slipping her hand in his. "Thank you for the biscuits."

They stood, holding hands, not moving or even breathing. Mitchell's hand was warm, and a tingling sensation traveled up her arm from his potent touch. This should not be happening. But it was, and she momentarily reveled in that comforting correlation. The sensation was far beyond comfort as her insides fluttered with excitement. Was this desire? Corrine grew hot all over. She released his hand, then stepped back, immediately missing the lost connection.

"You're welcome." Mitchell exhaled, placed his hat on his head, touched the brim, and headed for the door. Corrine hurried ahead of him and opened it.

"Saturday afternoon, then." Her voice sounded breathless to her own ears.

He hesitated long enough to slip on his gloves. "Until Saturday. Good afternoon, my lady."

Corrine quickly closed the door and leaned against it. Then, she laid her hand over her heart. It thundered in her chest.

Oh, this is not wise.

It occurred to her that they hadn't discussed Travis, nor did he give her any report, if there had been one.

Exhaling loudly, Corrine promised herself that she would speak to Travis soon. For she could not stay married to him if this attraction to Mitchell flared further.

CHAPTER ELEVEN

THE TEA PARTY was in full swing at the Duchess of Gransford's impressive residence, with the parlor transformed into a restaurant-type setting. The plush chairs and sofas were pushed against the walls, with round tables and chairs filling the floor. At the front of the room, a long table with a lace tablecloth held silver platters of savory sandwiches, fruit, biscuits, and loaf cakes. There were three Victoria sponge cakes, cream puffs, petit fours, lemon tartlets, and more. It was quite an elaborate spread. And what would a tea party be without scones and clotted cream?

An introductory tea was served first, and the ladies were encouraged to mill about the room and chat with each other before taking their seats. *Blast it.* Name cards were at the tables, so Corrine could not choose where she sat. She must gather the information now before the food was served. The servants were already filling the silver three-tiered trays.

About to survey the crowd, Corrine caught the Duchess of Gransford strolling toward her out of the corner of her eye.

"Baroness Addington, I am so pleased you came. I had hoped to speak to you a moment."

"Your Grace. Thank you for inviting me," Corrine replied politely.

"Drew tells me you were a nurse. So was I, back in the day."

Corrine tried to keep the surprise from her expression. The duchess had been a nurse?

"Drew also said you will be assisting him once a week," the duchess continued. "Thank you. We can use all the help we can get. However, I do have a favor to ask."

"Of course, Your Grace."

"We could use more volunteers at the free clinics; a couple of hours a week is all I require. I know approaching you this way is forward, but my nephew sang your praises. I would also like to invite you to our next board meeting so you can see what the foundation does. If it interests you, we can use you on our committee."

She had already decided to volunteer, but sitting on a committee? How could she refuse a duchess? She couldn't. Besides, Corrine wished to do something worthwhile. Why not join a meaningful project that utilized her talents? "Doctor Hornsby has already spoken to me about the clinics, and I plan to volunteer. And I think I'd like to attend your next meeting very much."

"Wonderful!" The duchess smiled. "I will send word next month. You are a dear. But now, I must resume my hostess duties. We will talk later, Baroness." The duchess lightly touched her arm, then moved toward another group of ladies.

"Corrine, is that you?"

Corrine turned to find a petite woman staring at her. Maybe not all that petite, as Corrine was barely four inches over five feet, and this woman was only an inch or two shorter. But this lady looked familiar. Very familiar, indeed.

The woman placed her hands on her hips, looking thoroughly exasperated. "Oh, come on. I'm Celia Gillingham. Although I'm now the Countess of Winterwood, more's the pity."

Celia was married to an earl? "Celia! Can you forgive me? It has been too long since Miss Langston's Finishing School." Corrine was genuinely pleased to see her. Celia always possessed a sunny disposition despite the tragedy of losing her parents at the vulnerable age of ten years.

They kissed each other's cheek. "Well, I have changed a little. I finally grew a few inches taller than five feet and lost most of that youthful plumpness."

"When did you marry?" Corrine asked.

Celia took her arm and led her to a more private part of the room, half-hidden behind a massive fern. "I stayed at Miss Langston's as long as I possibly could. I told you of my situation."

Yes, Corrine recalled the tragic incident that had brought Celia to the finishing school. Celia's parents had taken a moonlight trip along the east coast of England on the SS Princess Alice, where it had been struck by another ship. Over six hundred lives had been lost, including Celia's parents. After that unspeakable tragedy, Celia had lived with her aunt, The Countess of Darrington. While she'd come to like her aunt well enough, her cousin, Troy Buckingham, Viscount Shinwell, had tormented her constantly. Celia even confessed he had tried to enter her bedroom at night more than once. After that, she'd been sent away to school and rarely visited.

Corrine nodded. "Yes, I remember. Aan untenable state of affairs."

"Well, my uncle wasted no time marrying me off. I could have refused, but I did not want to return to that house as my cousin still lived there. So, I agreed. Winterwood is sixty-five now."

Corrine couldn't keep a gasp from escaping. Celia's husband was thirty-five years older than her? *My God.*

"Carlton is all right. We get on well enough," Celia continued. "I look after him, and he keeps a comfortable roof over my head. He isn't cruel. We are in London to see his doctor. Or so I surmise."

"Where do you live?" Corrine asked, completely caught up in the conversation.

"As far north as north goes, and still live in England—the hamlet of Marshall Meadows near the border to Scotland. Ever since Carlton's health started to decline, we rarely travel to London. He hasn't been to the House of Lords in years."

"How long are you here in London? You must come for tea."

"We leave tomorrow morning, but he will delay our departure by a day if I ask." Celia gave her a pointed look. "Why didn't you answer my letters all those years ago? Why did you ignore me?"

"I apologize. It was not well done of me. If you come tomorrow for tea, I will explain everything," Corrine said.

"Very well, I'll come. I know who else you can invite—another mutual school friend of ours, Selena Seaton. She is also married to an older man, the Duke of Barnsdale. I believe she's here at this party."

"Selena married a duke?" Corrine gasped, feigning her response since she already knew Selena would be in attendance. The three of them had been inseparable when they were younger. How tragic they had drifted apart. And much of that was Corrine's fault. "What do you know about it?"

"As I rarely come to town, not much. But if Selena hasn't changed, she will fill us in on the details. Come, let us seek her out."

Celia clasped Corrine's hand and gently pulled her into the multitude of ladies chatting along the room's perimeter. Her teacup rattled precariously on the saucer as she bumped into a few women.

"Selena!" Celia called out, attracting attention.

Selena, standing with three other ladies, turned and stared. Corrine nearly gasped at the cold expression Selena turned their way. Then she excused herself from the other ladies and came to stand before them.

"I see you haven't changed," Selena sniffed haughtily. "Still loud and rambunctious, Celia."

Celia tsked. "But it appears you have, Selena. Why so remote? Especially with us? We may not have all seen each other for close to fifteen years, but we *were* close friends."

Corrine gently touched Selena's arm, and Selena flinched in response. "What is the matter?" Corrine whispered. This was not like Selena at all. At school, she had been the leader of the trio, forthright and quick to smile and laugh. She'd often secretly raided the school larder, sneaking them biscuits late at night. Being a year older and taller, she'd often protected Celia and Corrine from some of the older girls' teasing, cruel ways.

A shuddering sigh escaped Selena's lips. "Please, leave me alone."

"We will not," Celia replied firmly. "Corrine has invited me for tea tomorrow. Why don't you come as well? Please. I want us all to be friends again. I am sorry we drifted apart. Little did we guess at the unexpected turns our lives might take."

Corrine removed her hand. "Please do come, Selena." It was apparent she would not be able to glean much information from anyone in this crowded setting.

"I will come," Selena said, her tone emotionless. "What is the address?"

"You will come? You're not just saying that to put us off?" Celia asked.

Selena's mouth twisted. "I do not lie."

"Thirty Wimpole Street, Marylebone. I recently married Baron Addington," Corrine replied.

"Please tell me he is at least younger than Winterwood," Celia exclaimed.

Corrine smiled. "Yes, a little. Come at two o'clock. I will have sandwiches and tea ready. Selena, do you still like shrimp sandwiches? I remember you saying you would ensure you had them every day as soon as you were married."

Selena inclined her head. "I do. I will see you tomorrow, then," she said, turning and returning to the ladies she'd been speaking with.

"Holy crow," Celia whispered. "What in the hell happened to her?"

Leave it to Celia to express her own thoughts so succinctly. "I do not know. But I believe it's quite possible she will not show up tomorrow."

Celia sipped her tea. "I think there's still a chance she will.

Behind the inaccessible mask, I saw a flash of sadness in her eyes. And loneliness. I can relate."

"Did you see that? How astute. I wonder if we dare ask anyone about her situation. Someone here tonight might know what's going on in her life." Then she looked closer at Celia. "But I am sorry you feel the same. In a way, I can relate as well." Perhaps more than she was letting on.

At that moment, the Duchess of Gransford called for attention. "Good afternoon, ladies. If you take your seats, luncheon will be served. You see the crystal bowl at the table by the door? I would appreciate it if you would leave a note of donation for the Hornsby-Wollstonecraft initiative. We sponsor free medical care for those who cannot afford it, along with education and legal services. Thank you."

The women weaved in and around the tables, finding their seats.

"I will ask around, and so should you. Something is wrong," Celia said. "And I aim to discover what is going on. I will come early tomorrow, before two, and we can compare notes."

"Yes, do," Corrine nodded. Besides finding out any information on Selena for her Galway investigative assignment, she was genuinely concerned for her friend. Was Selena cheating on her husband, the Duke of Barnsdale? It didn't seem possible. But then, did she really know her friend anymore?

AS PROMISED, CELIA arrived a little after half past one. Corrine led her into the parlor. "I will wait to see if Selena comes before I serve the tea. I'm sorry I never answered your letter after I left school. I discovered soon after my mother's death that we were nearly destitute. I had to find employment and take over the running of the finances. I will admit I felt shame over our reduced circumstances."

"What a terrible burden for a sixteen-year-old," Celia said, tsking. "It explains why you never answered our letters. You could have told us, though. We might have been able to help."

"I would never encumber my friends with such a burden. I will tell you more if and when Selena arrives. What do you know about her husband? Did you and Selena keep in contact?"

"I stayed at the school until age nineteen. They wouldn't let me linger about any longer, especially when my detestable uncle stopped paying the tuition. Selena left the year before I did. She is a year older than us. As soon as I married and moved to the Scottish border, I wrote you both, but I never received a response from either of you. As far as Barnsdale, I asked Carlton about him last night." Celia glowered, her brows furrowed in concern.

"Carlton said the duke must be near fifty-five years of age now. In the few dealings he'd had with him, however, Carlton found the man to be arrogant, vain, and thoroughly unlikeable. He'd also heard rumors that the duke had engaged in multiple affairs, even going so far as to attend those depraved parties where women are passed around as if on a dessert tray. There are no children. Well, there isn't with Carlton and me, either, which means nothing, really. Carlton is not sure when the marriage took place. Nine years ago or less?"

Multiple affairs? What bloody cheek for the Duke of Barnsdale to hire the Galway Investigative Agency to make inquiries concerning Selena when he was rumored to have indulged in varied extracurricular activities himself. Typical aristocratic men.

"It sounds as if you get on with your husband."

Celia shrugged. "As I said yesterday, Carlton's all right. We are friends of a sort. The age gap can sometimes be difficult, but we manage."

"Yesterday, I asked the ladies at my table about Selena. They told me she rarely attends social events, and when she does attend, she comes alone. 'Not a love match,' one lady told me."

Celia snorted. "I'm not surprised. What aristocratic marriage is a love match?"

Corrine was about to speak when the butler entered the room. "The Duchess of Barnsdale."

Corrine rose and immediately hurried toward Selena. She embraced her, but Selena stiffened as if she did not like being touched. Corrine stepped back and took Selena's gloved hand. "I am so very pleased you came. Thomason, bring the tea tray at once."

"Yes, my lady."

Celia also got up to welcome Selena. "I knew you would come. Here we are, all together again. The Bluebells are reunited. Remember how we fantasized about marrying handsome men who would become friends, and the six of us would live happily ever after?"

Corrine laughed. "Oh, yes. The dreams of young girls. I had forgotten that we had called ourselves the Bluebells. Was it our eye color?"

"Yes, and the fact that bluebells symbolize humility, constancy, and everlasting love," Selena replied sarcastically. "We vowed our futures would follow that path." She barked out a cynical laugh. "Well, none of that came true for me."

Corrine took Selena's arm and gently led her to the settee. "I'm not all that certain it came true for any of us." Celia sat next to Selena, and Corrine sat across from her. "I wish, first and foremost, to apologize for leaving school so abruptly, and not keeping in contact. You were like sisters to me, and yet I callously cut you both from my life."

"Well, we should have come to you to ask why," Celia murmured. "I must admit, I silently fumed. And I was hurt. Remember, Selena?"

The duchess nodded. "I felt the same."

Knowing she had hurt her friends cut to the bone. "I don't blame you both at all for not seeking me out. There is no excuse, but I'll explain why I did not answer Celia's initial letter all those years ago." Then she proceeded to tell her old friends a condensed version of her life over the past ten years.

Celia's eyes widened. "A nurse? It's a noble profession, but to take on the family's financial problems on your own. Was there no one you could turn to? Other family members?"

"No. There was no one."

Celia frowned. "Blast money. It's the cause of so much misery. But good for you for taking the money offered. And now you're separated from your husband? Any chance of a reconciliation?"

"There was not much of a bond between us to begin with. All I feel is shame for rushing into marriage because the family was near ruin." Corrine exhaled with a shuddering breath. "Still, my abrupt departure without explanation was not well done of me. We were girls, and our actions and reactions reflected our immaturity. Again, I do apologize."

"I accept, and we are sorry for not seeking you out. We should have known something was wrong," Celia replied. "Selena?"

"Yes, I agree and accept."

"Can we be friends again?" Corrine asked. "Please, let us promise to keep in touch. I have missed you both terribly. I will be honest; I have no other friends. I've been too busy to seek any."

Celia sighed. "Me neither. Especially since I live in near isolation in Northern England. Let's be friends again." They looked to Selena, who nodded. The relief Corrine felt was palatable.

"I would like to ask your advice on something rather personal, now that we're bosom friends again." She smiled, trying to gather her nerve. "It seems that…another man has caught my attention," she blurted. "Am I selfish for wishing to be free from my vows and see where this mutual attraction goes? I do not know what to do."

"What to do?" Selena exclaimed. "Engage a solicitor and come to an arrangement with your husband, even if it means you must return some of the money. Save yourself before you become a hollowed-out husk devoid of emotion. Like me."

Selena's stark words cut through Corrine's soul. Corrine wanted to love, and be loved. But who was to say she would find all that with Mitchell? She hardly knew him. Then again, she knew him better than her husband. Deep down, Mitchell appealed to her in every way. She looked carefully at her friend. Other than her situation, what had happened to Selena?

"What is it? Is it Barnsdale? Please talk to us, Selena," Corrine urged.

"Yes. We might not have been in contact the past ten years or so, but I thought of you both often," Celia said softly. "You can tell us anything, Selena."

The room was brimming with emotion, as if all their pent-up emotions of the past several years were escaping in a rush. The air fairly crackled with it. Selena's eyes shimmered with tears. "I hate him," she whispered miserably. "He is cold, cruel, and controlling. I have started doing charity work, just to get away from him. Mostly in the early evenings when he is home. I cannot bear to face him."

That was why Barnsdale thought Selena was having an affair. She was away most nights. Inwardly, Corrine was relieved. She could report to the Galway Investigative Agency that Selena was doing charity work. If the agency wished to investigate further, they had the option.

"Has Barnsdale—hit you?" Corrine asked softly.

"He wouldn't dare," Selena snarled. "I would put a bullet here." Selena pointed to her forehead, right between her eyes. "I have an appointment with a solicitor in two weeks' time, where I will be examining my options. I have had enough."

Corrine and Celia exchanged astonished looks.

"Good for you. You should take a lover," Celia stated firmly.

Selena shook her head. "After what I endured with Barnsdale? I want no other man to lay a hand on me ever again."

Thomason and Jonathan, the footman, entered the room carrying the tea service and the three-tiered tower filled with sandwiches, biscuits, and tarts. After setting up the afternoon tea on the table, the servants departed.

What Selena had related opened up all sorts of questions, but that was better left for another time. Corrine could see that just the little bit Selena had already confided had taken an emotional toll on her.

"Look—shrimp sandwiches. And Celia, I recall you prefer egg, salad cream, and watercress. There is also ham and cheese and beefsteak and onion," Corrine said.

"Brilliant!" Celia exclaimed as she picked up a plate and piled sandwich wedges. "I am famished. Selena..." Celia passed her a plate. "Tuck in."

Reluctantly, Selena took the offered plate and laid three shrimp sandwiches on it.

"I wish we were staying longer," Celia said, sighing as she laid her cloth napkin on her lap. "But Carlton is insistent we return to Marshall Meadows before the snow accumulates. I do not know when I will be back in London. But I am a prodigious writer. Promise me you will both answer my letters. We will exchange addresses before we leave."

Selena reached into her reticle, retrieved a lace handkerchief and dabbed at the corner of her eyes. Corrine studied her. Her friend had lost none of her fair beauty, and her golden-red hair still gleamed. But she seemed almost overwhelmed by sadness. And weariness.

"I will, I swear," Corrine replied.

"Yes," Selena replied shakily. "And so shall I."

Corrine poured the tea and passed the cups and saucers to her rediscovered friends. The years melted away, and they spoke as openly and honestly as they had when they were girls. Corrine was pleased.

Seeing Selena so miserable and Celia living in near isolation with a man almost old enough to be her grandfather convinced Corrine that she should do something about her marriage. Life was short. Why should she live it without feeling loved? If not with Mitchell, then someone else?

But she did not want 'someone else.' *Only Mitchell.*

Well. That was a firm admission.

She would do as Selena suggested, offering to return some of the money in exchange for a quick divorce if such could be achieved. Satisfied she had made the correct decision, Corrine smiled and sat back in her chair. It was the first time she had felt truly content in a long time.

Chapter Twelve

Mitchell decided the library would be a more appropriate place for his meeting with Corrine; it was a more public space than the office behind his bedroom. He had ordered tea and biscuits from Mrs. Evans and instructed her to bring them in about quarter past. And now, he stood at the window, waiting with breathless anticipation for her arrival. This was not good at all—longing for a married woman. Such powerful yearning made his heart ache like the devil. He now understood what the poets meant about describing love and pain within the same sonnet.

Speaking of his tortured heart, it leaped at the sight of a hansom cab pulling up by the front entrance. Mitchell pulled his watch from his waistcoat pocket and popped it open—she was right on time. Snapping it shut, he tucked it in his pocket as he headed to the door. He had to slow his stride to alleviate the numbing pain. Leaning on his cane for support, he opened the door to greet her.

"Good afternoon, my lady."

She wore a gray cape with a fur-trimmed hood. Her hands were tucked in a gray fur muff. It was chilly today, so the brisk air had brushed an attractive reddish-pink color on her cheeks. He stood aside to allow her to pass. "Good day, Sergeant."

"Right this way. We will have our meeting in the library. Doctor Drew is huddled in his study, and Mrs. Evans will bring us tea." Why had he said that? Mitchell supposed it was to reassure her they were not alone.

Once in the library, he assisted her with her cape, laying it on the chair by the door. Her afternoon gown had shades of dark gray and silver embroidery, complementing her lovely auburn hair. The fact that he noticed all this convinced him he was entirely smitten. After taking his seat facing her, Mitchell's heart flipped over again.

Say something. Anything to distract me from the fact that I want nothing more than to hold you in my arms and kiss you senseless. Until we both cease to breathe. Until the end of time.

"How was your afternoon tea? Any success with your assignment?" Mitchell asked, choosing a topic to divert his thoughts from his intense growing feelings.

"Yes. The duchess I was to observe and gather information on is an old friend from school. What are the odds? I gave my report to Althea nonetheless. A couple of good things came from the tea party. I became reacquainted with my old schoolmates—Selena, the aforementioned duchess, and Celia, who is married to the Earl of Winterwood. Also, the Duchess of Gransford enlisted me to attend a board meeting for the Wollstonecraft-Hornsby medical initiative and was happy to hear I'd already decided to volunteer a few hours a week at the clinic. The duchess was a nurse years ago. I had no idea."

"Damon told me about it. The duke studied medicine at Cambridge, which was unheard of for an aristocrat. He labored anonymously in an abandoned underground train tunnel, offering medical care to the destitute. He met the duchess in that clinic. She was in reduced circumstances then, though I am unaware of all the particulars."

Corrine's perfectly shaped eyebrows arched in surprise. "Well, that is impressive. An heir to a duke performing medical charity work? I—"

"Here we are!" Mrs. Evans announced as she hurried into the room. "Tea and biscuits as ordered." She plunked the tray on the table between them, and the china teapot wobbled precariously.

"Fresh out of the oven, they are. And the tea's hot. All cozy now? Good. I'm off." The housekeeper turned and exited the room so swiftly, Mitchell had no time to speak, let alone blink.

"*That* was Mrs. Evans."

Corrine giggled, and the blissful sound trickled across his heart. She leaned forward and poured their tea, preparing it as if she had done so for years. Holding her cup, she sat back in the chair. "I'm afraid I did not get a chance to inquire after the Addington barony. Now, I am all attention. What have *you* discovered?"

"The current baron has been sticking close to home. He has met with his solicitor, Mr. Dobson, twice more. He also spent two days at the railway office. His boss is Mr. Gregory McFadden, a wealthy industrialist. McFadden and Addington appear to be friends, as I observed them having luncheon at a nearby restaurant both days. The conversation was animated, and they seemed at ease with each other."

"Do you think there is more between them? I know Travis denied preferring men, but he would disavow it to anyone, seeing the legal ramifications of having an intimate relationship with the same gender. Such laws are so unfair."

Mitchell had liked her forthrightness, right from their first meeting. "I agree about the laws. It's a clandestine world, and it has to be. Serving time in prison for your desires is not appealing. As far as I know, Mr. McFadden has not been to visit, nor has Addington visited anyone or any place other than what I relayed to you." Should he mention Drew's a-sexual theory? *Best not.* "My guess from what I have observed is simply that they are friends. Nothing more."

"Any more sightings of the hooded man?" Corrine asked as she reached for a biscuit.

"Not on my end. You?"

"None at all."

Mitchell shook his head. "You must think me to be the most incompetent of detectives."

"Of course not. The man disappeared like a wisp of wind. That is no reflection on you," Corrine said, then paused for a moment. "There is a connection between the hooded man and Gilbert Addington; we've established that much. But what, I wonder? Will he turn up again?" she asked.

"I believe so," Mitchell replied. "Thomason said Gilbert did not invite the man in and left him on the stoop. Gilbert went into his study and returned minutes later. To retrieve something? Did he give something to the hooded man? Money, perhaps?"

Corrine's cornflower blue eyes sparkled. "Of course! Money! Brilliant! What else could it be? Correspondence? I doubt it. Why did he say he would return to talk to Travis, the new baron, unless he is owed something?" Then Corrine's brows knotted with worry. "What if he's dangerous? I should inform Travis of this as soon as possible so he can remain vigilant." Corrine caught his gaze. "I have something else to discuss with Travis. I'm going to ask for a divorce."

Mitchell could not believe his ears. His heart soared at the news. It took all his inner resolve not to smile. "Are you certain?" he asked softly.

"Seeing my old friends in loveless unions and their various levels of misery made me realize I do not want that for myself. I should have considered that before agreeing to marriage. I am hopeful Travis and I can come to some equitable arrangement." Corrine sighed wearily. "Do you think me inconstant? Flighty? For I am beginning to doubt the soundness of my decisions, as hasty as most of them have been lately."

"As you explained before, you were in an untenable situation. I'm sure the baron would understand if you presented your reasons to him as you described them to me. And no, I don't think you are flighty or inconstant."

Corrine reached for another biscuit and took a dainty bite, deep in thought, as she ate it. "Thank you for that. I'm about to be blunt again. Will you—wait for me? Oh, that sounds selfish on my part and terribly forward in making such an assumption."

Mitchell rose from his chair, grabbed his cane beside it, and joined Corrine on the sofa. Giving her an assuring smile, he gently took her gloved hand and turned it over. She wore white silk gloves with three small pearl buttons past her wrist. Slowly and reverently, he unfastened the buttons, then trailed the tips of his fingers across her upturned palm. A soft moan escaped her lips. Mitchell then tugged on her glove, removing it completely. Taking her hand once again, he lifted it to his lips and kissed the pulse point on her wrist. Corrine's moan deepened. That glorious sound spurred him onward. Turning her hand over, he softly kissed each knuckle while he caressed the top of her fingers with the pad of his thumb.

"Oh, Mitchell," she breathed huskily.

Mitchell laid her hand against his cheek, rubbing his face against her palm. The heat that moved through him was something he had never experienced before. Complete and utter bliss intertwined with a blast of desire strong enough to bring him to his knees. "I will wait for you for as long as it takes." He wanted to say so much more, to tell her he absolutely adored her. Though Mitchell had never felt this way before, he knew now was not the time to explain what was in his heart. For now, this was all he dared show and say concerning his prevailing feelings. Their acquaintance had only been for a few weeks. Were they progressing too fast? Many in society would claim so, but Mitchell didn't give a hang what anyone thought.

Corrine nuzzled his hand, then took it and softly kissed it before releasing it. "I will speak with Travis right away."

"Do you wish me to continue with the surveillance?"

"Allow me to speak to him first. If needs must, we will continue from there. I will tell him about the hooded man."

"Yes, do so. Gauge his reaction. Ask what he knows about his distant cousin, the late baron—if anything."

"I should go." Corrine stood as she gathered up her wayward glove. "Thank you for the tea and the lovely biscuits." Then she gave him a shy smile that jolted his heart. "And for expressing your feelings. For I feel the same."

Mitchell chewed on his lip, stopping him from saying more or pulling her into his embrace. He stood, leaned on his cane, and assisted her with her cape. For a brief moment, he leaned in and, barely making contact, gently nuzzled her neck, inhaling her evocative scent. Then he offered his arm. "I will hail a hansom cab for you." Walking her to the door, he felt a strange mixture of elation at her divorce announcement and her acknowledgment of reciprocated although vague emotions, as well as a subtle feeling of dread, as if their path forward would be fraught with obstacles—and possible peril. He tried to shrug it off. Sensing danger at every turn was just one of the hazards of being a detective.

Once outside, Mitchell hailed a hansom and assisted her, closing the folding doors behind her, then stood on the walkway until the cab disappeared from sight. With a sigh, he reentered the house to find Drew standing in the hallway, holding an enamel mug.

"Done with your appointment? Any tea and biscuits left?"

"Yes, there is. In the library."

Drew followed him into the room, sat on the sofa, and poured tea into his mug. He added milk and sugar, then snatched a biscuit from the plate. "Your case must be nearing its end, or is it?"

Mitchell sat, picked up his cup, and sipped the tepid tea. "I believe there is more going on than I've discovered. There is a mystery man who wears a long, hooded cloak and seems to want something from the baron." Mitchell explained the sightings.

"Curious," Drew murmured.

"What?"

"When I went to the police station to give the inspector an update on your condition after you had been shot, they took me into Inspector Stanhope's office. On his desk were a few items they retrieved from the scene. A pistol, a knife, and a long, hooded cloak, well-charred."

Mitchell's heart skipped a beat. "What? A cloak?"

"You might want to speak with Rett Wollstonecraft, Tensbridge's cousin. He was at the precinct giving his statement while I was giving my medical report."

Oliver's cousin? Right, he was there that night. But who wore the cloak? Danaher? If he had, it would have burnt to a cinder along with his body. But when Mitchell had arrived with the police officers at the crime scene, Danaher had *not* been wearing a cloak. Not that Mitchell had gotten a good look at the man. In fact, he couldn't have physically described him even if he tried. The room had been dim and smoke-filled.

Danaher was dead; Mitchell had heard his scream when he'd fallen through the floor into the flaming cellar below. Could it be Danaher's son looking for the baron, collecting on a debt belonging to his dead, criminal father?

"I will call on the viscount's cousin soon. It's quite the reach to connect the cloak found at the fiery crime scene to the man lurking about the baron's residence."

"But it has piqued your interest enough to look into it," Drew replied.

"Yes. It has."

Was Danaher alive? It was beyond all common sense. But Mitchell had learned early in his policing career to never rule anything out, no matter how fantastical. In Mitchell's experience, strange men showing up at one's door never led to anything good.

Right now, he had only one concern—to keep Corrine safe.

Chapter Thirteen

Corrine's hand still tingled from Mitchell's touch. Her confusing emotions had her doubting her decision-making abilities. Open flirtation with another man? She had not thought herself capable, but it appeared so. What were her feelings toward Mitchell?

Physical attraction caught her attention at first. There was no denying she found his fair good looks and sky-blue eyes appealing, along with his muscular build. She had caught a glimpse of his well-defined chest when she'd nursed him during his fever. But it was more than that. The man inside also fascinated her, and her feelings were growing deeper the longer she was around him. Mitchell was honorable and brave, and she believed that beneath the detective sergeant's stoic exterior, a passionate man existed, a side he did not show to anyone. But he had given her a glimpse of it today.

And it was because of all of that, that she must seek out Travis as soon as possible. It wasn't fair to either man for her to stay in this emotional limbo, torn between her intensifying desires and her dutiful vows and legal agreements. Corrine did her best to remain purposely vague whenever discussing emotions, and Mitchell did, too. It was apparent they were restraining themselves from making any hasty declarations or indulging in passionate embraces. But today was a decided step forward.

Remaining emotionally detached was also the way she dealt with her situation with Travis. Regardless of rapid decisions and regrets, the time had come to admit and rectify her failings. She liked Travis, what little of him she knew. But they could not go on like this.

The hansom cab pulled up in front of her home. She paid the driver and hurried toward the front entrance. As usual, Thomason was there to open the door.

"The baron awaits you in the sitting room, my lady."

Travis here? That would save setting up an appointment. She handed her cape and muff to the butler.

"Shall I bring tea, my lady?"

"Not at the moment. I will let you know." Corrine quickened her pace toward the sitting room, removing her silk gloves as she did. Upon entering the room, she found Travis staring out the window with his back to her.

"Travis?" she questioned.

He turned to face her, and his expression was maddeningly neutral, as always. "Good afternoon, Corrine."

Corrine closed the door and laid her gloves on the table. "Please sit. I was going to arrange a meeting with you, so I'm glad you are here."

Travis sat in the chair opposite her. "How business-like you sound, but I cannot fault you for it. What is between us began as a monetary agreement."

Corrine winced inwardly, her temper flaring to life. "If you recall," she said frostily, "you offered a marriage settlement. I did not demand one. Yes, I needed the money, and I took it. I am not ashamed. And if you will also recall, I was more than willing to make this a marriage in *all* ways." Perhaps her tone was biting, laced with a bitter sting, but she spoke the truth.

Travis crossed his legs. "Ah. That. I'm not sure how to explain it. It is not you."

"So you said before. Do try to clarify."

"I do not—experience—certain emotions concerning physical

relations with someone. I never did. Call it attraction or desire, I suppose. I have never encountered it. Not even erotic material stimulates me in any way. I mentioned it to my new doctor recently, as I have found it difficult to discuss throughout the years."

Corrine was stunned. Now, *that* explanation she did not expect. "What did your doctor say?"

"That I have a disorder and that I should undergo intensive therapy. More than one doctor has told me this, and I find that course of treatment to be extreme. I have concluded that I am just—different. There is no switch or mechanism to turn. I am what I am. Over the years, I have come to accept it."

"Then why seek me out for marriage?" Corrine asked incredulously.

"Of all the women I have encountered in nearly two decades, you were the only one who managed to cause a slight spark. I thought—I hoped—but alas, I cannot."

"Get hard, you mean?" Corrine said bluntly. "You have never stimulated yourself to completion?"

"I forgot for a moment you were a nurse and familiar with the workings of the human body. To answer your question, a few times over the past twenty years but not lately. Have you given yourself pleasure?"

"This conversation is unbelievable," Corrine murmured. "If you wish me to be frank, then yes."

"I have given it much thought over the past several weeks and have reached a conclusion. I want us to try to have a real marriage."

Corrine's head spun from this incredible conversation. "A real marriage in societal terms is sharing a bed and trying to conceive children. You just admitted you find sex abhorrent, so much so that you ran from this house when I suggested we try for a child. What makes you think now will be any different? Your proclamation makes no sense."

"I will try to clarify. Gilbert insisted I find a wife and have a child. The poor man was rather despondent over the prospect of dying without the possibility of an Addington heir taking over the barony. I felt sorry for him. So, I thought about my encounters with women over the years, and you sprang to mind. When I gave your name to Gilbert, he was vastly relieved."

"You pulled my name from a proverbial hat?" Corrine cried.

"Well, yes. He was pleased that you are Viscount Rothley's daughter. But not quite as much when he learned of your profession—he felt it beneath someone of your station. I did not mind; it showed purposefulness, and I told him so. Gilbert investigated your family and was also not terribly pleased with the financial state of the viscountcy."

My God.

She remained silent, for Corrine had no idea what to say to such a declaration. After several moments, she cleared her throat. "So that is why you offered the generous settlement right out of the gate. You played on my vulnerability and precarious financial situation. You knew I would not refuse."

"It's not as horrid as you say. Gilbert died happy, knowing I'd asked you to marry me. I only wished he'd lived long enough to meet you. It worked out for you, since you pulled your family away from the brink of insolvency. You see, I have come to agree with Gilbert about carrying on the name and the title. It's of paramount importance."

Corrine's eyebrows shot skyward. "And how do you intend to do that, considering what you have revealed to me?"

"I have pondered over that very quandary and found a solution. We can find a man that attracts you physically, and he can impregnate you." Travis smiled broadly, as if satisfied he had found the correct answer to a perplexing situation.

"I am not some brood mare!" Corrine retorted. "How dare you make such a lurid suggestion?"

Travis sat forward. "Please, do not be cross. Think about it logically. This is done more than you think. You get a child, I get an heir, it works out all around." He paused a moment. "What about the police detective? Thomason said he has been here quite often and that you have engaged in intimate conversations."

Corrine sprang to her feet. "Get out. I will not be a party to such doings."

Travis came to her side. "Easy. Steady now."

He spoke to her as if she were a skittish horse trying to escape the paddock. That blasted butler! Nothing was secret. Corrine pulled away.

"As I said, this happens more than you think," Travis continued. "There are many instances through the decades, perhaps even centuries, where the begetting of heirs through other means has occurred. We can have a good life. As friends and partners, we—"

Corrine had to keep her temper and retain her wits. She knew she could not allow overwrought emotions to send this conversation out of control, at least on her end. She pointed to the chair. "Sit, Travis. And listen closely to what I have to say." She kept her tone steady and firm.

"Very well."

"This marriage was too hasty on both sides. I was desperate, weary, and at the end of my rope physically and emotionally. I would have said yes to *any* man who offered to free me of my family's financial predicament. Once the die was cast, I thought, why not make a go of this marriage? I was upfront with you about what I expected. You initially agreed. I confessed about needing money to save my family from the first. I did not deceive you, sir."

"You were forthcoming on those points."

"Then why didn't you tell me any of this before we married? It's patently obvious that we cannot continue with this sham of a marriage. I will release you so you may find a woman willing to go along with your appalling heir scheme. We can come to an agreement, one where I will return a part of the settlement, for example. We can also agree on the grounds for the divorce. I know there are only a few that are allowed, but we can deliberate and choose one that will not damage your reputation and—"

Travis shook his head. "I do not want a divorce. It has taken me a while to puzzle this out, but I am confident I have reached the right conclusion. It's the only way forward, the only way to get an heir. I do not wish to find another woman. Once you think about this logically, you will see the common sense in such a partnership. Besides, you cannot afford to divorce me."

"I beg your pardon?" Corrine gasped.

"Your father came to me last week and asked for a loan—of twenty-five thousand pounds."

Corrine groaned. "Tell me you did not give it to him. I told you before we married that my father had sunk our family's fortunes. His careless disregard brought us so low that we were moments away from debtors' prison."

Travis sat back, crossing his arms. "Of course, I gave him the loan. He is my father-in-law. Your brother must have gotten wind of the transaction because he came to me to quash it but arrived too late."

There was no smugness in Travis's tone, but Corrine had the sick feeling he felt it, nonetheless. She had the overwhelming sensation of being trapped. *Checkmate.*

"Even if you return part of the settlement," Travis continued. "You will still be indebted to me for the loan. Your father signed the papers. If our marriage is dissolved, the loan comes due. The full amount."

Was that why the solicitor had been at Travis's residence in Camden Town? To draw up loan papers? Even if she returned the remainder of the marriage settlement in full, it would not be enough to wipe the debt clean. Corrine and her family would still owe Travis thousands and thousands of pounds. "I will make my father return it."

"It's gone. He invested most of it in some scheme or another. Or so he told me. I informed him there would be no more from me, not in loans or bailouts. Your careless father can sink or swim. And I told him thus. The man should be put away if your younger brother cannot control your father's imprudent impulses."

"You would keep a wife in such a way?" Corrine whispered. "Beholden to you, a captive under your thumb? Next, you will insist on an heir by whatever means, or you will call the loan due, ruining my brother's future."

"Come now. I would not sink so low," Travis said, tsking.

"But do you not see? You have already sunk several depths. There is nowhere to go *but* farther down. And I do not know you at all, it turns out."

"But you will come to know me better. I will sell my residence as soon as possible and move back here."

Corrine rubbed her forehead as a sharp pain tore through her temples. "No. You took time to work out your evil stratagem. At least grant me a few days to contemplate what you have told me."

"Evil? It's hardly that. I never thought you would be so overly dramatic. I had you pegged to be a sensible woman. But I will give you two weeks to give this some thought. You will see it is the best solution for all concerned."

Corrine could not believe this bizarre discussion. In turns, she felt disgusted and shocked. It would be prudent to change the topic before she said something she might regret. "I forgot to tell you something the last time we spoke. A man came here looking for the old baron. But he said he would seek you out soon. He wore a long, hooded cloak and seemed rather menacing. I thought I should warn you."

Travis stood. "That is quite the change in topic. Is this some veiled threat?"

"Of course not. I'm merely passing on information. Do with it what you will."

"I have not seen any hooded man, but thank you for the warning. I will call again in two weeks so we can discuss this further." He came toward her and took her hand. Corrine tried to pull away, but he held it tight. "We can make a go of this, I promise. I'm not evil, regardless of what you may say or think. You are my wife. I am your husband. Remember that." He released her hand and departed, closing the door behind him.

Corrine ran to the window and watched as a fancy carriage approached the door. Travis climbed in, and the carriage turned onto the street. It was then that Corrine allowed her pent-up anger to burst forth. She vented her spleen on the closest object, a porcelain horse figurine. With a swipe of her arm, she sent it careening across the room, and it smashed into bits on the wood floor. Yes, she'd acted overly dramatic, but this inconceivable situation warranted it.

Thomason immediately opened the door and entered the room. He stared at the shards and then looked at Corrine, a questioning look on his pinched face.

"An accident. Clear it away later. Leave me alone." To the devil with niceties. These servants were loyal to the barony, not to her. She would do well to remember it. Once the butler quit the room, she plopped onto the sofa and exhaled. What to do? If she returned what was left of the settlement, and set the divorce in motion, her family would be right back where they started before she accepted the marriage proposal. How could they ever repay it? Jeffery's salary would not be near enough to cover the payments. It may take months to find another satisfactory and well-paying nursing position. How would they live in the interim?

And Mitchell? Even if their relationship led to marriage, she would never saddle him with her family's debts. That tiny flicker of hope dissipated like a light breeze snuffing out a lit candle. She could send word to Mitchell to close the case, send the bill, and never see or speak to him again. But that was the coward's way out.

Jumping to her feet, Corrine rushed toward the desk, sat before it, and retrieved pen, ink, and stationery. Then she scribbled out a note.

Mitchell,

Starting tomorrow, continue with the surveillance on Travis. Please come here in four days, at two in the afternoon. There is much to discuss.

Corrine

She would need those four days to craft what she would say. It would be folly and unfair to drag Mitchell into this…mess. And it was a mess of her own making. But she would also be honest with Mitchell and tell him everything about her conversation with Travis. No matter what she yearned for, she could not place her family in financial peril again. But Corrine also had to think of herself. To be in a precarious pecuniary situation again would shatter her to bits.

A lone tear escaped the corner of her eye and trailed down her cheek.

It appeared she was destined to live out her life in a loveless, arranged marriage like her friends, and that bleak prospect broke her heart.

CHAPTER FOURTEEN

Later that night…

JEDI DANAHER STOOD in the parlor of the Earl of Darrington's garish flat. "I'm here as arranged. What have you got for me?"

"Right to the point," Darrington chuckled. "Sit, man. I will not bandy words standing in the parlor like gossiping ladies at a tea party."

Jedi looked about and plopped into the nearby wing chair. Darrington sat across from him, groaning as he took his seat.

"It took some doing, but I found some interesting information regarding the Addington barony. I had to contact—"

Jedi held up his gloved hand. "I don't give a flying shite how you gathered the facts. Just give me the pertinent points."

"You are an ill-mannered Irishman, I must say," Darrington sniffed. "But you always were."

"In the business we're in, politeness is not needed. Stuff your parlor manners."

"All right, then. I was shocked to hear just how robust the Addington fortune is. You would never know it from that shabby residence the old baron shut himself away in. Barely a step above middle-class. But the estate's worth? We are talking a few hundred thousand pounds. Can you believe it? I was told 'the low six figures, nearing the middle six figures.' It could be anywhere from two and a half to four hundred thousand pounds. I am all astonishment."

Jedi was also stunned. That greedy old muckshite of a father had given him only a couple of hundred pounds when, in actuality, he was swimming in obscene wealth. All those years ago, Gilbert Addington could have offered Jedi a proper upper-crust education and the upbringing to match it. Yes, the old baron had given money to Jedi's mother, but they'd lived on a precarious edge between the lower middle class and the upper end of the lower classes. His mother often took in sewing and the like for extra money. And that miserable git had money to burn? The shock turned to annoyance, bordering on rage. But he would not show Billy Buck what he was feeling.

"What else?" Jedi ground out.

"Travis Addington, the new baron, is staying at his previous address, at 7 Carol Street in Camden Town."

A smile tugged at the corner of Jedi's mouth. Now that he had the exact address, he could plan his next move. Jedi was owed part of the barony fortune. So, he would seek out the current baron. He didn't care about the legal aspect; morally, he had the right to some of that money.

"The talk is," Darrington continued, "he is there preparing the property to sell. I also heard about a temporary estrangement between him and his new baroness, but who knows if that is true? Besides buying a fancy carriage with two matched grays, he hasn't spent much of his fortune except on a large marriage settlement. I could not discover the amount. He married Viscount Rothley's daughter, Corrine. The viscount and his family have teetered on the edge of financial ruin for years. Rothley is a profligate wastrel, as he was when I knew him in his younger days. Always in debt."

"So the younger baron bought himself a wife," Jedi murmured.

"So it seems. Some years ago, I thought to join my family to Rothley's in a match between my son, Troy, and Rothley's daughter, but I'd be damned if I would take on his crippling debt." Billy Buck groaned and rubbed his ample thigh. "This damnable weather makes my bones ache like the very devil. Are we square now? My son told me of the incident that led to your supposed death." Darrington narrowed his eyes. "A good thing you released Troy when you did, or I would have got to you before the Wollstonecrafts."

Jedi did not doubt it, which is why he'd let that sniveling pustule of a viscount go instead of holding him for ransom along with Viscount Tensbridge's younger brother. What did it matter now? Jedi only cared about the present and ensuring he had a comfortable future. "Right, whatever you say. Anyway, we're square. I'll send word when I'm back in business."

"Make it quick, mind. Or I will go to Lucian Sharpe."

Jedi stood and quit the room. Once outside, he pulled the hood over his head. No use shillyshallying—he might as well visit the new baron now. Who cared if it was near ten o'clock at night? He waved at a hansom cab and climbed in when one pulled up beside him. "Seven Carol Street."

He arrived twenty minutes later. After paying the driver, Jedi immediately walked up and bashed on the door. It swung open, and he came face to face with the baron. "Well, hello, cousin," Jedi said.

"The hooded man. My wife told me about you. What do you want?"

"I don't do my business on the street."

The baron looked down his nose. "And I do not let strangers into my house."

"I acknowledged you as a cousin. Aren't you curious why?"

After a few moments' consideration, Addington stepped aside to allow him to enter. Jedi entered the hallway. "Any servants about? They always listen in, the bloody bastards."

"No. The maid has left for the day. Let's go into that room, the one to the left."

Jedi entered a modestly decorated sitting room or parlor and then sat. The baron sat opposite him.

"I know who you are. Jedidiah Danaher," Addington stated. "Gilbert left me a private letter with his will. You are his illegitimate son and the bane of his previous existence. My cousin said in his letter that you would look for a handout from me, as you have done from him your entire life."

"And who have you told about the letter?"

"No one. Not even the solicitor knew the contents."

Jedi's blood boiled, but he understood he had to stay calm. "I came to that sorry excuse of a man twice in the past forty years. After my mother died, he tried to put me in a foundling home to be hired out as cheap labor to whoever would pay. Feck that. I make my own way." Jedi lowered his hood. "See these scars? I earned every one of them out on the streets. I'm not a man to be crossed."

"So Gilbert said in his letter. He had you investigated, so he was well aware of your criminal enterprises. He also advised me not to pay you any extortion, should you turn up."

"Like a bad penny, yeah? Well, I had the barony investigated. You have hundreds of thousands of pounds that the miserable old sod tucked away. And some of that is mine. I deserve it. And so, I've come to collect."

The baron blinked rapidly, then laughed. "I think not."

Jedi flew out of his chair so swiftly that the baron gasped. He closed his hand around the man's neck and clasped it tightly, causing Addington to wheeze. "You will not mock me or dismiss my request if you want to live. After all, you have a pretty new wife. Maybe I should visit the baroness and show her what a real man is capable of."

Addington struggled but to no avail. Jedi gave one last squeeze before releasing his grip. Addington rubbed his neck as he coughed and sputtered.

Satisfied he'd gotten his point across, Jedi took his seat. "Now, let's discuss terms."

Addington glared at him, still rubbing his neck. "You're to stay away from my wife."

Jedi folded his arms. "Then pay me enough to stay away."

"Any amount I give you will never be enough. You will always come crawling back for more," the baron rasped.

Jedi shrugged. "That is a risk you will have to take. I won't be greedy and take it all at once. I'll come to you when I need it. Or better yet, let's start with a monthly stipend of a thousand pounds. You can pay me now."

"I do not keep money here," Addington retorted.

"I know toffs keep stashes of pound notes in hidden safes. I bet old Gilbert did as well. Maybe we should head over to Wimpole Street right now."

"No. I do not want my wife to know about any of this. Allow me to make arrangements when I know the baroness will not be at home."

"I don't want any servants about, either," Jedi demanded.

"That will take some doing. I need time."

"Don't try to stall."

"I'm not. I need to make arrangements. And I do not like the idea of a monthly stipend. It is too complicated to arrange meetings. Why not a yearly payment? I will make the first fifteen thousand pounds. What say you? We can negotiate further payments then."

Jedi eyed the baron shrewdly. He didn't trust this aristo as far as he could toss him. But fifteen thousand pounds was a good start. Then he needn't see this arrogant bloke again for a whole year. "I agree."

"How do I get word to you once I make the preparations for the meeting?"

Jedi thought for a moment. Where indeed? Perhaps it was time to come out of the shadows. "I will send a note to this address when I make arrangements on my end. Listen up, cousin. This had better not be a trap. Call in the coppers or anyone else, and I will pay that visit to your pretty wife. And she won't be so pretty when I finish with her. You follow?"

"Yes. Your threats are crystalline clear. I do not have as much money as you were led to believe, however. Most of it is tied up in ironclad investments that I cannot withdraw from. I also just lent my father-in-law a large sum. My cash reserves are not endless and I will not allow you to bleed me dry." The baron crossed his arms defiantly.

Jedi stood. "I won't ruin you. That's not to my advantage. I'm the baron's son, and it's past time I received my share. See to it. We're to meet at Wimpole Street, nowhere else. And you will hear from me very soon...Travis." Jedi laughed as he exited the room and out the front door.

Things were finally looking up. Speaking of illegitimate sons, it was time Jedi visited his own. Cillian, like the rest of London, believed Jedi dead in a pub fire. But he needed his son for his upcoming plans. With a low, raspy whistle, Jedi pulled the hood over his head and strolled down the walkway.

CHAPTER FIFTEEN

SINCE MITCHELL RECEIVED the note from Corrine three days ago, he had been watching the baron's residence on and off during the day, but not so much at night. The only activity he had noticed was the solicitor paying another visit. What could all the legal visits concern? Making up a will was what that man specialized in. Why now? To keep Corrine from being a beneficiary? Today was Thursday, so she would head toward Hallahan's place to assist Drew at ten this morning. Should he head there as well?

Since their restrained but emotional parting, he had been thinking of nothing else *but* Corrine. His fevered mind ran through all sorts of scenarios. Why would the daughter of a viscount and ex-wife of a baron give him—a lowly detective, a bastard son of a notorious duke—the time of day? But Corrine liked him and was attracted to him. She'd said so.

If he were to be honest with himself, he was already falling in love. *There.* He finally acknowledged and placed a name on the intense emotion. Mitchell's nighttime dreams were filled with snippets of domestic bliss. The two of them sitting in a parlor, drinking tea, laughing, and talking. But his nocturnal imaginings were also filled with sensual images of them in bed, Corrine riding him, her long auburn hair tumbling about her shoulders, a look of ecstasy on her face. Or him, behind, taking complete possession, wild, unabandoned—Mitchell scrubbed his hand down his face in frustration.

Taking one last glance at Addington's residence, he flagged a hansom. "Forty Brick Lane, Spitalfields," he said to the driver.

He climbed in, and the cab turned onto the road. Mitchell sat back and sighed, his cane laying across his lap. The streets passed in a blur, as he was still lost in thought. Would the baron release her? Strictly speaking, and even legally speaking, the marriage stood on dubious grounds since it was not consummated. Or was it? An idea struck him. He could stop by and quickly meet with Rett Wollstonecraft. Hadn't Oliver mentioned his cousin studied law? Besides, he had to speak to him about the cloak found at the scene. He glanced at his pocket watch and calculated the time it would take to make a slight detour. He could still make it to the East End on time if he was quick. Mitchell took his cane and banged on the trap door on the roof.

"Yes, sir?" the driver questioned.

"A slight detour. Five Hill Street, Mayfair."

It was not even nine o'clock. Hopefully, Rett was up already.

They arrived in no time at all. Mitchell gingerly exited the cab, then said to the driver. "Wait here, please. I will not be long."

The driver touched his forelock in reply.

Mitchell pulled on the bell, and the butler, Dalton, opened the door. "Good morning, Sergeant."

"Good morning. Is Mr. Rett available?"

The butler stepped aside. "He is in the dining room. I shall announce you."

Mitchell followed Dalton, who, once they reached the threshold, announced imperiously, "Detective Sergeant Simpson to see you, Mr. Rett."

Rett looked comfortable, reading his paper in his dressing gown. He jumped to his feet and came to Mitchell, holding out his hand. "It is good to see you, Mitchell." They shook hands. "Have you had breakfast? There is a veritable feast laid out."

Mitchell had to admit he felt a little peckish as he'd only had a biscuit. "I cannot stay long. I must travel to the East End in less than an hour, so I will keep my coat on. But I will have something, to be sure."

The butler bowed and left them alone.

Mitchell immediately tucked his cane under his arm and lifted the covers of a few silver chafing dishes. Piling his plate, he selected bacon, scrambled eggs, and roasted potatoes.

As soon as he sat down, Mitchell tucked in. Having toff friends was a decided advantage, especially regarding meals. Once he finished eating, he wiped his mouth with the napkin and laid it across his empty plate. "Sorry about that. I was hungrier than I'd thought. But I appreciate your willingness to speak to me, Rett. Tell me, how much do you know of the law?"

Rett sat back in his chair, nursing his cup of coffee. "It depends. It has been a few years since I studied it, and I have yet to take my Certificate of Laws, but ask away."

"First, I have a matrimonial question. If a couple does not consummate their marriage, is it null and void?" Mitchell asked between sips of tea.

"Not as such. In decades past, the church annulled marriages for such a reason. Now, it's done through the courts. This much I remember from my studies. It came about after the Matrimonial Causes Act of 1857. I recall there are three "I's" that are considered acceptable reasons for annulment: incest, impotence, and imbecility. Fraud is also considered. An annulment is not easy to obtain, and neither is a divorce."

Mitchell frowned. "In what way?"

"A man can ask for a divorce, claim infidelity by his wife without providing proof, and even name the man in question and sue him for monetary compensation. But if a woman files for divorce for infidelity by her husband, she needs grounds other than adultery. Grounds like cruelty, bigamy, incest, or desertion. That makes it very difficult for a woman to obtain a divorce."

"Not exactly fair," Mitchell murmured.

"When have laws ever been fair toward women and children? And all these court proceedings are public. I'm sure you have seen the newspaper write-ups for the more salacious cases. Only wealthy people can obtain divorces, especially the aristocracy, when bloodlines come into the picture."

"Yes. I see."

"Are you asking for a lady?" Rett raised one eyebrow. "As I said, it's very difficult. Her husband could make all sorts of false allegations, make it fodder for the press, convince the judge the divorce or annulment is frivolous, and that would be the end of it. The best way is to have the parties agree to the divorce and have the man apply for it. It would go much smoother."

"You are quite knowledgeable. Why did you not pursue a career in law?"

Rett smiled and placed his cup on the table. "Well, I have given it a good deal of thought lately. At twenty-seven, I should settle on a career. When I return to London next, I intend to work toward my certificate. Do you have other questions?"

"I do. It has to do with Danaher. He wasn't wearing a cloak when I showed up that fateful night. Did he have one on when you encountered him?"

"Danaher? There's a name I never thought to hear again. Yes, he wore a cloak with a hood pulled low over his eyes."

Mitchell's inner alarm began to stir. "I have never been face-to-face with Danaher. I only caught sight of him for a brief moment in the shadows when he shot me. How would you describe him physically since you faced him that night to pay the ransom?"

Rett crossed his arms. "I have to ask why you need to know this. You have piqued my curiosity."

Mitchell gave a condensed version of the hooded man's encounter with Corrine. He mentioned her name because he knew he could trust Rett to keep his confidence.

"That would be a fantastical twist in a mystery fiction book if Danaher was not the charred corpse in the cellar."

Mitchell snorted. "Yes, incredible fiction, to be certain."

"But you cannot rule it out."

"No, not entirely."

"At first, I only saw Danaher with the hooded cloak. When he removed it, I was able to see more of him. He had black hair and an ugly, mottled scar above his left eye, as if someone had cleaved open his forehead, and it had healed without proper stitches. There was also a thin scar from the left side of this mouth down part of his neck. I'd say he was in his forties, but who can be sure? His face itself would be considered good-looking enough if you ignored the scarring. Danaher stood about nine or ten inches over five feet, no more than that. Notice I mention him in the past tense."

Mitchell smiled. "An extensive description. Perhaps you should be a policeman instead of a barrister or solicitor." The smile faded. "Lady Addington saw scarring when the hooded Man briefly lifted his head."

"It cannot be him. Surely not," Rett gasped.

Mitchell grabbed his cane and stood slowly. "I'm beginning to wonder. I must take my leave as I have another appointment." Mitchell held out his hand, and Rett stood, came toward him, and took it. "Happy Christmas to you and your family, and get in touch when you return. I appreciate your help."

"I am glad to assist in any way. And a Merry Christmas to you. I hope everything turns out satisfactorily and you return to work soon. I cannot wait to hear how this concludes, including with the lady in question."

"Thank you, my friend." Mitchell hobbled toward the door. Then he stopped and turned. "I will tell you everything when you return. Safe journey to Kent."

Mitchell stepped out onto the walkway and hesitated. Traveling to Hallahan's to seek out Corrine, showing up unannounced, smacked of desperation. For God's sake, he would see her tomorrow. All these new and unwieldy emotions were wreaking havoc on his usually ordered mind. He climbed into the hansom cab and closed the folding doors. When the trap door opened, he said, "Forget Spitalfields. Forty-eight Gloucester Square, if you please."

"Right away, sir."

He would see Corrine tomorrow as planned. Yet, his inner alarm trilled insistently. *What did* she want to see him about?

CORRINE FINISHED HER nursing duties with Doctor Drew and headed into the restaurant. Her brother, Jeffery, was waiting in one of the booths. She had sent him a note two days ago asking him to meet her here at half past eleven. She slid across the bench across from him. Already, Jeffery looked contrite.

"This is about that damnable loan. Corri, I had no idea Father went to Travis with his begging cup out. I was gobsmacked when I learned of it," he said in a rush. "I immediately sought out your husband—"

"But it was too late," Corrine interrupted. "Or so Travis says."

A waitress came to the table. "Good day. Today we are serving roasted herb chicken, roasted potatoes, braised carrots, and green beans. We also have a nice lamb stew."

Corrine sighed. She hadn't eaten breakfast or much of anything the past few days. "I will have the chicken. And tea."

"I will have the same," Jeffery smiled. Once the waitress left, Jeffery's smile disappeared. "I'd no sooner canceled Father's accounts and paid his previous bills when I heard of this," her brother groused.

"Now you know what I have had to tolerate the past decade and more," Corrine replied sardonically. "And what I still suffer." She held nothing back and informed her brother of her recent conversation with Travis.

Jeffery's eyes widened the more she revealed. "That miserable bastard! You mean, you—and he never—" Jeffery paused as the waitress approached with a tray.

She placed a sizeable ceramic teapot, cups, and saucers before them, along with a milk pitcher and a sugar bowl. "Luncheon will be another ten minutes. Enjoy the tea."

Corrine nodded, gave a brief, polite smile, and turned slightly to watch the waitress return to the kitchen.

"No. We never. Now you know why I'm considering a divorce. His suggestion is beyond the pale. I would never involve myself with a stranger to have a child. I do not need or want a child that much," Corrine whispered fiercely as she poured their tea.

"We should have Father committed," Jeffery muttered crossly as he took the cup and saucer from her. "Look at what his irresponsible actions have caused. Is it possible to place someone in an asylum for monetary reckless behavior?"

"I doubt it. If so, the asylums would be filled to bursting. Jeffery, I need you to discover if Father put the money in some ill-advised scheme."

"As soon as I return from Manchester. I'm going to attend meetings at our branch there. I have heard rumblings I may be promoted—and transferred."

"No, they cannot do that. You're the heir apparent to a viscountcy. Who will watch over Father?" A sick feeling settled within Corrine at this unwelcome news. "I cannot deal with our father any longer. I cannot take over his guardianship. It will break me." Quite the confession, but true. Being a nurse, Corrine was well aware of the signs of someone near a complete collapse, and she was close to that point of no return just before Travis's proposal. The last few months of financial stability had managed to eliminate most of her anxieties regarding money and had made her feel somewhat safe from ruin. But how long would that fragile repair hold?

Her brother took her trembling hand. "Do not be distressed over this. I will refuse to take the transfer and tell the bank exactly why. That Father is not well and cannot be left alone and unsupervised. Nor can he leave London, not even temporarily."

Corrine exhaled. "Thank you. Will it place your status there in jeopardy?"

Jeffery released her hand, picked up his cup, and sipped the tea. "I am heir to a viscount. They will want to keep me on the payroll and keep me content. They will place me on the board of directors as soon as I inherit the title. They told me so. The bank is not all that large and prominent, so having a viscount on the board would be a feather in their cap. However, I must attend the meeting and may be gone for a week, perhaps more. But I will dive right into Father's loan when I return."

"I will ask Detective Sergeant Simpson to look into it as well. He is coming by tomorrow."

Jeffery placed his cup on the saucer. "I do apologize for what I said about Sergeant Simpson. Good for you for hiring him to follow Addington. Yes, have him investigate Father's actions, as well. We must untangle you from this imprudent marriage. But how?"

Corrine sighed. The marriage was impulsive, rash, irresponsible, and whatever other synonyms fit. "I'm not sure it is possible. But we must try."

"Thank you for confiding in me."

Corrine smiled warmly. She loved her younger brother dearly. He had still been a child when their mother had passed away, and in reality, Corrine had brought him up since their father hadn't wanted to be bothered.

Just then, the waitress returned with the food, setting heaping platters before them. Then she hurried to another table.

"Look at this. Absolute perfection," Jeffery marveled as he stared at the golden breast of chicken.

"The chef here is very talented. Nothing fancy, just basic meals that excel. He is a half-brother to Detective Sergeant Simpson."

Jeffery sliced into his chicken. "I take it there is an interesting story there."

"But it is not mine to tell. When are you going to Manchester?"

"In two days. I will come and see you as soon as I return."

Feeling relieved, Corrine speared some roasted potatoes onto her fork and ate them.

When they were nearly finished with their meals, the waitress came to the table and placed a platter of tarts, fancy biscuits, sliced seed cake, and other assorted petit fours before them. "Liam said this dessert assortment is on the house, in thanks for your help with the nursing. I will bring you plates and a fresh pot of tea. Enjoy the rest of your luncheon."

"This looks fancy enough to grace an aristocrat's table," Jeffery exclaimed.

Corrine laughed, then leaned in and whispered, "They came from an aristocrat's table. Mr. Hallahan sells them to his customers to raise the needed money to feed the unfortunates of the neighborhood every morning before he opens."

"Well done. I *am* impressed." Jeffery took her hand once again. "I have a feeling everything will work out for you, Corri. Wait and see."

Will it? Corrine was not so confident. But with her brother on her side and Mitchell there as well, perhaps she could have some semblance of hope. All she knew was that she looked forward to seeing Mitchell tomorrow. He made her feel safe. But more importantly, alive.

And Jeffery was correct. She had to detach herself from this irresponsible marriage as soon as possible.

CHAPTER SIXTEEN

CORRINE WAS *NOT* looking forward to this visit with Mitchell only because she loathed to tell him the details of her husband's bizarre suggestion. This entire situation was mortifying. She had considered more than once breaking it clean with Mitchell, paying his fees, and stating that they could have no further contact as she had decided to stay in the marriage and offer no further details. But in the end, Corrine could not do it. It would be cruel to the extreme. Not only that, but never seeing him again would permanently scar her soul.

Regardless, she had puzzled and ruminated over Travis's completely inappropriate proposal. If she agreed to stay with him, what would he do? Bring what he deemed suitable men to parade before her? Like she was at Tattersalls, choosing a prime bit of horseflesh. It would not do. The fact that Travis even recommended it wiped away any semblance of goodwill she felt toward him.

But the money. Blast money and all the problems associated with it!

What a damnable muddle.

Thomason entered the room. "Shall I bring tea, my lady?"

Corrine whirled about to face the butler. "How do you know I'm having company?"

"Your note to the sergeant was not properly sealed, my lady. The footman told me. I run this house and need to know the particulars to carry out my duties efficiently."

"Like informing the baron of any visitors while he stays at his former residence?" Corrine replied sarcastically.

"I do not take sides, my lady. The baron asked if anyone had come here since he departed, and I would not lie to him. I gave him the sergeant's name and nothing else. Nor would I lie to you. I am aware you and the baron are having difficulties. I do live downstairs. But I assure you I have not spoken of it with anyone. That is the business of this house and no one else. I do not allow the servants to gossip while under this roof or outside of it. I would dismiss them immediately."

"Thank you, Thomason. I appreciate your discretion. You may bring a tea tray if you please."

Thomason gave her a slight bow, then quit the room.

Corrine believed the butler as his tone was firm and absolute. But she had more significant problems than gossiping servants. It was past time to acknowledge her feelings toward Mitchell.

They were more than friends.

If this was what falling in love felt like, it was a miserable experience. But only because she could not speak her heart to anyone and could not fully accept her feelings toward Mitchell as long as she remained married. However, in this quiet moment, she wholly embraced the rush of emotions. It brought misery because of her situation but also a surging torrent of bliss, filling her heart to near bursting. Her insides fluttered as if butterflies had been let loose whenever she saw him. Corrine wanted him with a yearning so fierce, she knew not how to contain it.

So, when Thomason announced Mitchell's arrival, all restraints temporarily melted away. Once the butler left to fetch the tea tray, Corrine ran to Mitchell's arms. He was shocked at first, then his cane hit the floorboards with a clatter, and he immediately pulled her into his embrace. His strong arms wrapped around her, and Corrine laid her head against his chest. His heart beat as rapidly as hers.

Mitchell gently smoothed her hair. "What is it? What has happened? What can I do to make it better?"

The last question caused tears to shimmer in her eyes, and she felt the fluttering within her turn into rolling waves. The sensation felt like she was falling off a cliff, which she was—falling more deeply in love with this exquisite man. "Just hold me," she whispered shakily. Corrine could stay like this until the end of time, but Thomason would return with the tray at any moment.

Mitchell pulled her closer and softly kissed her forehead. In that tranquil paradise of mutual affection and tenderness, Corrine lingered in his giving warmth—until she heard the footfalls of the butler. Reluctantly, she stepped back, already missing the comfort of his embrace. "Thomason," she whispered.

Mitchell immediately picked up his cane and sat on the sofa, while Corrine sat in the wing chair opposite him. The butler entered the room, placed the tray on the table between them, and left without a word. It was as if he could sense the intense emotions swirling about the room.

She caught Mitchell's gaze. "If only I had met you first."

His brow furrowed. "I do not like the sound of that."

She shook her head. "It's not a dismissal, although I very briefly considered it. So much has happened since we last spoke, and I hardly know where to begin. When last we parted, I came home to find Travis waiting to speak with me." Corrine told him everything about the conversation, including her innermost thoughts. As she poured their tea, she revealed her husband's twisted scheme and the reason he'd proposed it. Then, when she passed the plate of sandwiches, she told him of the latest loan and her brother's late discovery of it. Corrine also gave Mitchell her father's address.

Mitchell listened intently, slowly nibbling on the cheese and onion sandwich between gulps of tea. For once, he did not keep his emotions hidden. The rapidly changing expression on his face ran from concern to disgust, then anger. "That deviant. To make such a grotesque demand and tie it to debts and your family's financial survival. Addington's behavior is questionable, and I doubt his sanity. Regardless, I'm sorely tempted to visit him and pound some sense into him. With my fists. Your father, as well."

"I'm tempted to encourage you to do that very thing. But we cannot sink to his level. I agree that he's not acting in a way that is considered normal. What kind of man makes such a twisted proposal? And why? All his blather about heirs, and he is content to have another man's child be the heir?"

"It makes no sense. He wants society to know he can produce an heir when, by his own admission, he clearly cannot. It appears that becoming a baron laid responsibilities at his feet, and he has no idea how to handle them." Mitchell's look turned thoughtful. "Perhaps we can sink to his level—to a point. He has given you two weeks to consider his offer. That gives me time to investigate this loan of your father's, if it even exists."

Corrine sipped her tea. "Why would he lie? We can easily check. Besides, my father admitted the loan to Jeffery, though he would not say what he did with the money nor show my brother the supposed loan papers. Perhaps my father lied to Travis when he said he put everything into a financial scheme." She placed her cup on the saucer. "I agree with your observations on Travis's character. How can I extricate myself from this mistake of a marriage?"

Mitchell exhaled. "I have asked a friend who studied law at university. The prospect will not be an easy one."

Corrine listened as Mitchell laid out the options open to her regarding annulment and divorce. She grew more horrified the more he revealed. "Oh, lord. I am truly stuck. Travis will never agree to terms. He made it quite plain that he wishes the marriage to continue and wants an heir."

"I once heard of a story of an earl and his countess desperate for a legitimate heir. They found out that they couldn't have children but announced to society that they were expecting, and then the countess was whisked away to an isolated manor in Scotland. She returned seven months later with a baby boy. The heir was an orphaned baby from a tiny village in the Highlands that no one had ever heard of. These types of elaborate secret baby schemes have been done for centuries. This particular tale occurred over one hundred years ago, but the practice is still done. I have no doubt."

"I've heard various stories, too. Yet, the Highlands tale you relayed leaked out, nonetheless. And something like that would have been easier to conceal in the Georgian era."

"Perhaps. But as you say, there is always gossip about one's aristocratic lineage. The thing is, the earl and the countess got away with it. You could use this idea to stall Addington."

Corrine's eyebrow raised. "Stall?"

"As I said, you have to fight fire with fire. For example, tell him to wait on selling his residence until after Christmas, that it's difficult to shift a property during the holidays, and that he should stay there until it can be sold. Or anything you can think of. Tell him you need more time. Tell him there are other ways to get an heir, and they need consideration."

Corrine frowned. "I'm not well-versed in lying. And that is what I will be doing."

"I'm not one for deceitful actions either. Frankly, I cannot believe I proposed this. Dismiss it out of hand. If you wish for a divorce, you will have to claim adultery and add cruelty or desertion. You must prove it in court, and the details will become fodder for the newspapers. Or you can go for an annulment and claim him impotent."

Corrine shook her head. "That is no choice at all. It will bring scandal and ruin down on my family and the Addington barony." She smiled shakily. "We could always run away. Then Travis would have no choice but to divorce me for adultery and desertion. But again, the shame of it all. I honestly do not know what to do."

"Find a competent solicitor? Stall for time, and allow me and your brother, when he returns, to find all the information we can. Do not give up. Not yet." Mitchell gave her a crooked grin. "I must admit, running away is tempting. For us to be alone, to explore our feelings? I cannot imagine anything more enticing."

"Thank you for saying that—about us escaping," she murmured. "It *is* vastly enticing."

"But?"

Corrine sipped her tea thoughtfully. "Even if I manage the divorce, there is the matter of the money owed. I would never ask you or anyone to take on the debt of tens of thousands of pounds. As I said, I am stuck." Her voice sounded miserable to her own ears.

"One thing at a time. Let's meet in three days. I will ask Drew to pick you up in his carriage and bring you to Hallahan's restaurant. We will do it under the cover of night. I think it prudent that we no longer have private meetings at our residences. Why give your detestable husband any more ammunition to use against you?"

Mitchell was right. They could not meet alone like this again. "Doesn't Hallahan's become a pub and gaming room in the evenings?"

"There are still tables set aside at the back for those wishing an evening repast. It's basically leftovers from luncheon, or so Hallahan tells me."

A smile tugged at the corner of her mouth. "He is very shrewd, using every last crumb he can." Corrine sighed. "Yes, I will meet you at Hallahan's. What time?"

"Tell Thomason that you are meeting with Doctor Drew Hornsby to discuss your charity nursing work and will be gone two hours. I will have Drew pick you up at seven sharp."

"That is clever. Well done."

"Being a detective has its advantages. It appears I can lie when necessary."

"And what about…us? Can there be an us?"

MITCHELL'S HEART CONTRACTED in pain at her words. When she

ran into his arms, he thought he was dreaming. But Corrine felt real, soft, and utterly glorious in his embrace. He never wanted to let go. He also had a physical reaction, but he managed not to make it obvious. Any barriers he had placed between them came tumbling down as he held her close to his rapidly beating heart. "Yes. We must keep the faith that it will work out." He stood, for if he lingered any longer, he would pull her into his arms again. "We will talk more at dinner about the other aspects of your case. As for now, I will look into your father's loan immediately."

Taking his cane, Mitchell came to her side. "Do not get up." He took her hand and laid a tender kiss upon it. "One day at a time," he murmured. "We will get through this."

Turning, he exited the room as swiftly as his aching leg would allow. Nodding to Thomason standing in the hallway, he exited onto the walkway. He loathed leaving her, but he had much to do. Not only concerning her case but also dealing with her father. Corrine was distressed, and Mitchell did not want to add more to her troubles today by telling her what he suspected about the hooded man. Perhaps he'd break the news of the possibility at dinner, in a more relaxed setting. First things first: Corrine's wayward and reckless father.

Mitchell waved down an approaching hansom cab. "Sixty-nine Baker Street, Marylebone." It wasn't a high-end address, but a fashionable one, nonetheless. Seven minutes later, he arrived at the residence to find two men arguing on the front step. The tall, younger man had brown hair shot with dark red, the same shade as Corrine's hair, or near to it. This had to be Jeffery, her brother. The older man, a few inches shorter, had white-gray hair with bushy white whiskers, and his physicality was lean. He had his arms folded in defiance.

With a disgusted look, the heir apparent turned on his heel and stormed into the house. The viscount strode toward Mitchell's hansom, motioning to the driver. Mitchell could not hear the conversation, but the viscount must have understood the cab was occupied, for he hailed another cab. Mitchell took his cane and tapped the roof again.

"Yes, sir?"

"Follow that cab at a discreet distance."

They were off. The viscount's cab eventually turned onto Westbourne Grove, a chic shopping area in Notting Hill. The busy street was filled with horse-drawn omnibuses, carriages of all sizes, hansom cabs, and several automobiles. The viscount's cab pulled up in front of Whiteley's Department Store. The store consisted of a row of shops containing seventeen departments. The viscount exited his cab and entered one of the boutiques. Mitchell grabbed his notebook and pencil from his inside coat pocket and took notes. Rothley had gone into the perfumier and beauty department showroom. Was he buying for a woman, perhaps? Mitchell made a note to return and question the staff.

Rothley wasn't in the shop long and was soon in his cab traveling out of the West End. Mitchell's driver followed at a distance. At last, the cab stopped in front of a modest row house. A maid answered the door and let him in. The cab departed. Mitchell wrote the address in his book. Ninety-four Old Street, in northeast London. Then he tapped the roof.

"Yes, sir?"

"Back to Whiteley's, if you please."

Once they arrived, Mitchell paid the driver. He gave him a little extra for his deft navigation of the overcrowded London streets and keeping an inconspicuous distance from the viscount's cab. Mitchell stepped across the threshold of the perfumier shop and was inundated with a blend of evocative scents. The place was fancy and reeked of money, decorated with white Grecian columns, glass display cases, and electric lighting overhead. Female shop assistants manned every case, and many were waiting on customers.

A well-dressed gentleman came toward him, no doubt the floor supervisor. "Good afternoon, sir. May I direct you?"

Mitchell wasn't keen on flashing his division card again, but technically, he was still among the ranks. Reaching into his side coat pocket, he fetched his leather card case and flipped it open. "Detective Sergeant Simpson. Viscount Rothley was just in here."

"Yes, I served him myself. Is something the matter, Sergeant?"

"Is there someplace we can talk privately?" Mitchell asked solemnly, giving the supervisor a reason to take the conversation elsewhere.

"Of course. Follow me. Natasha, you have the floor." The supervisor led Mitchell down a narrow hallway and into a cramped office. "Her name isn't Natasha; it's Annie Jones, but fancy names give the customers a dash of class."

Good. The man was chatty. Which meant he might reveal all sorts of things. Mitchell sat in front of the desk facing the supervisor. "And your name, sir?"

"I am Colin Peterson. How may I help you?"

Mitchell gave him a crooked smile. "I'm sure you've said those words many times through the years."

Peterson laughed personably. "Very clever, sir. Yes, I have."

"Viscount Rothley, why was he here?"

Peterson sobered. "I am not certain I should discuss such an important client."

"I would not ask if it were not imperative and integral to my case. Of course, I am unable to discuss it."

"Of course."

"I assure you that anything you tell me will be under the strictest confidence. Your name will never be mentioned."

"Well, in that case." Peterson reached into his desk drawer, brought forth a hefty ledger, and flipped through the pages. "The viscount opened an account with us last year. He ran up quite the bill—several hundred pounds, in fact. I was vastly relieved when his son came into the store about six days ago, paid off the arrears, and closed the account. He informed me not to give his father any more credit. I just informed the viscount that the account was paid in full and would be unavailable to him in the future."

"And what was his reaction?"

"Understandably angry. He cursed his son, calling him 'an interfering young buck with no business sticking his nose in his business.' The viscount demanded I open another account, and I politely refused. He fumed but eventually placed an order and paid cash."

Mitchell scribbled in his notebook. "And what did the viscount usually order?"

"All sorts of perfumes, lotions, creams, soaps, cosmetics, only the best quality." Peterson leaned in and squinted at the ledger. "All deliveries were to a Mrs. Robson, ninety-four Old Street."

So Rothley kept a paramour. Was that where all the money was going? At least in the last year or so?

"The viscount came into the shop with Mrs. Robson about seven months ago. He placed a huge order," Peterson continued, warming up to the subject. "I heard from supervisors from other departments that the viscount spent hundreds of pounds on ladies' clothing, like leather gloves, expensive undergarments, and the like. Do not get me started on the jewelry."

Rothley had a mistress, all right. "How would you describe Mrs. Robson?"

"Early forties, much younger than the viscount. She was dressed stylishly and had an air of quality about her. It was hard to tell if it was real, or if she was putting it on. I have seen men of means come in with their side pieces, sometimes with those of the lower classes. Giggling and rubbing up against the men. Mrs. Robson did not act that way. She had dignity."

Mitchell tucked away his notebook. "You have been most accommodating, Mr. Peterson. Thank you."

"I appreciate that I was able to take a short break."

Mitchell grabbed his cane and stood. "This is to be kept under the strictest confidence," Mitchell reiterated gravely.

"Of course."

Mitchell touched the brim of his hat and departed. Once out on the walkway, he gazed up and down the street. Mitchell waved to an approaching hansom cab and gave the driver the address. He might as well grab the bull by the horns and confront Rothley. Right now.

Chapter Seventeen

MITCHELL BANGED ON the door insistently. At last, it opened, and the maid gave him an annoyed look. He didn't give her time to speak, but merely pushed past her and into the front hall.

"Here! You cannot just come in here like that. Who are you?" the maid whined.

"Where is Rothley?" Mitchell demanded.

The maid lifted her chin and sniffed. "I don't know who you mean."

Mitchell was not going to get anywhere with this woman. He only hoped there weren't muscular footmen lingering about because getting into a brawl was not on his agenda. Assessing the layout, he assumed the couple may be upstairs. Barging into a bedroom while Rothley was alone with his mistress was not ideal, but he had to do what needed to be done. He climbed the stairs as swiftly as his aching leg would allow.

"Mrs. Robson!" the maid screamed. "A strange man is in the house!"

Mitchell kept going, and when he made it above the stairs, a woman stood in the hallway in a pink silk dressing gown.

"Who are you?" she cried, her hand above her heart. On that hand and arm were expensive rings and bracelets. At least, Mitchell assumed they were expensive. The lady was as Peterson described. Mitchell took her arm, pulled her into the room, and slammed the door. Lounging on a chaise was Rothley. Thankfully, he was still dressed. He had removed his coat, and his shirt and waistcoat were undone, exposing his chest. He looked incredibly fit for a man in his early sixties. He held a brandy snifter, looking comfortable in his surroundings.

"Don't get up," Mitchell said sarcastically. "I'm here to collect the loan Addington gave you."

Rothley's annoyed look turned to one of shock. "Loan? Who sent you?"

"Where is the twenty-five thousand pounds?" However, as Mitchell looked about the room, he could see where some of the previous money had gone. The room was lush, with crystal chandeliers, expensive art, and electric lighting. Gold embossed wallpaper as well.

While Corrine had worked her heart out the past ten years, trying to keep her family from the brink of financial ruin, her father had been investing in various schemes and keeping his mistress comfortable. The miserable wretch.

"I do not have the money on me," the viscount sputtered as he placed his snifter on the table beside him. "Did Addington send you? Those were not the terms I agreed to. He has no right to ask for it back."

"For nearly fifteen years, your daughter has worried and scrimped, selling artwork and trinkets to keep food on your table. Lady Corrine became a nurse and toiled long hours to pay your bills. And when your son was old enough, he also found work because of your extravagant lifestyle. Have you ever given them any thought at all?"

Rothley's eyes narrowed. "Corrine and Jeffery sent you? The ingrates."

Mrs. Robson gasped. "Son? And a daughter?"

Mitchell did the one thing his police training warned against: he'd become personally involved. *Too late.* Mitchell dropped his cane and, with two hands, grabbed fistfuls of the viscount's open shirt, bringing him to his feet. "Ingrates? Your daughter made an impulsive marriage of convenience to pay your outstanding bills since the family was close to being imprisoned for your debts. Were you even aware? Did you even care?" Mitchell's voice rose with each question. How disconcerting to learn that he was close to giving a deserved beating to this heartless aristocrat.

"James? Is this true?" Mrs. Robson cried, clearly distressed.

A small voice arose from the doorway. "Mama? Papa?"

Still holding on to Rothley, Mitchell swung about to find a small boy rubbing his eyes as if he'd just woken. Mrs. Robson rushed to the boy, dropped to her knees, and hugged him tightly. The lad looked no more than five years of age.

"It's all right, my dear. Come back to bed and finish your nap." Mrs. Robson looked up to find a shocked maid standing in the archway. "Mary, please take Master James to his room."

James? They named the child after Rothley. Of course, the small lad called him 'Papa.'

With the child escorted from the room, Mrs. Robson closed the door and faced the viscount. "You told me you were wealthy and that it was no hardship to see to my comforts. Those were your words. I objected to most of your improvements," she said, pointing to the ornate chandelier. "But you said you could well afford it. What else have you lied about?"

Mitchell could see the mixture of anger and hurt glistening in her eyes. He released the viscount, who visibly slumped. Disgusted, Mitchell pushed him into the chaise longue.

"Flora, my love. Let us not discuss private business in front of this over-muscled thug," Rothley soothed.

Mrs. Robson turned to face Mitchell. "I ask again, who are you?"

Mitchell grabbed his leather case and flipped it open for her to see. "Detective Sergeant Mitchell Simpson."

"The police!" she cried.

Rothley buried his face in his hands.

"I'm temporarily on leave, ma'am, and working as a private investigator. I was hired to recover this ill-conceived loan.

Naturally, I cannot reveal who hired me."

"James, where is the money?" Mrs. Robson demanded. "The truth, for once."

"You told Addington you'd placed it in some scheme and had already lost most of the money. Is that true?" Mitchell interjected.

"No," the viscount replied wearily. "He threatened to call in the loan if his marriage to my daughter faltered. I told Addington I'd lost it so he would not ask for it back. I have lost money before in such dealings, so I concluded he would accept that explanation."

"Where is it?" Mitchell growled. He was swiftly losing his patience.

"I have it tucked away. But I have already spent six thousand pounds."

Had the idiot spent that much in less than ten days? What a sniveling, thoughtless bastard. Mitchell grabbed his cane from the floor. "Go and get it and bring it here."

"I will not!" Rothley sniffed haughtily. "This could be some elaborate plan to fleece me of my money. I will lay coin my son is behind this. How dare he go all over town, cancel my accounts, and tell the shops not to give me credit? And my daughter? She hounded me endlessly for years about my lifestyle. How dare she? I am a viscount—"

Mitchell gave Rothley a backhanded slap. It was not very gentlemanly, but Mitchell had never claimed to be a gentleman. At least it silenced the viscount. "Collect the money. You have thirty minutes. I will stay right here. And do not think about doing a runner. I will have the Metropolitan Police on your trail, and you will be found and arrested for fraud. Think of the scandal. Go now."

Silently, the viscount grabbed his coat and marched from the room, slamming the door behind him.

Mrs. Robson wobbled, and Mitchell took her arm to keep her from swooning. He escorted her to the wing chair and sat opposite her. "I had no idea about any of this," she whispered.

"When did you become involved with him?"

"Six years ago. I was a singer in an upscale West End theater. He asked me out for a late supper. I nearly refused since he was so much older, but I found him charming and handsome. He is sixty years old but hasn't changed since I met him. Except his hair is whiter." She frowned, looking quite miserable. "He lied to me all this time. James said he was a wealthy but lonely widower with no children. I fell in love with him."

"He is a widower, and his family lived on the edge of financial ruin for years because of his thoughtless, spendthrift ways. At first, he invested in one business scheme or another and bought creature comforts for himself without ever thinking of his son and daughter."

Mrs. Robson pulled a lace handkerchief from the sleeve of her dressing gown. She dabbed at the corner of her eyes. "Then, when he met me, I became his new scheme. He spent money on me. I did not ask for any of the lavish gifts or fancy furnishings. Then James came along—"

"The boy is his, then?"

"There has been no one *but* James. Ever. We never talked about marriage. I supposed I liked things as they were. I had no desire to be a viscountess. I regretted that decision after my son was born. I should have looked out for his future. He could have been the heir—so I thought. But James has another son, after all. Perhaps, deep down, I didn't trust James. I always felt he kept things from me. Now I know." She caught Mitchell's gaze. "And why am I telling you all this? Because I believe one of his children hired you. Please explain to Lady Addington and her brother that I had no idea about any of this. You *do* believe me?"

"Yes. I believe you. Your reaction to the news was not counterfeit. What will you do now?"

"What choice do I have? Regardless of his lies, I suppose I still love him. He is the father of my son. I will try to forgive, but he broke the thin line of trust between us. I'm not sure it can be mended." Mrs. Robson looked about the room. "He bought this residence—or so he claims. If so, I will make him sell it along with the garish furnishings. It is time I thought of my son's future. Marriage, with James claiming his son and giving him his name however it is legally done, would be a start—if it can be done at all. Where we go from there, I know not."

"I will tell Lady Addington about this. And Jeffery Edgeworth, her brother. They are good people and have suffered for years from their father's reckless ways."

"This Addington person James spoke of, Lady Corrine's husband?"

"He is a baron. She entered the arranged marriage to settle her father's debts."

"Oh, dear God. What a muddle."

They fell silent after that, both lost in their thoughts. Mitchell felt sympathy for Mrs. Robson. She had much to consider. And so did Mitchell. Even if Corrine and her brother paid back most of the loan, there were still six thousand pounds to consider, as well as the money spent from the marriage settlement. It could cost Corrine close to ten thousand pounds to be free of Addington. And that was only *if* he would even agree to a quick divorce—with him claiming that he committed adultery. The man would likely never agree to it.

Financially speaking, Mitchell could not help. He had six hundred pounds in his account, meant for his retirement—and borrowing ten thousand or more from his few nob acquaintances, whether family or not, was out of the question. Most of them were not overtly wealthy and had little money to spare. Mitchell could never ask for such a huge favor.

The door burst open, and Rothley strode through, tossing a silk bag at Mitchell. "It is all there. Take it and get out."

"Not until I count it."

Mrs. Robson dragged over a small round table and positioned it before Mitchell. He nodded, then pulled the paper notes from the bag. Dividing them into denominations, he tallied up the money. "There are eighteen thousand pounds here. You said you spent about six. You are a thousand short."

"I need to live!" Rothley sputtered.

Mrs. Robson held out her hand. "Give it here, James."

"No," he replied petulantly, like a small child being told to give up his favorite toy. "You will give it to *him*."

Mitchell shook his head. "If Mrs. Robson has it, I will not take it. She needs it for your son."

Rothley handed the rolls of notes to Mrs. Robson.

"Sit, James. We have much to discuss. Is that all, Sergeant?"

"For now." He touched the brim of his hat. "Good day, Mrs. Robson."

He took the bag and his cane and departed. He didn't envy Mrs. Robson's upcoming conversation. But Mitchell had more important considerations—Corrine, for one. Her father might be lying about spending the six thousand; he could have all or part of it tucked away elsewhere. It was lucky Mitchell managed to retrieve this much. He could rush to Corrine's and tell her the news about the money, but there had been enough drama for one day. Meanwhile, he had to secure this money safely. Hopefully, Drew owned a safe. Then, he would travel to his police precinct and ask to see all the reports relating to Danaher and the fire in Notting Dale. He needed proof that what he suspected could be true. Whatever he found, he would compile a full report and present it to Corrine. Things were moving at a rapid pace, rushing toward a conclusion.

Whatever the future held for them, Mitchell and Corrine would face it together.

CHAPTER EIGHTEEN

CORRINE SAT IN Drew Hornsby's carriage as the horses' hooves clomped steadily toward the East End. She glanced at Mitchell's newly discovered half-brother. He looked very young, earnest, yet self-contained. But, as Corrine knew all too well, medical professionals had to keep a detached air when dealing with patients and humanity at large, or one could fall to pieces. Witnessing tragedy and heartache took its toll. It had done so with Corrine. Staring into Doctor Drew's lovely blue eyes—so similar to Mitchell's—she could see the shadows lurking beneath his serene countenance, as if he had seen too much already.

"It must have been quite the blow to learn the identity of your biological father," Corrine said quietly.

"It was, rather. In the back of my mind, I knew it must be bad, as my mother changed our last name and moved us about until she became sick. I asked her once about my father, and all the blood drained from her face. She firmly stated I was never to mention him again, that he was a bad man who was looking for us. She refused to tell me the reason. To sell me, perhaps, as he had so many others? Once the Hornsbys adopted me, I assumed I was safe. But life takes unexpected turns."

Corrine sighed. "Yes, it certainly does. Do you resent your viscount father for telling you the truth?"

"No, my lady," Drew replied softly. "I love him too much to resent him about anything. I understand that he made a deathbed promise to my mother, that he would not tell me the truth of my birth. I accept that, as I have witnessed enough of them in my occupation. I also recognize my bloodline and the various siblings that come with it."

Corrine nodded. "I think Mitchell is having difficulty accepting the shocking revelations."

"When a loving family adopts you, you let down your guard and believe yourself secure. It's difficult when something comes along and upends that precarious sense of protection. I am still dealing with it. My family has been nothing but supportive. Alas, Mitchell does not have that, as both his parents have passed. It's one of the reasons I asked him to move in with me for a while. We are assisting each other in our own ways."

"I think that is brilliant. Well done."

Drew answered with a slight smile and an incline of his head. The plush carriage stopped in front of Hallahan's.

"Why not come in and join us for a late supper?" Corrine asked. "Please, Drew, if I may call you that. And I would like you to call me Corrine. We will be working together at the free clinic now and then, after all."

"You have much to discuss with Mitchell, and I assume some of the conversation is private."

"Then come in for a drink, at least."

"Very well, Corrine. I shall." Drew banged on the roof, and the sliding window opened.

"Yes, sir?"

"Wright, park the carriage. I shan't be long."

Drew assisted her from the carriage, and she took his arm as they entered Hallahan's. The place was alive with vibrant conversation as a haze of tobacco smoke hung over the area. Every table was filled with patrons playing games of cards. Coins and pound notes littered the tables' surfaces, along with mugs of beer, goblets of wine or port, and overflowing ashtrays. Servers moved skillfully between the tables, gathering empty glasses or delivering platters of finger foods. Corrine's mouth quirked. They were no doubt leftovers from aristocratic meals.

A waitress came to stand before them. "Hello. I recognize you both. Are you here to meet the detective?"

"Yes, we are," Drew replied.

"This way, if you please."

Weaving in and around the tables, the waitress led them through a door into a private room. Mitchell stood.

"I will not stay long," Drew said. "Corrine invited me for a drink." Drew pulled out a chair for Corrine across from Mitchell and sat beside his half-brother.

"My name is Enya. What would you like?" the waitress asked.

"I will have a glass of white wine," Corrine answered. "And please bring us a platter of those tasty-looking finger foods."

"Right away. Gents?"

"I will have a pint of Bass pale ale if you have it," Drew replied.

"We do. Detective?"

"The same, if you please."

Enya gave them a warm smile. "I'll return directly."

Mitchell's eyebrow cocked as he glanced from Drew back to her.

"You may speak of generalities of the case in front of Drew," Corrine said, guessing Mitchell's thoughts.

"Very well. I have recovered part of the loan Addington gave your father."

Corrine was utterly shocked. "I am impressed. Well done, you. How did you manage that?"

Mitchell gave her the details, following her father from an expensive shop to a residence on Old Street and how he forced his way in and found her father with his paramour.

"Wait, there is a young boy?" Corrine whispered. "My father led a double life the past seven years, taking mine and Jeffery's earnings and spending it on Mrs. Robson? Where is the money now?"

"In Drew's safe."

The waitress returned with their drinks and placed a platter and small plates in the middle of the table. "There are lobster puffs, a mushroom one, and I think one has goat cheese. Have fun discovering the flavors."

"Thank you," Corrine replied absently, still in shock.

"Thank you," Mitchell said. "We will order dinner in about an hour."

Enya departed. Corrine's eyes rimmed with unshed tears at the information Mitchell had revealed. "That poor woman and her child. It seems they are victims of my father's blatant selfishness as well." She looked up at Drew and Mitchell. "I have a half-brother. I now understand the shock of learning such information."

Mitchell took the platter of canapes, placed a few on his plate, and then passed it to Drew. "Mrs. Robson gave me the impression that she still loved your father, but trust would be a major concern in the future. Whether she stays with him, I cannot know."

Corrine took a trembling breath, then exhaled. "I will ask my father about all this soon enough or when I can bear to face him. I'm vastly relieved you recovered as much as you did."

"I've discovered more. You might want a sip of fortifying wine. The hooded man? It may be a villain I had dealings with in Notting Dale. His name is Jedidiah Danaher, and he is a rookery boss. He was believed killed in a pub fire."

"Believed? This is the man that shot you that night?" Drew asked, his expression incredulous.

Corrine gasped. How could it be possible? And why? Why would a rookery boss seek out Addington and have possible ties to the previous baron?

Mitchell explained how he'd stopped in to visit Rett Wollstonecraft, who was also there that night, although Mitchell stated he could not talk about the details. Then he told them of the detailed physical description Mr. Wollstonecraft gave. "Yes, that is it," Corrine interjected as she touched her forehead. "The scarring I saw for a fleeting moment was on the forehead and temple. What connection could this criminal have to the barony?"

"*That* is the mystery. Let's assume that Danaher is still living and lurking about the streets. I traveled to Notting Dale yesterday, and the side of the street where the pub was located has been completely razed. The place has had multiple loads of dirt delivered to fill in the craters caused by the fire. There were men still working on it when I was there. One of the laborers told me that more buildings will be pulled down in the new year. A complete clearance will be in full swing come spring."

Drew took his last sip of ale. "So the plans for a mix of public and private housing will go ahead then? There will be no place for Danaher to return, will there?"

Mitchell shook his head. "No. Which may make him desperate. Still, how on earth am I to find him in this city? It will be damn near impossible."

Drew stood. "On that note, I will take my leave. Enjoy your dinner. I will have Wright take me home, and then send him back for you. Take your time. Good evening."

"Good night, Drew," Corrine smiled.

After the doctor's departure, Enya returned. "We have roast beef with all the trimmings, including Yorkshire pudding."

"That sounds wonderful," Corrine replied. Mitchell nodded. The waitress gathered up the empty plates and hurried away. "After what you have relayed, I do not feel safe. Danaher could show up at any time and demand to see Travis. I warned him that a hooded man was looking for him. He acted unconcerned."

Mitchell frowned. "Perhaps you should return to your father's home until this situation resolves itself."

"No. I will never return there. I'm so angry and disappointed. My father was always an egotistic creature. Even Mother said so. But this? To have a mistress and a child? I worked my fingers to the nubs, and my brother logged in long hours at the bank. only to keep him and his second family in comfort! Why didn't my father tell us about them? I can never forgive—or forget."

"I do not blame you. Not in the least."

"Tell me about your parents, the Simpsons. Surely, they were better than my father. I want to hear about your childhood. It might cheer me up."

Mitchell sipped his ale. "Charles Simpson was fifty-eight, and my mother, Clara, was fifty-six when they adopted me. They could not have children of their own. At the time of the adoption, I was about four years old, with no memory of my past life. I cannot recall my biological mother at all. Anyway, my father retired from the Met Police when I turned seven, and they gave me all the love and attention I could ever want. They encouraged my education and extensive reading, and when I told my father I wanted to be a policeman like him, they encouraged that, too."

"They sound perfect. When did they pass away?" Corrine asked, her voice soft.

"They died within two months of each other just after I turned twenty-one—the downside to having older parents. I still miss them terribly. I cannot fathom what my life would have been like if they hadn't taken me in. When I was adopted, my name was Mitchell Evercreech. I asked my father once why my last name wasn't Simpson. He said I should keep the name I was born with and be proud of it." Mitchell shook his head. "Only I wasn't born with that name. It was made up using my given name and the place where I was born. Damon showed me the entry in the ledger."

"That is horrible."

"That was a common practice in some orphanages, work-houses, and foundling homes. It was Damon who suggested I take my parents' last name. So I did a few months ago. I should have done it long before now." Mitchell sighed. "I always meant to find a proper flat to live in, as I have my parents' furniture, household goods, and my books in storage. I could not bear to part with them. I have been living in rented rooms since they died. I figured I would use the items if I ever got married. In the meantime, I've been trying to save money."

"Money. It's always at the core of things, isn't it?"

"Unfortunately. I'm sorry your mother died. That must have been difficult."

Corrine sighed. "It was. My childhood ended the day she passed. I was taken out of school and forced to take over the running of the viscountcy. My father refused to do it. My home was not a loving one like yours. My parents barely spoke near the end of her life. I am not sure what she died of—I was never told. Perhaps she was just weary of it all. The debts. My father's reckless ways. Well, I inherited it all and am still dealing with it."

Mitchell took her hand. "You do not have to deal with it alone. Not ever again."

Taking his hand, she rubbed it against her cheek, reveling in his warmth. Smiling at him, she then released it. "Thank you. That means the world to me."

"Now, to a thoroughly unpleasant topic—Danaher."

Corrine took a sip of wine, but the taste of it felt bitter on her tongue. "Is Danaher someone I should be frightened of?"

Mitchell sighed. "He pointed that revolver at Tensbridge without a moment's hesitation. I saw it and pushed my friend out of the way. The bullet caught me in the leg."

"You are a hero," Corrine whispered, admiring and loving Mitchell all the more.

"Not as long as Danaher is possibly still breathing. I assume he may blame me for showing up and ruining his kidnapping/extortion scheme. You are associated with the barony. Danaher wants money from the baron. We have to be vigilant. Anyone caught in Danaher's orbit is in danger."

"WHY ARE WE here, on Wimpole Street?" Cillian asked.

Jedi wondered why he'd even told his illegitimate son he still lived. Granted, the boy was barely twenty years of age, but he might prove useful. "Do you remember me telling you about my father?"

"Aye, some baron or such."

"Well, he owes me money. Or rather, his estate does. He died some months back. I've come to collect the first payment, and I want you standing beside me. I'll give you a small cut. Watch this dodgy bloke for any sudden moves. You have that knife I gave you?" Jedi asked.

"Aye, it's in my pocket."

And safely tucked away in Jedi's coat was his revolver. Jedi gazed at the night sky as they strolled along the walkway toward the baron's residence. It was overcast tonight with a brisk breeze. If they had to escape, the cloud cover would work to his advantage. Jedi banged on the door.

When Addington answered, he pointed at Cillian asked, "Who is that?"

"My son. You didn't say to come alone. Did you give the butler the night off?"

"I did as you requested. He's gone to the pub."

"And your wife? Off on her appointment?"

"She is."

"Well, let us in, Travis. As I told you, I don't conduct business on the street."

With a barely concealed grumble, Addington stepped aside to allow them to enter. Once in the hall, Addington pointed to the room on the left. "In there."

Jedi glared at Travis with narrowed eyes. "This better not be a trap. If anything happens to me, I have men in place to see that you and that pretty wife of yours pay with your lives."

"It's not a trap. I want this transaction out of the way, and you and yours out of my life. I have decided to pay you twenty-five thousand pounds...*if* you sign a paper saying you relinquish all claims to the estate and will never come near me again."

Cillian looked puzzled. "Relinquish?"

"Excuse my son. Not much of an education. It means surrender, abandon, withdraw, or retreat. Release."

"Bugger that," Cillian snorted.

"I'm inclined to agree with my son, but I can be reasonable on occasion. I'm genuinely hurt that you don't want a family connection, Travis. I am deeply wounded." Jedi gave the baron a counterfeit look of anguish.

"I doubt it." Addington strolled into the room, and Jedi and his son followed. A fire blazed in the hearth. Bookcases lined the room's perimeter, and an ornate desk stood at the front. A large portrait of a country setting by a lake was on the wall behind it.

"Where is the money?" Jedi snarled, growing impatient.

Addington stood behind the desk and pushed a large brown envelope toward him. "Sign this."

"After I get the money."

Addington opened the envelope, laid the paper on the desk, and pushed the ink set toward Jedi. "Sign first. I demand a show of trust. For this amount of money, I do not think it is too much to ask."

Jedi cast a glance at Cillian, who gave him a questioning look. "I don't sign anything without reading it." Jedi sat in the chair before the desk, snatched the paper, and scanned the text. Jedi looked up from the document. "Who wrote this? Who else knows about this transaction?" Anger began to churn deep within Jedi. This was not the agreement they'd decided on. If there was one thing Jedi could not abide, it was dodgy dealings, especially with the snotty upper crust.

"My solicitor," the baron said, sniffing arrogantly. "He knows about this meeting, so if anything happens to me, he will call the police immediately."

This bloke was not as vacuous as Jedi had first surmised. No matter. Jedi dipped the pen into the ink bottle and scratched his name at the bottom of the document. Then he stood. "My end of the bargain is done; now do yours. And be quick about it."

Addington turned to face the large painting, touched the bottom corner, and it opened like a door, revealing a wall safe.

These toffs always had hidey holes to stash their valuables. Realizing that he'd soon land a large amount of money made Jedi slightly giddy—enough that he let down his guard for a moment.

Addington reached into the safe and twirled about, showing a revolver. Without hesitation, the baron pulled the trigger. At almost the same instant, Jedi was shoved out of the way by his son, who grabbed his side and collapsed to the ground. Addington froze, as if shocked. Every survival instinct Jedi possessed roared to the surface. He pulled out his pistol and fired twice at the dumbfounded bastard, who groaned, then crumpled to the floor.

Jedi stepped over the bleeding baron and inspected the safe. Empty, except for a small wad of pound notes. Jedi snatched them and shoved them in his coat pocket. That miserable bastard had had no intention of paying. He'd lured him here to kill him. Jedi glanced down at the man and spat on him, then shoved him hard with his boot. Dead—or close to it. *Good riddance and all.*

Best to escape. The neighbors had no doubt heard the commotion. Jedi grabbed the contract paper on the desk and headed toward the door. There was no use leaving any evidence around.

"Wait! Don't leave me here!"

Speaking of evidence. His son.

Jedi came to stand before him. "Sorry, my boyo. As I told you before, it's every man for himself. You should have remembered that. The coppers will be here soon. They will try to get you to help their investigation. No mentioning my name or anything else." Jedi held up the paper. "And don't mention this deal. You follow?"

Jedi didn't wait for a reply; he was already out the door and down the hall, looking for the back entrance. Once he located it, he ran through the rear yard and onto the street. Leaving Cillian meant leaving behind a loose end. His criminal instincts said he should have put his son out of his misery and also protected his own hide, but for some strange reason, he couldn't bring himself to do it. Damn that baron to a fiery hell. By the looks of him, he was already halfway there. But Jedi couldn't let this go. If the baron kicked off, there was more than one way to skin a cat. It may take careful planning, but he would get his money.

After all, there was always the pretty soon-to-be-a-widow baroness.

Chapter Nineteen

Mitchell strolled along the walkway with Corrine proudly on his arm. This would be the last time they spent alone, which filled his heart with sadness. He would miss the ease with which they conversed—and the potent attraction that grew stronger whenever they were close. There was so much Mitchell wanted to say and do, but Corrine had made it clear that as long as she was married, she could never—and he ultimately agreed.

"What do we do next?" Corrine asked, drawing closer to him. "I cannot believe Christmas is only ten days away. It does not feel like the holiday season with everything going on. I do not want to share a meal with my father or husband."

"Understandable. You could always come and share a repast of turkey or roast beef with Drew and me," Mitchell suggested hopefully.

Corrine squeezed his arm, causing a blast of desire to tear through him. "I would love that, but I had best not."

Disappointing, but she was correct. "As to what we do next? See about a solicitor. I will ask Drew. That is a start. We will take the rest as it comes."

They located Drew's carriage, and Mitchell assisted Corrine inside. He climbed in after her, biting his lip to stem the jolt of pain tearing through his leg. Though he faithfully followed Drew's daily rehabilitation exercises, he had not seen any improvement, at least not enough to make a marked difference.

Sighing, he knocked on the roof. The window slid open.

"Yes, Sergeant?"

"Thirty Wimpole Street."

At that, the carriage lurched forward. Corrine patted the bench seat beside her. "Is it terrible that I wish you to sit beside me? And hold me?"

"Not at all." Mitchell crossed the small space and slid his arm about Corrine's shoulders, pulling her close. Try as he might, he couldn't resist kissing her forehead.

Corrine sighed softly. "I feel safe when you are near like this. I never thought a man would ever make me feel this way."

"I will do anything to keep you safe. Anything," he whispered fiercely.

They held each other close until the carriage slowed. Reluctantly, Mitchell moved over to the opposite bench. Pushing the curtain aside, he peered out onto the quiet street.

"Your place is in darkness."

"It's past nine. Thomason may have gone to his rooms."

A tug of caution pulled at Mitchell's gut. "I thought butlers didn't retire for the night until everyone in the house was accounted for?"

"That's true in a larger household. Not so much ours, especially where the other servants do not live in. I will be fine. I have a key."

"I should come in with you."

"You had best not. Someone could see. A strange man coming into my house past nine o'clock? I do not want to give Travis anything to use against me. Believe me, neighbors see all sorts."

"It's pitch black outside. No one will see much of anything at all." Mitchell frowned. "But I will not argue the point. I will stay here until you give me the all-clear sign. Just come out on the front step and wave, then I will depart."

"Very well. Send me a note once you talk to Drew about the solicitor." Corrine took his hand and squeezed it affectionately. "Good night."

Mitchell watched closely as she unlocked the door and stepped across the threshold. But what momentarily caught his attention were the number of people coming out of their residences on either side of Corrine's. And across the street. How odd. It seemed she was right about being seen. But something told Mitchell this was more than just a case of meddlesome neighbors. Something had occurred on this street, and everyone was looking in the direction of Corrine's house.

CORRINE REMOVED HER gloves and stuffed them in her cape pocket as she inched along the hall. Blast it, it was dark. "Thomason?" How strange that he wasn't nearby. "Thomason?" she called out loudly.

The only reply was a drawn-out groan. Corrine followed in the direction of the wounded animal sound. *Travis's study.* As she reached the doorway, a distinct odor slammed her senses, a smell she was well familiar with. *Blood.*

When exposed to the air, blood took on a copper or iron metallic smell. That salient fact was one of the first things she'd learned when studying to be a nurse. And in this room, the scent was overwhelming. Corrine took three steps toward the gas light wall sconce when she slid on something and lost her balance. Down she went, falling hard on her side. When she got up, she realized she'd fallen into a pool of blood on the floorboards. And now, she was covered in it. Horrified, she came to her knees and crawled into the hall, then managed to stand.

As she raced for the front door, she glanced downward. Part of her gold gown was coated in blood. She stood on the front step and yelled, "Mitchell! Come here!"

He was out of the carriage and at her side at once. As he took her arm, a voice called out, "Baroness, we heard loud booming sounds from your house not more than a few minutes ago."

"Do you have a telephone?" Mitchell asked the man who stood wearing a coat over his dressing robe.

"Yes, I do."

"Then call the police immediately."

The man turned and hurried into his house as more neighbors converged on the walkway.

Mitchell escorted her inside and closed the door. "Where are the lights? Do you have electric ones?"

"Only in the parlor. There is gas lighting in the study. It's where I heard a groan—and I fell." She pointed to her gown and cape. "Blood."

"Stay behind me," Mitchell whispered. "And do not touch anything."

They made their way a short distance in the hall when Corrine grabbed the back of Mitchell's coat to make him stop. Taking a handkerchief from her cape pocket, she covered her hand and turned the gas light on. Illumination filled the hallway. Then she pointed to the doorway on the left. "In there."

When they reached the entrance, the overwhelming odor hit her again, but she managed to stay against the wall's perimeter until she reached the gas light. Turning the knob, the yellow flame flickered to life and revealed a scene of horror. Two men lay on the floor. One of them was Travis.

Tossing her cape and the handkerchief aside, Corrine's nursing training came to the forefront, and staying well clear of the pooling blood, she laid two fingers against Travis's neck artery. His chest was not rising and falling. He had no pulse.

She turned her attention to the other unconscious man. He still breathed. Looking about, she pulled the drapery from the window and folded it several times. "Mitchell, hold this against his wound. It's there, on his side. There is a revolver at Travis's feet. I have to check Travis once again. He has been shot as well, more than once, I think."

When she returned to Travis's lifeless form, it was plain that any lifesaving skills she had learned, like sternal compressions, would be pointless. Travis had been shot in the chest and above his right eye. There would be no bringing him back. Even though she had wanted out of this marriage, she'd never wished it to end like this. How utterly horrifying.

Corrine turned, looked at Mitchell, and sadly shook her head. "He's gone."

Mitchell shook the unconscious man until he groaned. His eyes fluttered. "Someone was here with you. Who was it? Who left you to bleed out? Give me a name!" Mitchell demanded.

"Left me," the young man rasped. "He left me."

"Who?"

"Father. The bastard." The young man started coughing, and a thin trickle of blood dripped from the corner of his mouth.

"Don't die and let him get away with it. Give me a name," Mitchell urged.

But the young man had fallen unconscious again. Corrine pointed to the hallway. "I am going to ring for an ambulance wagon."

"It will be too late. The constables can take him quicker. This house is located in Division D, Marylebone, number two district. I know some from this region. Listen, we will be taken in for questioning right away. We tell the truth, but we will leave the loan out of it. They won't keep us overnight. I assume you do not want to come back here."

Corrine shivered. "I will never stay in this house again."

A wagon pulled up to the front door, the bell clanging loudly. "Here, hold this against the wound. I will let them in," he said.

They exchanged places, and Mitchell grabbed his cane and headed toward the front entrance. Corrine pressed hard against the wound; already, the drapery was soaking through. The bullet may have nicked a vital organ. She could hear a muted discussion in the hallway, and then four constables ran into the room, along with a man in a derby hat and a long wool coat. He was dressed similarly to Mitchell, meaning he was undoubtedly a detective.

The detective pointed to the young man. "Take him to St.

Mary's Hospital."

Two constables came forward to grab the young man's arms and legs.

Corrine stepped back. "You must keep pressure on the wound on his left side. There might also be internal bleeding, possibly in his intestines. Be careful with him."

"Keep him alive, lads. I want a statement," the detective directed. "And the other man?"

Corrine sadly shook her head.

"Take the wagon, and Wilson, you stay at the hospital," the detective continued. "Murphy, stop by the station and tell them we need a photographer and an ambulance wagon for the body."

Corrine cast a glance at Travis. She still couldn't believe it. All he was now was a corpse to be hauled away.

"Yes, sir." The constables picked up the young man and headed toward the door.

"The baroness was a nurse for over a decade," Mitchell interjected. "Lady Addington knows of what she speaks."

"Tell the doctor or surgeon everything the lady said," the detective commanded.

Once the men departed, the detective reached into his pocket and took out a notebook and pencil. "So, you're on leave, you say?" he asked Mitchell.

"Medical leave, temporarily working as a private investigator. Lady Addington, this is Detective Reid Mahone. Detective, Lady Corrine Addington."

"My lady," Mahone murmured. He pointed at Travis. "Your husband?"

"Yes. Baron Travis Addington."

"My condolences. Who was the young man?"

"I have no idea," Corrine answered.

"The man was not here alone,' Mitchell stated.

"Oh? Why?" Mahone asked.

Corrine was curious to know how Mitchell had come to that conclusion as well.

"There is only one revolver at the scene. Multiple gunshots were exchanged since both men were shot. The second man took the gun and escaped, probably only mere minutes before we arrived. People were already gathering on the street when we approached the door. The neighbor heard 'booming sounds,' meaning more than one shot." Mitchell pointed to the wall. "It could be a robbery. The wall safe is empty."

Corrine spun around. Wall safe? She had no idea Travis had one.

"But even more damning is the fact that the young man said he'd been left behind…by his father, whoever that might be."

Mahone furiously took notes. "Is there somewhere we can talk?"

Corrine spread her arms. "I would like to change. And before you ask, I came into a dark house. I called for the butler, but he was not there. I heard a groan in the study, entered the room, and slipped in that pool of blood. I crawled to the hall, stood, and called for Sergeant Simpson. He came in, I turned on the gas lights—I had a handkerchief wrapped around my hand—and it was then we saw the bodies. I felt for a pulse on my husband, but there was none. His injuries were fatal."

Mahone's mouth quirked. "That answered several of my questions, but I have more. Many more. And I believe it best we make this official at the station. So, yes, my lady, you may change, but bring the gown to me. I will need it for evidence."

Corrine took one last glance at Travis's lifeless form. "I hired Detective Simpson to follow my husband. I believed he was cheating on me. We only married a few months ago, but it was not a love match. If you are wondering why I'm not sobbing uncontrollably, I have learned to keep my emotions in check in stressful situations, medical or not. I am sure it will hit me later. And you should also know that I had a meeting tonight with Doctor Drew Hornsby. I work with him at the free clinic, volunteering as a nurse. Detective Simpson was there also, to discuss my ongoing case. There were dozens of witnesses." Good lord, she was rambling. Perhaps the stress had already taken its toll.

"My lady," Detective Mahone said firmly. "You are not a suspect."

"Yet, you mean." Corrine blew out a shaky breath. "Ignore that. I will go change."

"I *will* have to corroborate your story, my lady. It's part of my job. But I'm acquainted with Doctor Hornsby and have heard of Sergeant Simpson's sterling reputation. My asking questions does not mean I believe you guilty of anything."

"I understand, Detective." Corrine nodded and hurried upstairs. Her cheeks were hot. She could feel it. She had to keep a cool head and not take offense to any inquiries.

Oh, Travis. I am so sorry this happened to you. What were you up to?

CHAPTER TWENTY

THEY FINALLY EMERGED from the Harrow Road police station shortly after one in the morning. Mitchell gently grasped Corrine's arm as they slowly navigated the steps. The temperature had plunged during the past few hours; their breath hung in the air in frosty puffs.

"Where can I take you?" Mitchell asked quietly.

"Not to Wimpole Street. Not to my father's," Corrine replied firmly.

"To a friend's place, perhaps?"

"My nursing friends have no room to put me up. And as for my recent reacquaintance with my school chums, well, Celia has returned to Northern England, and Selena has enough problems without me adding to them."

"Perhaps a hotel, then? The Savoy? Brown's Hotel?"

"I prefer your suggestion of staying with friends. Do you and Drew have a spare room? Just for a night or two until I get my bearings."

"Drew has a few rooms in the rear he will let in January. I'm certain he will allow you to stay there. It is a separate small flat."

"Do you think he will? I would be ever so grateful." Corrine looked down the street. "Wright is not still here? The poor man, waiting all this time."

"I came out two hours ago and sent him home. He will tell Drew to wait up for me. So we should catch a hansom cab. They are about at all hours. Here comes one now." Mitchell flagged it down, then assisted Corrine inside. Once seated, he took her gloved hand and laced his fingers through hers. She held tight.

"Poor Thomason. To come upon a murder scene, then find police tramping all through the house.... He told the police that Travis had insisted he take the night off." Corrine shuddered. "And now, he has to oversee the cleanup, the poor man." She gazed outside the window. "Why would Travis schedule his meeting when I had an appointment, and tell Thomason to take the night off, unless he wanted to be sure there would be no one around?"

"That is what it looks like—a private meeting that ended in murder and a possible robbery. I suppose it is up to Mahone and his men to track all leads. I have a feeling one of them might include a mysterious man in a hooded cloak."

"So you believe the hooded man was meeting Travis tonight?"

"I do. He is at least the top suspect."

"A terrible thought just came to me. My father. Maybe he confronted Travis over the loan!"

"I thought that as well, but I'm not sure your father is capable of killing someone. And the young man said his father left him. Unless your father has more children than you know of, I think it's fair to say he wasn't involved. Still, I'll keep that information private for now, and tell Mahone about the loan soon."

"You will continue to pursue this on your end, correct?" Corrine asked.

"I will. It's possible the hooded man brought someone—his son?—with him as backup, and since the safe was opened, it involved money. A payoff? Blackmail? One possibility is that the baron had no intention of paying. He opened the safe, brought forth the revolver, and fired. He might not have had any idea the hooded man was armed, too. And the younger man must have got in the way. Or maybe the younger man did the shooting." Mitchell exhaled wearily. "It might be wise for you to stay with

Drew and me. The hooded man may still want money from the estate. And who else can he get it from than the widowed baroness?" At her stricken look, he added, "I am sorry to be so blunt. I don't wish to frighten you."

Corrine squeezed his hand. "No. I like it when you are honest with me and discuss everything. I want that to continue. We have to consider every possibility."

"Exactly. We also have to consider the possibility that the hooded man may be Jedi Danaher."

"Good heavens. What happens next?"

"We should visit the solicitor, Mr. Dobson, first thing tomorrow and find out the reason for all those visits to Addington. How long is your brother away for?"

"A week or more. He said he would send word when he returned. Oh, but I will not be at Wimpole Street, though I will keep the servants on the payroll until I know more. Thomason can send on any inquiries and correspondence." Corrine laid her head against Mitchell's shoulder. "I am so exhausted, yet also wound up inside. I'm not sure I can sleep tonight. The scene we came upon will haunt my dreams for the foreseeable future."

Mitchell's, as well. It was one of the bloodiest crime scenes he had ever come upon. Mahone had told him they'd dusted for prints, a relatively new procedure, but Mitchell figured it would not do much good. Still, one selfish thought filled his mind.

Corrine is free.

Free from her imprudent marriage and, hopefully, any financial obligations. It would depend on what they found in the will—if there was one. Would Addington be bitter enough to leave Corrine nothing at all or place a codicil, demanding the loan be paid in the event of his death? Or would he exclude her altogether? Surely not. Even if Addington left her no money, there was still the eighteen thousand pounds in Drew's safe. Mahone knew nothing about that. Yet. Did they dare risk keeping it from the detective? All Mahone had to do was speak with Viscount Rothley, his son, Jeffery Edgeworth, or Mrs. Robson and he'd know the truth. Mitchell frowned. Perhaps he should have mentioned it after all. He would have to give it further consideration after they saw the solicitor.

"Who was that injured young man?" Corrine asked softly, interrupting his disturbed thoughts.

"It could be Danaher's son. He said his 'father' left him. I read about him in the police reports. He was wanted for questioning concerning Danaher. The son wasn't there the night I was shot, but he might have been involved in the abduction of Miss Claudia Ellingford. He fits the general description. Then again, it could just be an accomplice."

"His own father deserted him. How heartless. But then, he killed Travis, so it is not surprising. I cannot quite accept Travis is gone." Corrine let out a quivering breath. "I suppose we will have to wait until the accomplice regains consciousness and answers questions before we know of his identity."

"If he awakens at all." Mitchell pulled Corrine closer.

They remained silent during the trip to Gloucester Square. Mitchell saw lights blazing in the bottom flat when the hansom pulled up by the front door. As requested, Drew had waited up. After paying the cab driver, Mitchell opened the folding doors and assisted Corrine out, and to the house.

Drew greeted them. "Come into the parlor. I have a fire going and brandy at the ready."

Once situated in the parlor, Drew passed the filled brandy snifters to Mitchell and Corrine. "Wright mentioned a crime scene, the police, and a body under a tarp being carried out. Addington?"

Corrine nodded as she swirled her brandy.

"I am sorry for your loss, Corrine."

She gave Drew a wan smile, then motioned toward Mitchell. "Tell him what we came upon."

Mitchell relayed a condensed version of the events. Drew's eyebrows shot skyward more than once through the brief narrative. "My God. Corrine, I absolutely agree it would be best if you stayed here with us. In fact, I prepared the small flat for you. It was recently renovated and has a bedroom, water closet, sitting room, and a small kitchen with a gas cooker. You are welcome to stay as long as you wish. It's rather cozy, if I say so myself."

"Thank you so much. I will pay you," Corrine answered, her voice wobbling. After sipping the warmed brandy, she placed the snifter on the table.

"At the end of the month. We will discuss terms later," Drew replied kindly.

"Corrine will need a solicitor or barrister to navigate the legal waters regarding Addington's untimely death. Can you recommend anyone?"

"You may think it forward of me, but when Wright told me what had occurred, I sent word to a school chum of mine—Baxter Chambers. He is a solicitor and will be here at ten in the morning."

Corrine erupted into tears. As she had predicted, tonight's happenings suddenly caught up with her, and a rush of emotions burst forth. Mitchell gathered her into his arms. She calmed but still sobbed softly against his coat sleeve. Mitchell smoothed her hair, whispering comforting words.

Drew stood and held out his hand, offering a set of keys to Mitchell. "For the flat upstairs."

Mitchell took them. "Thank you, Drew. For everything."

His half-brother gave him a brief smile and left the room. It was the first time Mitchell had thought of Drew in that context. How extraordinary.

Corrine sniffled, then sat upright, laying her head against his shoulder. "I usually do not go to pieces like that. I'm not much of a crier."

"I feel a little like crying myself," Mitchell murmured. "It has been a stressful night. And it is not over. There are more hurdles to overcome. Would you like to go to your rooms? Or stay here by the fire?"

"By the fire. With you holding me. Drinking brandy. And

just—being together."

"Then we shall." Mitchell reached for her glass and handed it to her. Then he retrieved his own. They sat together in quiet contemplation and companionship for two more hours. It was half past three when he finally escorted her to the rear flat.

The next few days would be difficult, but Mitchell would be by her side as long as she needed him. He loved her with his very heart and soul and would do so until he breathed his last.

THEY COULD NOT get an early appointment with Mr. Dobson but obtained one at half past one in the afternoon. Mitchell gave the reason for the meeting, although the murder was splashed across the morning papers. It was a good thing Mitchell—with Corrine's permission—had sent word early in the morning to Thomason to pack a valise with some of her possessions and clothes and bring them to the rear entrance at Gloucester Square. The butler had informed Mitchell that reporters were already gathering on the front walkway, eager to glimpse the grieving widow. *The vultures*.

Surprisingly, Corrine managed to catch a few hours of restful sleep. When she awoke, she felt as if some of the weight she had been carrying had been lifted off her shoulders. Then, she immediately felt guilty. Travis's death should not give her a sense of relief—but it did. In a small part, but it was there, nonetheless.

Mr. Chambers arrived promptly at noon, and they gathered in the parlor. After introductions, Drew said, "Bax, take care of my friends. I am off to the clinic."

Then they were left alone with the solicitor. Mr. Chambers placed his soft leather case on the table and pulled out papers and a pencil. "Now, my lady, Sergeant Simpson. Tell me everything. I'm your solicitor, and everything you relay to me will be kept in the strictest confidence."

Over the next fifteen minutes, Corrine and Mitchell took

turns in the narration. They told the solicitor everything, including about the loan, her thoughtless father, Travis's horrible proposition, and the hasty marriage itself.

"And did you tell the police all of this?" Mr. Chambers asked.

"No," Mitchell replied. "Not everything. Nothing personal like the loan or the entire truth of the state of the marriage. Corrine told them that the baron was living at Carol Street to prepare it to be sold. It was the truth."

"And you have possession of the eighteen thousand pounds?" Mr. Chambers asked.

"Yes. It's in a safe," Corrine replied.

"I suggest we allow Mr. Dobson to reveal the will's contents before deciding anything else. Is there an heir presumptive?"

Corrine shook her head. "Not that I am aware of. But then, Travis and I had not conversed much since the hasty marriage."

"If no heir exists, the entailed property and money passes to the crown. If the baron did not mention you in his will, there is not much I can do. Such are the laws. I would suggest we not mention the loan unless we have to. I do not recommend keeping it, but we will remain quiet until we know more."

"Who will the money belong to, legally speaking?" Corrine asked.

"This loan could be a legal muddle. If your father raises a fuss and actually has legal papers to back up the loan, it may have to be returned to him. However, he will still owe the barony, if the terms are stated as such. But we will deal with that when the need arises."

"About those loan papers… They might not even exist. My father has been known to tell falsehoods over the years, if they served his purposes," she said.

Mr. Chambers took a few notes. "Noted. We'll look into that. And how much was the marriage settlement that the baron paid?"

"Twenty-five thousand pounds, and after paying my father's massive debts and giving him and my brother monthly incomes, there is about ten thousand remaining. As far as I know, Travis put it in a trust that only I can draw on.

"Good. I can safely say that settlement will not be part of the entailed estate. The remaining money is yours, my lady. You have a contract for that money?" Corrine nodded. "Good. Now, we had best head to Mr. Dobson's office and see what's what."

FIFTEEN MINUTES LATER, they were shown into Mr. Dobson's plush office. After introductions and taking their seats, Mr. Dobson opened his desk drawer and put on gold spectacles. "Right. I have all the relevant papers before me. My condolences, my lady, for your loss. First, let me state that there is an heir presumptive."

Corrine gasped. "Travis never said. Not ever."

"We only learned of that fact recently, my lady. It is standard practice to investigate the family tree, and I did so the moment Travis Addington became the new baron. It's called agnatic primogeniture. A male heir is discovered by tracing shared descendants through the male line. I found one. His name is Patrick Addington-Wells, and he is currently living in Ireland. I mailed a letter to him last month. He replied swiftly, stating his shock, and agreed to the terms."

"Terms?" Corrine asked.

"That when he becomes baron, he drops the Wells part of his name and only goes by Addington. There are other issues to iron out, like a deed of settlement. He is twenty-five and recently married into a well-to-do family. They are the ones who insisted he add Wells to his name. Many wealthy families do so when all they have are daughters. It is a way to carry on the name."

"Married?" Corrine whispered. "So what does that make me?"

"Lady Corrine, Dowager Baroness Addington."

How many more shocks could Corrine endure? If Travis had recently learned of this, why the push to advance his heir scheme? It made his suggestion all the more sordid. It also explained his haste in trying for an heir, by whatever means. To deny an actual relative a chance to be the heir for one that did not have

Addington blood was decidedly selfish. It proved she didn't know Travis at all.

"Mr. Dobson, when did you tell Travis of the discovered heir?" Corrine asked.

"Only last week, my lady, when I received Patrick Addington's reply. I wanted to have all the details in place before I informed his lordship," Mr. Dobson replied.

So Travis had been told *after* he'd revealed his scandalous heir plan. Would he have kept this newly discovered information from her? She would never know.

"Before I go over the relevant part of the will," Mr. Dobson said, bringing Corrine out of her thoughts, "there is something I must reveal. The baron asked me to do so in the event of his death. When we read Gilbert Addington's will, the old baron attached a letter." He held it out toward Corrine.

"Could you read it aloud?" she asked.

"Are you certain, my lady? There are personal revelations within."

"Mr. Chambers is my solicitor, and Sergeant Simpson is my trusted protector and advisor. Please, read it."

"Very well. 'To Travis Addington. The barony is now yours, and with it, the responsibility of producing an heir by whatever means necessary. As we discussed, this is of paramount importance. There might be another heir out there. I never bothered to have it investigated. But concerning this particular branch of the family tree, you are the last man. See it done. I left you plenty of money and investments. Use them well to ensure the family's future. Speaking of family, I have a confession to make, a shame I have carried with me for more than forty years. A thorn in my side. I have an illegitimate son. Have a care. He is a loathsome human being and a criminal besides. He may come looking for money. Arm yourself. He is dangerous. His name is—Jedidiah Danaher.'"

Chapter Twenty-One

MITCHELL CAME OUT of his chair so swiftly that his cane clattered to the floor. "Danaher? Jedi Danaher?"

Mr. Dobson looked up from his papers. "You know of the man, Sergeant?"

"Unfortunately. Danaher was the rookery boss in Notting Dale, better known as The Potteries and Piggeries. The area is located within my police division. He supposedly died in a fire, but there was no way to identify the charred corpse the firemen came upon. Still, the Baroness and I had reason to speculate that Danaher might still be alive, and that he contacted Travis Addington, looking for money. Now we know the reason why." Mitchell could not believe this. Gilbert Addington's illegitimate son? He sat and then glanced at Corrine. She had gone as white as a sheet. He briefly squeezed her hand before turning his attention back to Mr. Dobson.

"I notice that you said 'know' the man and not 'knew,' Mr. Dobson," Mr. Chambers stated. "You are aware of Mr. Danaher's current situation?"

Mr. Dobson sighed. "Yes. I am aware. His lordship recently informed me that Mr. Danaher had made contact, seeking money as the old baron had predicted. I immediately urged him to go to the police. But the baron wanted to pay him a lump sum to be rid of him once and for all. So I drew up a legal paper stating Mr. Danaher, in accepting the payment, would not be entitled to any further money from the estate."

As far as Mitchell was aware, no such document had been found at the murder scene, but he would have to check with Mahone.

Mr. Dobson flipped through the sheaves of papers. "Ah. Here it is."

"May I see that, Mr. Dobson?" Mr. Chambers asked. He took the document and quickly scanned it. "The amount of money being paid has been left blank."

"Quite so. The baron was to get back to me with the amount. Although he said something strange before he departed. He said, 'I have ways to make Danaher sign'."

"Did Travis take the money out of the account?" Corrine asked.

"That I do not know, as he did not ask me to do it, my lady. I will speak to the bank immediately. Before the baron left our meeting, I urged him again to go to the police. He said he would think about it. I assumed he was still considering it because the baron did not contact me to withdraw money. Unless he did it himself."

"Mr. Dobson," Mitchell interjected. "As you saw in this morning's papers, the baron was murdered. Of that, there is no doubt. You must tell Detective Mahone, D Division, about Danaher."

"I will contact him once this meeting is concluded. Now, we come to the will. I only finalized it last week."

Mr. Dobson read through the legalese, which had Mitchell's mind drifting to more critical matters. Danaher? *My God*. And the letter from Gilbert Addington stating, "Arm yourself." Had Travis taken that advice literally? Obviously. There was a good chance Danaher did not get the money after all. Perhaps, instead of giving in to the extortion, Travis had planned to shoot Danaher to be rid of him. This meant Danaher could still come after Corrine for what he felt he was owed. Every worst-case scenario was coming to pass. Another part of the letter caught Mitchell's attention. Getting an heir by 'whatever means.' Chilling. It explained Addington's loathsome heir arrangement.

"Mitchell?" Corrine said, gently laying her hand on his arm.

"I'm sorry. What have I missed?"

"I am to keep whatever is left in the trust," Corrine replied. "And that is all."

"Not quite all, my lady," Mr. Dobson said. "There will be a small stipend every month until you remarry. It will continue for the rest of your life if you do not. But that will be up to the new heir. You may stay at Wimpole Street until the new baron arrives. That may take a few months, or he may arrive sooner. I am not certain."

Corrine shook her head. "No. I will not return there ever again. I have found temporary lodgings. What about the servants at Wimpole Street? I strongly suggest they be kept on. Thomason and Mrs. Morris have been there for decades. Jonathan, the footman, has been there eight years."

"I have discretionary funds to handle such expenses, including the funeral. I will employ the servants until the new baron arrives, and when he does, I will suggest he keep them on. But that will be up to him. I will also pay your lodgings until we finalize the monthly stipend with the new baron. I'm afraid the remuneration will not be a large amount. Your husband suggested thirty pounds a month. It may be less than that, or it could be a little more."

"That is more than sufficient, Mr. Dobson. I do not live extravagantly. I never have. You may pay ten pounds to Doctor Drew Hornsby. I will send you the particulars."

"Would you wish me to plan the funeral, my lady?"

"Yes, please, in conjunction with Mr. Chambers. Considering the tragic circumstances, it should be as private as possible." Corrine stood. "I will leave Mr. Chambers here and allow you to make the necessary plans, including retrieving the body from St. Mary's. And I would like a summary of exactly what I am entitled to in the will—in writing."

The men stood. "I will report the funeral plans to you as soon as possible, my lady," said Mr. Chambers. "Leave the details with me."

"I will also need to collect the rest of my belongings. Can you arrange that, Mr. Chambers? And inform the servants of the situation?"

"Between the two of us, we shall handle everything. Do not distress yourself, my lady."

After Mitchell gathered his hat and cane, he took Corrine's arm, and they departed. Stepping out into the bright December sunshine, Corrine gave a trembling breath. Mitchell immediately steered her into a nearby alley. Shadows engulfed them, giving them privacy from the busy street.

She leaned against the wall, and Mitchell moved to stand in front of her. Resting his cane against the bricks, he cupped her face. Hang decorum and the fact her husband was not even in the ground yet. He caressed her flushed cheeks with the pads of his thumbs. Mitchell was not wearing gloves, and the touch of her silky-smooth skin had his nerve endings pinging like mad. "I will not let Danaher near you," he whispered fiercely. "If necessary, I will finish the job Travis started. I will protect you with my very life."

Then Mitchell captured her lips with his and kissed her fiercely, with all the pent-up desire rising within him. For a moment, Corrine seemed shocked but then enthusiastically returned his kiss, her tongue seeking his. They ended the kiss, staying in each other's arms. All he wanted to do was hold Corrine close. But nearby voices brought him back down to earth.

Slowly and reluctantly, he took a step back. From the illumination of the sun's rays, he could see Corrine's beautiful face and the desire in her eyes. She brushed her fingertips across her well-kissed lips. "Mitchell," she whispered. "How I have longed for you to do that. And how I want you to do it again. Right now."

He groaned and trembled from the emotions overtaking him.

"And do not apologize," Corrine continued, her breathy voice huskier than he had ever heard. "Or say we should not have done it, that it was not respectable. My marriage was not real. And Travis is dead, as terrible as that fact is. I'm no longer married. I am free." Corrine took a step toward him, then cupped his cheek. "We are free, at least in this respect. Free to show our feelings, at least when alone. And I am rambling again."

Mitchell turned his head slightly and kissed her palm. "I adore your ramblings. I adore…you. I have since the moment we met. From the first time I saw you. It was as if a thunderbolt hit me."

Corrine cupped her hand around the nape of his neck and pulled him in for another passionate kiss. She took the lead, and Mitchell loved it as she explored every inch of his mouth. More voices drew near, and he stepped away again. "I should take you to your flat."

They glanced about the street, then stepped out of the alley. Mitchell hailed a hansom. After they were inside, he took her hand and held it.

"What do we do next?" Corrine asked.

"You mean, regarding Danaher?"

Corrine nodded.

"We watch and wait. He will no longer use the hooded cloaks, or so I surmise. Perhaps he will use another disguise. We also wait to see if Addington withdrew money from the bank in the past few days beyond the loan he gave your father. If there was another withdrawal, we can assume Danaher got his money and will go to ground. After the murder, he would be wise to disappear. That is *if* he got the money."

"And if he did not?"

"Then Danaher will likely still want what he feels he is owed. He may wait until things die down, or he could be desperate enough to take a chance and demand it, sooner rather than later."

Corrine sighed. "And what do we do about the loan?"

That was a quandary. If they handed it over to the solicitors, it would be given to the new baron. Or worse, to her spendthrift father. After the emotional distress Addington had put Corrine through, and what she'd had to endure from her self-centered father, Mitchell felt she was entitled to the money.

"This goes against every fiber of my morals, but I believe we should say nothing for now, as Mr. Chambers suggested. If the loan is the only withdrawal on record, the law and the police will assume it was money paid to Danaher."

Corrine shook her head. "My father supposedly has papers for the loan, stating that the full amount is due if Travis and I divorce."

"After talking with your father, I concluded he is a bit of a dunderhead, as well as an incredibly selfish person. Sorry to be so direct."

"It is the complete truth," Corrine replied.

"I think Addington fabricated the paper your father supposedly signed. He planned to use the document and the loan to make you amenable to his twisted heir plan. He threatened you with it in your last meeting with him. I'm sure it was politely put, but still a threat, nonetheless."

"Yes, it was a threat. When I feel sorry for Travis's tragic end, I recall his machinations, and any pity I might feel all but melts away. He held that blasted loan over my head. How horrible. Would he have told me about the discovered heir? Who knows?"

Mitchell laced his fingers through Corrine's. "You are free. If the loan document existed, Mr. Dobson would have mentioned it today."

"You're right. He would be duty-bound to mention it."

"We hope. I suggest we say nothing for now, as Mr. Chambers suggested. If the law comes to inquire, we can deal with it then. Obviously, we will give it back."

"And if no one comes to inquire about it?" Corrine murmured.

"My first instinct is to say that you should keep it as compensation for all you have endured from your father and, more recently, your husband. However, that is an opinion from my heart, not my head."

Corrine sighed. "Even though your reasons are sound, it would not sit well with me."

"Honestly? Not me either. My common sense says to return it to the barony. But waiting until the solicitors work out the details is still the wise thing to do."

"I feel—strange. I am not sure what I should be feeling. And because of that, I should not be making any decisions right now. I agree, let's wait."

Those words arrowed straight to Mitchell's heart. Corrine was speaking of the money, but it also could be said of what had passed between them in the alley. Any emotional declarations from him should be delayed. So should any outward displays of passion beyond a kiss. Adding to her overcrowded plate was the last thing he wanted to do. There was a time and a place—and this situation was not it, no matter how much he yearned for her.

"After dropping you at Gloucester Square, I will go and see Mahone. He needs to know about Danaher and everything we learned at Mr. Dobson's office today. Mr. Dobson said he would contact Mahone, but I would feel better if it came from me first. Besides, I want to know if the young man lived through the night, and if they discovered his identity."

"Yes. I still cannot believe everything that has unfolded during the past twenty-four to thirty-six hours. Danaher as Gilbert's illegitimate son? Remember what Thomason revealed? About a man with scars coming to see Gilbert? I guess Danaher came for money, just as you said. The fact that Gilbert never allowed the man at the door inside spoke of his disdain. The old baron paid Danaher and dismissed him."

"Yes. Exactly that." He looked outside. "And here we are." Mitchell waited until the hansom stopped, then climbed down and assisted Corrine. "Do you have everything you need?"

"I will need to get a little food in, and some dishes and such, but all I want now is to sleep."

Mitchell kissed her hand. "Yes, rest. I will see you tonight. Come downstairs for supper later if you wish."

"I will. Just bang on the door if I do not come down before half past six."

Mitchell escorted her through the rear yard entrance and watched as she climbed the wrought iron stairs to the second level. Corrine unlocked the door, turned, and waved. Maybe he should have checked the small flat, but Mitchell believed it unlikely that Danaher would have any idea where Corrine would be staying. Likely, he was lying low at the moment. Though how long he would stay secreted away was another matter....

Once he returned to the hansom, he told the driver, "Marylebone Lane police station."

After he met with Mahone, he would travel to the Lancaster station and inform his inspector of the developments. The more police officers looking for Danaher, the better.

CHAPTER TWENTY-TWO

A UNIFORMED POLICEMAN brought Mahone and Mitchell steaming mugs of tea, then closed the door and left them alone.

Mahone took a sip. "Nice and hot. Now, about the young man. He's still alive, but the doctors are not sure he will fully recover. As the baroness surmised, his intestines were nicked by the bullet. There was a great deal of internal bleeding. After hours of surgery, they removed the bullet along with several feet of gut. They say he is young and strong and may recover if he lives through the next few days." Mahone took another sip of tea and opened his folder. "A woman showed up at the hospital. She would not say how she discovered the young man had been injured. Her name is Erin Quinlan, and she says her son's name is Cillian Quinlan."

"Danaher's son," Mitchell stated. "I remember the name Cillian from my precinct's reports."

"She admitted that much and said the boy had no connection to his father until about a year ago when Danaher showed up out of the blue. Against her strong objections, Cillian has been following him around like a loyal puppy ever since. The young man just turned twenty years of age."

"Danaher must have sent word to her about Cillian's injury. Have you questioned the young man by chance?"

Mahone shook his head. "No. He's been unconscious since

coming back from the operating theater. The hospital will contact me when or if he wakes. What have you learned since we last spoke?"

"The late baron's solicitor, Mr. Dobson, will be in touch with the details. But we discovered a possible motive for Danaher to have been at the baron's estate that night at the meeting earlier today. He is the illegitimate son of the previous baron." Mitchell went on to explain about the demand for money and the supposed document.

"The inkwell set was on the desk and freshly used. We dusted it for prints. Danaher could have signed a paper, legal or not, and taken it with him. I will reach out to the Lancaster Station and warn them about Danaher."

Mitchell sipped his tea. "I will see them as well. If Cillian recovers, I assume he's in legal trouble. Cillian is already wanted for bodily injury. He was in a knife fight with Miss Ellingford and also may have assisted his father in holding her against her will. You can use those charges to obtain information from the young man—if Inspector Stanhope agrees to reduce the charges in exchange for information. I don't see why he wouldn't. He is anxious to have Danaher off the street."

"I will certainly mention that when I speak with Stanhope."

Mitchell took a sip of the hot tea. "And what about the baroness?"

Mahone arched an eyebrow. "What about her?"

"She could be Danaher's next target if he didn't get the money he wanted from Addington."

"Then it's good that she has employed you, Simpson. I've no men to spare. You know what the staffing levels are. When the police department was formed in '29, London's population was one and a half million. It is now closing in on seven million, and recruitment efforts for the police have not kept up." Mahone opened his desk drawer and brought out a sheath of papers. "Since PC Baldwin's murder in October, there has been a public outcry for the police to be armed with revolvers."

"Perhaps we should. I know it is optional for detectives." Mitchell shook his head. "I put in for one shortly before I was shot. Talk about irony."

"Do you have it now?"

Mitchell shook his head. "I took the test shortly before being injured. Stanhope is keeping the revolver for me until I come off leave. I can try and collect it from him."

Mahone pointed to the desk drawer on the right. "I also have one. It's locked in here. I do not need it, but you, on the other hand, may. We know Danaher is armed and dangerous. I will do what I can on my end to locate him—I know a detective at the CID at New Scotland Yard headquarters—and will arrange a city-wide search." Mahone stood, went to a cabinet, and unlocked it. "You might be better served carrying the British Bull Dog revolver. It fits nicely in a coat pocket." Mahone placed it on the desk. "And here are two boxes of Webley .442 caliber cartridges. I got this from a search in an opium den. It hasn't been cataloged. Take it. As you are aware, there are no rules or registration regarding guns for the police or the public."

Mitchell stood, palmed the pistol, and slipped it in his coat pocket. It was a good fit and well-hidden. "Thank you. I appreciate it. We will keep each other informed of any developments?"

"We shall."

A uniformed constable knocked and entered. "A note, detective."

Mahone took it and read it. "It's from the solicitor, Dobson. He wants me to come and see him tomorrow, no doubt to tell me about Danaher. Have a care, Sergeant. Stay safe. And do not hesitate to use your weapon. We know Danaher has no qualms. He tried to kill you already."

Mitchell picked up the boxes of cartridges. "Actually, he was aiming for my friend. I shoved him out of the way and caught the bullet instead. But your point is well taken. We know what Danaher is capable of. Believe me, I will not hesitate."

"Jedidiah Danaher is wanted for questioning for this crime.

We have no solid proof he pulled the trigger as we have no weapon, and the one eyewitness is unconscious and may not recover. However, he is wanted for kidnapping and extortion in Notting Dale. I would prefer we arrest him. I want him to serve time in prison, at the very least. But if he leaves us no choice—"

Mitchell nodded. "I understand. Goodbye, Mahone."

Taking his cane and tucking the cartridges under his arm, he exited the police station. The afternoon sun was setting, but he had enough time to travel to Lancaster Station and bring the inspector up to date on Danaher. Soon, the entire force would be out looking for him. Mitchell could only hope they pulled him out of whatever dark hole he was hiding in before he came near Corrine. But if he did, Mitchell would be ready.

No one would ever threaten Corrine. Not while he breathed.

CORRINE AWOKE SUDDENLY, sitting upright in bed. She blinked rapidly, her eyes adjusting to the light. Rays from the setting sun poured in through the sheer draperies. It took a moment for her to recall where she was—Doctor Drew's rental flat. Because her estranged husband had been murdered. The horrific image of the murder scene formed in her sleep-groggy mind, but Corrine shook it away. The sight was not something she would soon forget.

Regardless of recent events, at least the bed was comfortable, and she had slept soundly. It was the first time since the murder that she had been alone with her thoughts. In less than six months, she had gone from being an impoverished nurse and daughter to a viscount, to a baroness, to a widowed dowager baroness without a home. At least she had some money. But it must be budgeted, and the generous monthly stipend to her father and brother would have to be reduced or eliminated. Her father would rail about that. Still, it was time he changed his ways, especially now that he had a young son and Mrs. Robson to support.

And that was yet another shocking revelation. How could her self-seeking father not tell her and Jeffery of the boy's existence? Or of Mrs. Robson? It was becoming clear that it was time for Corrine to think of herself, her future, and let her father take care of himself.

And that future will include Mitchell Simpson.

Corrine closed her eyes and sighed. Oh, the kisses in the alley. Just thinking of the passion that had flared between them had her insides doing somersaults.

She was in love; there was no denying it.

Exhaling, Corrine stood and slipped on her gown, then her cape. A thought struck her as she snatched the key from the bedside table. Nearly ninety pounds were in the sitting room desk drawer at Wimpole Street. The key was in her jewelry box in her bedroom. She remembered placing the money there when Travis had given her a roll of pound notes for the household and her expenses. She had given Thomason ten pounds to settle any outstanding accounts and to order more groceries.

Corrine would have to ask Mitchell to go to Wimpole Street to retrieve the money, for she would not cross that threshold again. What would she do without Mitchell? All he had ever done was offer assistance, comfort, and protection. Independent she might be, but having him as her stalwart support meant the world to her.

Once in the lower yard, she slipped through the rear entrance. The hallway was lit, so she called out, "Drew? Mitchell?"

"In here," a voice called out. It sounded like Drew. "We are in my study, three doors down on your right."

Both men stood when she entered the room.

"Good evening. I am unsure of the time." She smiled, removing her cape.

Mitchell assisted her, the brush of his hands across her shoulders sending her heart tumbling. "It is fifteen minutes past six.

Did you manage to sleep?"

"I did. What a comfortable bed and cozy rooms. Thank you, Drew, for allowing me to stay here. It may be several weeks."

"Stay as long as you like. Mr. Dobson sent me a ten-pound note this afternoon for your rent. Very generous. He also included another ten for your incidentals, food, dishes, and the like. What can I get you to drink before dinner?"

Mitchell escorted her to the leather sofa and sat beside her.

"Do you have sherry?" she asked.

"As a matter of fact, I do," Drew replied. "I recently added a few choice spirits and liquors to my sparse cupboard." He strolled over to his cabinet, opened the doors, and located the bottle of sherry. Taking a crystal glass from the shelves above, he poured a generous amount and then handed it to her. "Mitchell and I were discussing Christmas when you came in."

"Oh, good heavens. I nearly forgot," Corrine murmured as she sipped the sherry.

"We would be honored if you joined us for a holiday meal," Drew said, smiling.

"Nothing too elaborate," Mitchell interjected. "Mrs. Evans will cook a turkey and a few side dishes on the twenty-fourth. All we will need to do is reheat it. Drew and I have become experts at doing that."

Corrine smiled. "I am also proficient at reheating. Between the three of us, we can manage it. I would love to join you." Her smile slipped away. "It seems so strange to smile and talk of holidays and festive dinners with Travis at the morgue."

Mitchell took her hand and squeezed it assuredly. "It is, no matter the circumstances. Saying life goes on sounds rather odious, in light of recent events, but it is the truth. What also came from Mr. Dobson, besides the money, is a letter to you." Mitchell released her hand, then took the sealed note from the table and gave it to her.

Corrine broke the seal and scanned the contents. "How very swift and efficient. The funeral will be in three days, on the twenty-second. There will be no wake. There will be a hearse with four horses decked out in plumes of ostrich feathers, along with two mourning coaches, ten men marching alongside acting as pages. There will be a brief, private funeral service, then the procession to the cemetery, about one and a half miles from the church. Tradition says I am not to attend the graveside burial, but as Mr. Dobson states, many mid-century traditions are not always followed now."

"Who will be attending the service?" Drew asked.

"Mr. Dobson says he will be there, as will Mr. Chambers. And myself. That is it. Because of the murder, Mr. Dobson suggested we not turn the funeral into a possible gawking spectacle. Though I suppose curious onlookers will watch the procession. I must buy a black mourning gown as soon as possible."

"This is just a suggestion, but perhaps you should send word to your brother to cut his business meeting short so he can be at your side through the funeral service and burial. It would not look appropriate if Drew and I attended."

"I will do that first thing in the morning. Yes, Jeffery should come home." Corrine folded the note and laid it on the table.

"And your father?" Mitchell murmured.

"I do not want him there. His support would be all for show, as he has never given me any facilitation before. I cannot abide hypocrisy."

Drew stood. "Allow me to check on dinner. Nothing too elaborate, a beef stew."

"That sounds delicious," Corrine said, sighing.

Drew left them alone.

Corrine turned to face Mitchell. "I have a favor to ask. There are over ninety pounds in the sitting room desk drawer at Wimpole Street. Can you retrieve it for me? Travis gave me the money about three weeks ago."

"I will go first thing in the morning."

"The key is in my jewelry box in my room, not that I have much in the way of jewelry. I managed to hide a few brooches that belonged to my mother from my father. He sold the rest over the years. The key is located under the shelf within the box. I will write a note you can show Thomason to allow you into the room. Hopefully, they haven't packed it yet."

"A note is a good idea. Would you like me to contact the bank where your brother is employed? They can get word to him sooner."

"Would the murder make the papers in Manchester?"

"A murder in London? Not usually, as they have enough of their own crimes to fill the papers, but since the victim is a baron, possibly."

"Yes, I would appreciate it. It's the Strand Provincial Bank, 210 Piccadilly."

"I will make the stop tomorrow."

Corrine took Mitchell's hand. "Thank you for being here for me."

"If you haven't guessed already, I would do anything for you. Anything."

Corrine threw her arms around Mitchell's neck and embraced him. She loved him fiercely, and as soon as the funeral was over and Travis was laid to rest, she would tell Mitchell just that.

Life, indeed, did go on. And Corrine was not going to waste a moment of it.

CHAPTER TWENTY-THREE

WHEN MITCHELL AWOKE the following day, he discovered snow had blanketed the ground overnight. It was only a few inches but would not melt anytime soon since it was blasted cold. After pulling his wool scarf tightly about his neck and his wool coat collar upward, he stepped outside and shuddered as the brisk wind whipped about his legs. Reaching into his coat pocket, he grabbed his fur-lined leather gloves and, once situated, retrieved his cane from under his arm and started along the walkway, keeping a wary eye out for any possible ice. All he needed to do was to take a tumble and injure his leg further. Finally, after close to a month of diligent rehabilitation exercises, Mitchell was starting to notice some improvement in flexibility over the past couple of days, and the occasional pain in his leg was not nearly as intense or as often as it had been. Or maybe the lightness in his step was Corrine.

The prospect of a future with her had him hoping as never before. But many obstacles still stood in their path. Mitchell reasoned that anything was possible as long as they faced it together.

A hansom cab traveled toward him, so he flagged it down. "Thirty Wimpole Street," he called out to the driver as he climbed in and closed the folding doors. Now that winter was here, many of the cabs had a windowed enclosure to give some protection from the elements. Mitchell had heard, through his peerage acquaintances, that petrol cabs would replace horse-driven carriages in less than ten years. Perhaps that would be one venture Mitchell might consider, although he couldn't invest much. Less than ten minutes later, he paid the driver and was left standing before the Addington residence. Mitchell glanced up and down the street, concentrating on the surroundings. Since it was cold this morning, there were few pedestrians or costermonger carts. Mitchell's focused observation fell on a shivering young boy standing across the street, holding out a battered cap, hoping people would drop in a penny or a half-penny.

Mitchell crossed the road and dropped a shilling in the cap. "Best to get in out of the cold, lad. Buy yourself a hot meal."

"Thank ye, sir. I will. Yer kind and all." The boy, dressed in ragged clothes, quickly snatched up the coin and placed his hat on his head. With an exaggerated bow, he loped off down the street and disappeared around the corner.

Looking both ways, Mitchell crossed the street. A black mourning wreath hung on the front door of the Addington residence, and black crepe was wrapped on the door knob. He barely rapped on the knocker when Thomason opened the door to greet him.

"Sergeant Simpson. Do come in."

The scents of turpentine, carbolic soap, and beeswax inundated his senses. "You were left with a hell of a cleaning job, Thomason. How did you fare?"

Thomason led him to the study where the odors were more potent. The rugs were gone, and the furniture had been moved against the wall. "We managed, Sergeant. However, the maid quit as the task was too gruesome and stated that she could not work in a house where a murder had taken place. I fear the footman and the housekeeper-cook are also contemplating taking their leave."

Mitchell looked around. You could hardly tell it had been a grisly murder scene. "I will inform Lady Addington. Can you hire another maid?"

Thomason shook his head. "I doubt it, Sergeant. Jonathan and Mrs. Morris are only here because all peerage and wealthy homes are cutting back on staff levels. They would be hard-pressed to find gainful employment in service. I know this is a selfish request, but do you know what will become of us?"

"You're to be kept on for the time being until the new baron arrives and—"

Thomason visibly staggered. "New baron?"

Mitchell probably should not have revealed that, but one of the first things Dobson or Chambers should have done was inform the servants. The way staff was treated always angered him. Mitchell had seen it many times in his capacity as a policeman. *So, to hell with it.* "Lady Addington was shocked by the development as well. The young man was only recently identified. He comes from another branch of the family, apparently one that Gilbert Addington had no contact with. Gilbert never informed Travis Addington that the Irish branch existed. It was the solicitor who made that discovery. The new baron is a young man in his twenties, recently married."

"I am in shock. I do not know what to say."

"I'm sorry to be the one to tell you. The young baron will need servants, so chances are you will be kept on. Lady Addington suggested that very thing. But that will be Patrick Addington's decision." Mitchell looked about the room. "Personally, I cannot see the young man bringing his new bride to a house with such tragedy attached to it. But that will be for the solicitors and the new baron to work out." Mitchell reached into his side pocket and passed Thomason a note. "Lady Addington asked that I retrieve a few items. The rest will be collected later. The solicitors will arrange it."

Thomason opened the note and read it. "Of course. Whatever the baroness needs. Do thank her for speaking up for the staff." He hesitated. "There are some items in storage downstairs, such as dishes, a clock, and extra bedding. Could the baroness use them? No one has taken an inventory as yet. I take it Lady

Addington will not be returning here."

"No, she will not. As for the items, thank you for the suggestion. She is renting a small flat from a friend of mine and could use various household materials. She will appreciate the assistance."

Thomason shook his head sadly. "I never should have gone to the pub that night. But the baron insisted. He even gave me two pounds for a steak dinner and a couple of pints."

"How were you to know?" Mitchell murmured. "Do not feel guilty."

"Come this way, Sergeant." Mitchell followed Thomason upstairs and into Corrine's bedroom. It wasn't overly large but well decorated with light blue and gold shades—very much Corrine's colors.

"Her ladyship has trunks in the next room. They were never fully unpacked. Her jewelry box is there." Thomason pointed to the light oak dressing table. Mitchell opened it and, digging under the shelf, located the key to the sitting room desk.

Thomason followed him to the sitting room. Unlocking the desk drawer, Mitchell readily found the roll of notes. He peeled off five pounds and handed it to Thomason. "For any delivery charges and anything you feel the baroness will need. She has a small kitchen, so it will require a kettle and a few pots and pans, I imagine. Also, she might appreciate the bedding from her room. It may bring her comfort."

"Leave it to me. I will see it is delivered this afternoon, Sergeant."

"Good man."

"A Merry Christmas, Sergeant, and to the baroness as well."

Mitchell slipped the roll of notes in his side pocket, then pulled on his gloves. "The same goes for you and the staff, Thomason. From the baroness as well. Try and enjoy the holiday. The detective on the case, Mahone, is very competent. Look out for suspicious characters hanging about and let Mahone know immediately."

They headed toward the front entrance, and Thomason opened the door. "I will, Sergeant. You can count on me."

Mitchell touched his forelock and stepped out in the cold air. He glanced about the street again. Since he found no one lurking about, he waved down another hansom cab. "Seven Carol Street," he instructed the driver.

Once they arrived, Mitchell banged on the roof.

"Yes, sir?" the driver asked.

"I will only be a moment. Then I will need to go to the bank."

Mitchell stepped onto the walkway and stared at Addington's residence. The door had boards nailed across it. Mahone must have had it secured. Would the new baron keep this residence? It hardly seemed likely. It was too middle class for the likes of a wealthy baron. Travis Addington had been going to sell it anyway. Mitchell scanned the street. Good, the baker's cart was here.

Once he stood before the wagon, he touched the brim of his hat. "Good day. Are you the owner of this cart?"

The man, who was in his late thirties, gave Mitchell a wary look. "Aye. My wife and I do the baking early each morning."

"An acquaintance of mine owns a restaurant in the East End. I would like to give him your name. He might be interested in buying some of your goods."

The wary look deepened to one of skepticism.

Mitchell reached in his side pocket for his division card. "Detective Sergeant Simpson. This is not a scam. Baroness Addington sings your praises and wonders if you would be amenable to us putting your name forth."

"I have no idea who the baroness is, Sergeant, but thank her." The man held out his hand. "My name is Royce Eckley, and my wife is Rosa. She does the biscuits and cakes. I do the breads and scones. We also do tarts when the fruit is in season."

Mitchell shook Eckley's gloved hand. "Then you had better give me three of everything so I can send samples to my acquaintance and a dozen ginger biscuits and six scones. I'm not guaranteeing that the man who owns the restaurant will be in contact, but if he does, I will have him use my full name and today's date. That way, you know he is on the up and up."

"Thank you, sir!" Eckley immediately started bagging up everything. After Mitchell paid, he lifted the stuffed paper bag and tucked it close as he headed toward the carriage. His wandering gaze came upon a parked hansom. Mitchell stopped, his inner copper alarm beginning to peal. But he could not see anyone sitting inside it. Just his overactive imagination, perhaps.

Once situated in the cab, the driver pulled out onto the street, and Mitchell glanced back through the small rear window to see if the cab was following him. It was not. Overactive indeed. Mitchell settled in the carriage, and his thoughts turned to Corrinne. The sooner he was done with these errands, the sooner he could return to her. But before he went home, he had another stop to make—to the Galway Agency to bring them up to date on the case status. He should have seen them before, but these past weeks had been a whirlwind of activity and emotion. He also owed them their share of the Addington fee. Should he take on any new cases? Or wait until Corrine's current situation calmed down? He looked out the side window. Snow flurries fluttered downward from the gray sky above. He had enough money to live for a few months and would tell the Galway sisters he would be available again when Corrine released him.

Mitchell hoped that would never happen. Because he was deeply and irrevocably in love with Corrine.

One hour later…

"WELL, CHARLIE?"

The young lad stood before Jedi, twisting his cap between his fingerless gloved hands. "A man came to the house. He were in there twenty minutes or more. Before he knocked on the door, he came over and gave me a shilling. I saw him up close. Later, I snuck closer to the house and heard the butler call him sergeant summat or other."

Sergeant? A soldier? Or a copper? "Give me a description, Charlie. A good one."

"He were tallish, wearing a long wool coat with a gentleman's hat. He weren't no slubber, or skinny either. I reckon he could win a fight easy—muscles and all. The gent walked with shoulders back, determined-like. The git had light hair, not gold as such, and blue eyes like the sky. He weren't old, and not ugly. But what do I know about it? Oh, and he were lame. He used a cane to get about."

Lame? Could it be Simpson? The description fit. What in the hell was he doing at the baron's, back on the job, already? The baron's house wasn't even in that peeler's territory. Simpson was fast becoming a thorn in his side. First, he'd assisted in foiling Jedi's ransom plan close to two months ago. And now he was somehow involved with Addington? "And then what?"

"I followed him. You said to follow anyone who came to the house. He went to Carol Street. Stood in front of number seven for a tetch, then walked over to a seller's cart and bought all sorts, bread and the like. He looked over at the cab I was in, but I ducked down quick. He didn't see me."

"You're sure of that?"

"Aye, I'm sure. He looked away and got into his own cab. Then he went to a bank on Piccadilly, The Strand. Again, he were only there a few minutes. He were going all over. Then he stopped at a place on Cleveland Street." Charlie twisted his cap nervously. "After that, the driver got caught in traffic, and we lost him around Paddington Station. I'm sorry, Jedi. I tried my best. Don't cuff me one."

"I'm not going to hit you, Charlie. Considering all the bloke's stops, you did all right. How much money have you got left from what I gave you?" Rumor had it that Charlie was his, but Jedi didn't care one way or the other. The lad was clever. That was why he used him in this capacity.

The boy reached into his pocket and pulled out a handful of coins. "After paying the driver? Some florins and pennies, plus the shilling the lame bugger gave me."

"Here's half a crown. I'll be in touch at the usual places. Remember, tell no one I'm alive or that you've seen me, you follow? You know what will happen."

Charlie snatched the half crown and swiftly tucked it and the rest of the coins in his pocket. "Aye, I know and all." The boy ran off, leaving Jedi in his hiding place. It was a condemned building in Notting Dale, but a few people still lived there. Rumor stated the place would be pulled down next month. In the meantime, it afforded him a safe room in the basement, with its own door leading into the alley. It had a functioning fireplace running along the side of the building. Since other people were using it, so did Jedi. It kept him warm.

But he knew he couldn't stay here long.

And he dared not venture out. Not just yet.

Jedi had no idea how Cillian was doing or if he'd grassed him to the coppers. He hadn't known his son that long. Would he crack under pressure and give up the goods? Maybe he should send word to Erin and give her a warning only he knew how to deliver, just to ensure his son's silence. He could sweeten the deal by offering her money and asking her to check out the Cleveland Street address for him.

Jedi threw more coal on the fire and sat back in the rickety chair, folding his arms. Paddington Station. That was in the Tyburnia area, where mucky-mucks lived. Why would a copper be traveling over there? Maybe he would make Charlie prowl the streets looking for the lame man. The area wasn't that big. Perhaps he could contact his informant at the Lancaster Station where Simpson worked and discover the detective's status. The more he thought about it, the more Jedi was convinced it *was* Simpson. And he'd make sure the sergeant would regret interfering in Jedi's plans again.

He sat there for a moment, trying to figure out what to do next. He hadn't heard anything about Addington's funeral. Nothing had been in the papers, at least from the ones he found in rubbish bins. The murder was splashed all over, but nothing more. Jedi would be a complete nutter to show up there, in disguise or not. He curled his lip at the thought of the baron. What an idiot to pull a gun out of the safe and shoot. It just went to prove you couldn't trust any toff.

Well, he paid the price of double-crossing me.

The smart thing to do would be to leave London immediately and not look back. But to do that, he'd need money. If Addington had just paid him, he would have been gone already. Granted, he still had close to two hundred pounds left from his stash, but that wasn't enough to live on for the rest of his days. And there was still a chance he could collect... He just needed to devise a way to do precisely that. He was *owed*. Jedi could not let that go. Not when it concerned money. Not ever.

And this time, no one had better stand in his way.

Chapter Twenty-Four

THE NEXT DAY was a flurry of activity. Corrine was pleasantly surprised when she received a delivery from Wimpole Street in the late afternoon. Inside the boxes were dishes, pots, glasses, bedding, a clock, and some of her clothes and toiletries. This had to be Mitchell's doing, she surmised. He was looking out for her once again. Earlier this morning, he'd traveled to a local grocer and placed a food order: sugar, tea, bread, and other sundries. Plus, she had the ginger biscuits and scones he'd purchased yesterday.

She'd also received a telegram from her brother, Jeffery. He was catching a late afternoon train and would return to London tonight. He would come to see her at Gloucester Square immediately.

Mitchell handed her a bag of Yorkshire tea to place on the shelf in her tiny kitchen. "After this, I will head to The Crowing Cock with the baked goods."

"I am tempted to come with you. I do not like that my life must come to a standstill because I'm a widow. The black mourning gown is not being delivered until tomorrow morning." She rubbed her chin thoughtfully. "I can wear the nurse's uniform and the veil."

Mitchell shook his head. "I am not certain that is a good idea. Danaher may be lurking about. As I said last night, I felt I was being followed yesterday."

"I need to stay active. I cannot sit here alone with my thoughts."

"Then, by all means, come with me." He came toward her and cupped her face with his hands. The pads of his thumbs caressed her cheeks, sending waves of desire through her. "Know this. I will never dictate to you how to live your life. I only expressed doubt because of your safety."

"I know. Thank you for keeping me safe."

"There will be a time—and very soon—for us to discuss what happens in the future. In the meantime—" He swooped in and captured her lips, kissing her passionately. Corrine replied with a soft moan as her insides turned to custard. Exploring, he delved deep, caressing every part of her mouth. To her disappointment, Mitchell ended the kiss and stepped back. "We had best head to Hallahan's before we become swept away."

Corrine was tempted to grab his lapels, pull him in, and kiss him fiercely. They were alone. Why not allow themselves to be swept away? *Because the time was not right.* Corrine laid her hand against his cheek. "Then we should leave immediately." She whirled about and headed to her bedroom. "I won't be a minute!"

CHANGED INTO HER uniform along with the veil obscuring her face, they hailed a hansom. After paying the driver, they stood in front of the restaurant. It was three in the afternoon and, thankfully, not too busy. Fluffy snow flurries tumbled from the sky but melted as soon as they hit the ground.

Taking Mitchell's arm, they stepped inside. On her opposite side, she had the paper bag tucked in close. A waitress came toward them. "Hello, detective. Here to see Liam?"

"If he can spare a few moments."

"I will fetch him."

The waitress disappeared out back, and moments later, Mr. Hallahan opened the swinging door and motioned them to come toward him. He led them through the kitchen, where young lads were chopping carrots and potatoes, another lad was scrubbing the counters, and a woman sorted through trays of food. The scents had Corrine's mouth watering: frying onions, gammon steak, plus the sweet smell of chocolate and buttercream.

He led them into an office and closed the door behind them as they took their seats. "My condolences, Baroness. I saw the newspapers." Hallahan said gruffly as he sat.

Corrine pulled back her veil. "Thank you. I'm a dowager baroness now. There is an heir—a surprise to everyone. But I would much rather you call me Corrine when we are alone. Or Lady Corrine, whatever makes you comfortable." She handed him the stuffed paper bag. "We discovered this costermonger selling baked goods. We think they are superb. We thought you might like to sample them and throw some business the man's way."

Hallahan emptied the bag and placed the food before him.

"We got it yesterday, so not exactly fresh, but you will get the idea," Corrine added.

"Enya!" Hallahan yelled, causing Corrine to start.

The waitress that had served them the other night stuck her head in. "Yes, Liam?"

"Bring us three mugs of tea and four small plates. Any customers?"

"Nothing we can't handle. A few ladies ordered tea and cakes."

With the waitress gone, Hallahan tore off a piece of bread, prodding it with his fingers. "Nice and light, not doughy. I can't bake bread to save my life." He tore off a piece and chewed. "It's delicious."

"I told Royce Eckley that if you were interested, you would contact him using my name and yesterday's date. I told the man the decision is yours," Mitchell said. "Both he and his wife do the baking. They sell on Carol Street."

Hallahan cocked a thick eyebrow. "Why are you doing this?"

"Why not?" Mitchell immediately replied. "The man and his wife are talented, and so are you. Why not arrange something that can benefit you all? Isn't that the purpose of our group?"

"I don't know, is it?" Liam questioned. "You've asked me to join this club and gave me a vague outline. What's next?"

"I suppose a vague outline is all we have at the moment. I've been busy with another case."

"I'm afraid I am the case Mitchell is speaking of," Corrine said with a small smile. "I have taken up all his time and some of Drew's as well. I believe doing good works is the foundation of The Duke's Bastards, either with the members or those outside of it. Do I have the right of it, Mitchell?"

"You are correct," Mitchell replied, giving her a warm smile.

Enya entered with a tray. She then placed the plates and mugs of tea on the table, along with spoons, napkins, milk, and sugar.

"Cheers, Enya. Take a sample of everything on the table and hand it out to the staff. I want your opinions," Hallahan stated. She did and hurried into the kitchen. "Help yourself. Fix your tea and take samples." Hallahan piled one of everything on the plate. He bit into the ginger biscuit. "Aye, these are exceptional. I will get in touch with the man. I definitely will want the bread and perhaps some of the others. I don't get daily deliveries of the nob food. The one you saw in the kitchen was the first in a week. So I can use some baked goods to fill the gaps."

Corrine realized that was the most she had ever heard Mr. Hallahan speak. It meant he was a little more at ease around them. They ate in silence.

"Liam?" Corrine asked.

Hallahan's head shot up at the mention of his name.

"Did you receive the shoes and mittens I sent over a week ago?" she asked. "They are for the people who come for the free soup each morning."

"Aye. I'm sorry I didn't send a thank you. It slipped my mind. I'm not well versed in expected society manners," he replied frankly.

"I don't care about that. I am glad to help. I would like us to be friends."

Liam snorted and looked at Mitchell. "Can you believe this?"

Mitchell took her hand and kissed it. "Yes, I can. Corrine is kind, generous, and a good friend to have. She likes you, although I am not sure why." Mitchell gave Liam a crooked grin.

"I'm sorry I even agreed to see you and the earnest young doctor," Liam grumbled. "All I can say is I'll try. Thank you—Corrine."

Corrine beamed. If she could do her part to soften Liam's gruffness and make him amenable to accepting assistance and friendship, not only from her but also from Mitchell and Drew, then that would undoubtedly help her forget, for a while, all the stress in her life.

Later that evening…

THE DOORBELL CHIMED, and Mitchell stood. "I will get it."

"It is probably Jeffery. He did say in his telegram he would be coming here right from the train station," Corrine said.

Drew stood as well. "I will leave you to visit with your brother."

"No, please. I want you both to stay for now," Corrine insisted.

Drew sat again, and Mitchell headed down the hall to the entrance. He opened the door, and a young man holding a valise stood on the stoop.

"Mr. Edgeworth?"

"Yes. And you must be Sergeant Simpson."

Mitchell stepped aside. "Come in. Your sister is anxious to see you."

Edgeworth swiped snowflakes from his shoulder before stepping inside. "How is she doing?" he murmured.

"Keeping a brave face. Corrine is a courageous woman."

Her brother gave him a side glance when he mentioned her

first name. "Yes, she is. More than I ever realized."

"Let me take your coat and hat. You can place your case there on the hall tree seat." After he hung Edgeworth's coat and hat on the hook, he led him down the hall to the sitting room. When Edgeworth entered the room, Corrine came to her feet.

"Jeffery!" Corrine ran to her younger brother's open arms. He enveloped her in a comforting embrace.

"I am so sorry, Corri. So very sorry." Edgeworth's voice shook on the last words.

Mitchell and Drew exchanged looks. This was decidedly a private family moment. Perhaps they shouldn't be here after all. But Corrine stepped back and swiped the tear trickling down her cheek. "Jeffery, I want you to meet my good friends. Detective Sergeant Mitchell Simpson and Doctor Drew Hornsby."

The men exchanged handshakes. "Hornsby?" Edgeworth questioned. "Related to the Duke of Gransford?"

"Yes," Drew replied. "He is my uncle. Viscount Hawkestone is my father."

"Jeffery, sit here on the sofa near the fire. You must be chilled to the bone. How about a brandy, or would you prefer scotch?" She chuckled. "Listen to me. As if I am the lady of the house." Corrine smiled.

"Well, you are," Drew replied. "What can I get you, Mr. Edgeworth?"

"A brandy sounds perfect," he replied, sitting on the sofa beside his sister. "Can you tell me what happened?"

Drew handed Edgeworth a snifter and then sat in the chair opposite him. Mitchell sat next to Drew. There was a small table between them, and since they already had their drinks, Mitchell picked up his tumbler of scotch and took a sip.

Corrine sighed. "I'm not sure where to begin. I was at dinner with Drew and Mitchell at The Crowing Cock—" Corrine went on to tell her brother of finding Travis dead, the injured man, and what they had discovered at the solicitor, as well as the fact that there was an heir.

"I cannot believe this. And Travis did not know about the Irishman until a week ago?" Edgeworth said incredulously. "Where does that leave you?"

"Not as well off as before. We will have to tighten our belts. But that is a discussion for another time. I need to tell you about Father and the loan."

Drew and Mitchell stood. "On that note," Mitchell said, "We *will* leave you alone. Mr. Edgeworth, we have sandwiches left over from afternoon tea. Would you like some?"

He nodded. "Thank you."

Drew left the room. Mitchell hesitated, then laid his hand on Corrine's shoulder, and squeezed it in consolation and affection. She looked up at him and smiled. God, how he loved her. He departed and closed the door behind him.

AFTER DREW DELIVERED the platter of sandwiches, he left them alone. Jeffery grabbed one and ate it. "There is something between you and Simpson," Jeffery said, "More than friendship."

"There is—now. But that is not up for discussion. Mitchell did, however, follow Father several days ago. Right to the home of our father's mistress."

Jeffery's mouth dropped open. "What? You cannot be serious."

"Oh, I am. Her name is Mrs. Robson, and she has a son of about four or five years of age. His name is James, and he called Father 'Papa.' His affair only occurred in the last seven years, but to have a secret life and foolishly spend money first on himself and ill-advised business schemes, then on his paramour and his son—hundreds of pounds in expensive gifts—I'll never forgive him. Blast the retail shops for not itemizing what was on the bills. And all that money came from our hard work. Our sweat and worry."

Jeffery sprang to his feet and began pacing about. "That miserable, thoughtless bastard. And the wh—"

"Do not say that loathsome word. Mitchell says Mrs. Robson was genuinely shocked to hear Father had other children. He also told her he was wealthy and could easily afford all the extras he bestowed. Mitchell recovered some of the loan Travis gave Father."

Jeffery stopped pacing. "How much is some?"

"All but seven thousand pounds."

Jeffery groaned and slumped into his seat. "The new baron will want the money back."

"That is so," Corrine replied quietly. "The solicitor I hired, Mr. Chambers, said to wait before we mention it. There is still much to be ironed out."

"So not only am I to see to Father's care, but also a woman and her son? It cannot be done, even if I manage a promotion. And as dowager, your income will be next to nothing."

"And since the heir is not blood-related to me, he is under no obligation to give me any income at all. Everything is up in the air, as usual. More uncertainty. More stress. But beyond our problems, Travis was murdered. That is the worst of all."

Her brother caught her gaze. "And here I am thinking of myself, once again. I do apologize. Perhaps I'm more like Father than I realized. A sobering thought. I'm also sorry you witnessed the aftermath."

"Yes, it was terrible—something I will not soon forget. Will you go with me to the funeral? Stand at my side? Outside of the procession, it's to be private. The solicitors and me. And you, if you agree."

"Of course, I will be there for you. I—"

The doorbell trilled.

Corrine started to get to her feet, but Jeffery was already striding toward the doorway. "You stay seated. I will get the door."

A few moments later, Corrine could hear a muffled conversation. Then, the voices got louder. Suddenly, her father burst into the room with Jeffery behind him, trying to grab their father's arm.

"Get your hands off me, boy!" her father growled at Jeffery.

"How did you find me?" Corrine gasped.

"I took a page from your book. I hired a private investigator. I want my money back. I saw Addington's murder splashed all over the papers. So the loan repayment is no longer necessary."

Jeffery scoffed. "Who gave you that asinine advice?"

Mitchell and Drew came into the room.

"Ah, you have your muscle here. And another man, besides. I will not inquire about your living arrangements. You are not my concern, Corrine. Even though you stuck your nose into mine. Just keep your bully boy away from me. He had the audacity to slap me!"

Corrine looked at Mitchell, then back to her father. Mitchell did that? *Good.* "You deserved it."

Her father snorted as he reached into his coat pocket. "Here are the loan papers. Now give me the money at once."

Jeffery snatched them from his father's hands and scanned the contents. "This is not a legal document. Neither the bank nor the solicitor have signed off on it. Nor is it notarized."

"I will have you know it's a promissory note. Addington said the legal papers would follow. Now that he is dead, the money is mine."

Corrine noticed Mitchell and Drew stayed by the door. She was glad of their presence but also mortified they were witnessing her father's arrogant behavior.

"In case it slipped your self-seeking mind," Jeffery ground out, "I work at a bank and have a vast knowledge of loans and the clauses therein. Legal promissory notes are written by banks. Any other note is useless. This..." He pointed to the paper. "...will not stand up in court."

Corrine came to stand beside her brother and glanced at the note. "This is Travis's handwriting. He also says it must be paid back in ten years at an agreed interest rate of two percent. Or the entirety of it was due in the event of our divorce." So Travis *was* going to hold it over her head. Her opinion of Travis dropped several more notches. Yes, he died needlessly and tragically, but he had every intention of making her life miserable. Not any longer.

"What do I care about ten years from now?" her father bellowed, bringing Corrine's attention to the present. "I may not even be alive, then. And I knew you would never divorce him as we need his money. The terms were favorable to me," her father said with a sniff.

"GET THIS THROUGH your head," Jeffery snarled, clearly losing his patience. "This is *not* legal. You will have to pay the money to the new baron. Where is the rest of it? The seven thousand? And do not lie. For once in your egocentric life."

"I have it. I spent close to a thousand." Her father crossed his arms defiantly.

"Here is what is going to happen. First, you will leave Corrine alone. She has dealt with your reckless ways long enough. Second, you will marry Mrs. Robson and move her and your son into the town house. Did you buy that house on Old Street as you told Mrs. Robson?" Jeffery demanded.

"No, of course not!" her father snapped. "I bought the furnishings and fixings."

"Then you will sell all of it and give me the proceeds. You see, Father, from this moment forward, I will be in charge of the finances for the viscountcy. I have found you a position."

The horrified look on her father's face looked like a man condemned to death. "Work? Me? The peerage does not work!"

"You will. You are now on the board of directors for The Provincial Strand Bank. They are rather keen to have a viscount on the board as it will raise their profile. Since I work there, I will take your place when the time comes. It works out for everyone. You will attend weekly meetings and avail yourself when needed for any promotional needs, all for a yearly stipend of one hundred and forty pounds."

Her father was shocked. "I cannot live on that!"

"Many people live on that very well. And many, many more would kill to have that yearly income," Jeffery replied firmly. "There will be no further allowance from Corrine, so get used to making your own way. You will be placed on a budget and will have to start living within your means."

"You are making me part of the burgeoning and insufferable middle class!" her father whined.

"Upper-middle-class. Come, Father. We are going home." Jeffery shoved their father none-too-gently toward the door. "Corrine, send me the information on the funeral, and I will be there. We will talk more then."

Corrine ran to Jeffery and kissed him on the cheek. "Thank you for this."

Jeffery nodded to Drew and Mitchell as he pushed his father through the door. There was a muffled conversation in the hallway, and then Corrine heard the front door slam.

Mitchell came to her side. "Are you well?"

"Yes," she smiled. "More than I have been for quite some time."

No more worrying and fretting over her family. Corrine took Mitchell's hand. And this glorious man would be with her every step of the way.

CHAPTER TWENTY-FIVE

MITCHELL WAITED FOR Corrine to return from the funeral. Usually, it rained on the day of a funeral; at least, that had been Mitchell's experience. Today, it was overcast, with the sun occasionally poking through the gray clouds. He sat in the main sitting room, nursing a scotch. He loathed not being able to be there for Corrine, but at least her brother was by her side. Mitchell had to admit he was impressed by how the young Edgeworth had stepped up and taken control of the wayward Viscount Rothley. Corrine had carried the burden long enough.

The doorbell clanged. He did not rise to attend to the door, as Mrs. Evans was here today—at least for the next half hour. Moments later, she entered the room and announced, "Mr. Edgeworth, to see you, Detective. I'll leave as soon as I'm done the washing up."

"Thank you, Mrs. Evans."

She nodded, wiped her hands on a tea towel, and returned to the kitchen.

Edgeworth removed his hat. "Corrine is upstairs changing."

Mitchell stood and shook the man's hand. "How did it go?"

"Mercifully swift. A few pious words, a blessing, and into the ground. There were certainly onlookers aplenty for the procession, but the solicitors arranged that no morbid curiosity seekers could enter the cemetery. Mr. Dobson told us he received a telegram from the new baron. He is coming to London right after

Christmas. He should be here on the twenty-seventh, or later, if he decides to stay at an inn before catching the train."

Mitchell raised an eyebrow. "That quick?"

"Steamer ships and railways. He will be here in less than fourteen hours when, just a decade ago, the journey took over a week. Listen, Simpson. What is going on between you and my sister? I know it is none of my business. Corrine made that clear. All I ask is that you be patient and kind. But Corrine informed me you were all that and more. She invited me here for Christmas dinner. Is that satisfactory to you and the doctor? I do not want to intrude."

"I have no problem with it, and neither will Drew. What about your father?"

"He will spend the holiday at Old Street with his new family as he should. There will be many adjustments come the new year. Meeting our half-brother will be one of them. But we shall take it as it comes."

Mitchell nodded. "Wisely spoken. Are you staying for a drink? Tea?"

Edgeworth shook his head. "No, thank you. I will see you all on the twenty-fifth." He touched the brim of his hat. "Until then."

"Goodbye, Edgeworth."

Well, at least that portion of Corrine's problems had concluded satisfactorily. Now, there was just the rest of it. A few moments later, Mitchell heard the rear door bang shut and Corrine glided into the room like a heavenly vision, having changed into the red rose and blue gown that he adored. Her beauty took his breath away.

Mitchell immediately stood and assisted her in removing the cape. "Your brother stopped in to see me before he departed."

Corrine sat on the sofa. "He told you?"

"About the funeral? In general terms."

"I know this sounds awful, but it is as if a further weight has been lifted from my shoulders. I felt it the moment they put Travis in the ground. I'm eager to move forward."

"That is good to hear."

"I think my past—dealing with my father, our financial woes, my stressful occupation—has helped me deal with this latest burden. I am handling Travis's death far better than I thought I would."

"Many people would have gone to pieces under the circumstances. You are more courageous than you know." Mitchell picked up an envelope from the mantel. "This was delivered from Carol Street. Thomason sent it. It is addressed to you. There are other condolence messages as well. But I thought you might like to see this one."

Corrine opened the note. "It's from Selena, the Duchess of Barnsdale. She sends her condolences and offers her friendship. I will answer her tomorrow and arrange for us to see each other in the new year. I will write to Celia as well." Corrine sighed. "The three of us were very close in school. Like most young girls, we dreamed of falling in love and marrying. As it turned out, none of us married for love. We called ourselves the Bluebells."

Mitchell smiled. "That is quite precious. Why the Bluebells?"

"Well, the color of our eyes, first and foremost," Corrine laughed.

Mitchell chuckled.

Corrine sobered. "Also, bluebells symbolize humility, constancy, and everlasting love, and we pledged to follow that creed. But life had other plans for us. When my mother died, I was pulled out of school, and my life changed forever. I was so ashamed of our reduced circumstances that I never answered my friends' letters. How foolish the young can be on so many fronts."

"I'm sorry you all grew apart. Not just the young are foolish. Look at your feckless father."

Corrine nodded. "How true. And I *am* glad the Bluebells have reconnected. I have missed them terribly."

"How about a cup of tea? That I can manage to make."

"I would adore one."

Mitchell stood. "Then you relax and allow me to serve you."

"I could get used to this," she teased.

"So could I," Mitchell replied huskily. With the tip of his finger, he caressed her cheek, along her chin, and across her bottom lip.

Corrine grabbed his hand, kissed it, and rubbed it against her cheek. "I have fallen for you, Mitchell Simpson. Head over heels, tumbling, plummeting, whatever description fits."

Mitchell swiftly brought her to her feet and kissed her deeply. Passionately. With a profoundness that had his heart soaring. He then laid kisses along her chin, down the part of her neck that was exposed, and back up to capture her lips again. "And I have fallen for you. I love you, Corrine. With every fiber of my being."

Corrine smoothed a lock of his wavy hair. "You do? Truly? I love you, too. So. Very. Much."

They kissed, and Mitchell trailed his hand along her spine, then looped it around her waist, bringing her close. There was no denying his feelings, as he was hard as oak. It would be easy to become carried away but Drew would be home in an hour or so. He stepped back. "I will fetch the tea."

Beaming and happier than he had been in a long time, Mitchell first headed down the hall to lock the rear entrance, then descended the nearby stairs to the kitchen. His lady wanted tea, and he'd give her anything she desired.

WITH A SHUDDERING sigh, Corrine pulled the draperies aside and gazed out the window. Things were moving at a swift pace, and by rights, she should embrace a period of calm and rest after everything that had transpired. But more than anything, Corrine wanted to place all this behind her. With Travis's burial came freedom, an unfettered sense of relief, and an anticipation for the future. And Mitchell was very much a part of that. Corrine could not contain her joy; she twirled in a circle with her arms outstretched. When she came back around, she gasped as a man stood in the doorway—and he held a revolver.

"Not a sound," he murmured menacingly. "Who else is in the house? Servants?"

"No servants," she whispered.

The man stepped into the room and quietly closed the door. It was then she could see clearly. Scars. Dark hair. It was Danaher.

"How did you get in, Danaher?" Corrine whispered.

"Baroness," he tutted. "I'm a thief. I know how to pick a lock or two. I'll make this quick. I've come for the money. I visited your father yesterday, and he told me of a muscled cripple who assaulted him and took his loan money. Money he got from the barony. Eighteen thousand pounds should be adequate. A proper settlement for a son long ignored."

Corrine fought to keep her shock from showing outwardly. Her father had told Danaher everything and did not warn her? What kind of person was he? She was suddenly very glad that she'd decided to have nothing to do with him.

"I know who owns this house—I have ways of finding out what I need to know. And I know Simpson lives here. What does that annoying copper mean to you?" Danaher hissed through clenched teeth.

He means everything. "Sergeant Simpson is on medical leave, working as an investigator. I hired him to follow my husband. You know, the one you killed?"

"Watch your tone, Baroness. Sit over there." He waved his revolver toward one of the wing chairs facing the door. "Your gobshite husband fired first. My son pushed me out of the way. So, I fired back, defending myself."

Corrine sat in the chair. "Then tell the police that. At least there is a chance you will not swing from the gallows if you claim self-defense. If your son recovers from his injuries, he can corroborate your story."

Danaher snorted. "You sound like a copper."

"Or maybe you don't care if your son recovers, since you never asked how he is doing."

"Whether I do care or not is none of your concern. Now, the money...." Danaher murmured, watching her closely.

"Money? Let me tell you right now that I have none. I'm a dowager countess who will soon have only a small monthly stipend to live on. So I can't help you." She took a deep breath, trying to calm herself. "How did you discover where I was?"

"I hired a clever lad to watch the funeral procession for me. He was in a hansom cab and followed you. He stopped long enough to pick me up on the next street. And now, here I am. Who was the man with you at the funeral? It wasn't Simpson since he uses a cane."

"It was my younger brother."

"Any chance he will show up here?"

"No. He left a short time ago."

Danaher frowned. "You're lying about the money."

Corrine blinked rapidly. "I have no idea what you mean."

Danaher growled. "I can tell when someone is lying. Besides, I was told you were given a generous marriage settlement. We can start there."

How did Danaher discover that? "That is long gone. I had to pay my father's debts. It was the reason I married Addington in the first place." Another lie, as she still had part of the settlement left, but Danaher couldn't know that.

"Then let us move on to the loan money. It's here in this house, isn't it? I'll wager there was no time to take the money to the bank or the solicitor, so it must be tucked away in a safe. Hornsby's family are aristos, and those toffs always have places to hide their treasures."

Dear heaven, Danaher had guessed correctly. Corrine raised her chin defiantly, determined not to show any fear, though her insides fluttered like mad. "As I said, I haven't the faintest idea what you are talking about. Even if there was a safe, I don't have the combination."

Danaher's eyes narrowed. "How convenient. Then, I suppose I will stay here until Hornsby returns. Just how many men do you have under your spell, Baroness? The viscount's doctor son and the crippled copper. Where *is* Simpson? And don't tell me he went out. He wouldn't leave you alone and unprotected."

"If you leave now, I will not tell the police you were here. They are looking for you—the entire force. News of your criminal escapades have reached Scotland Yard and the Metropolitan Police headquarters. You should leave London. Tonight."

I must keep Danaher talking.

"Are you trying to scare me? It's not working, Baroness."

"What will happen if Doctor Hornsby returns and opens this fictitious safe, and there is nothing there? Have you thought of that possibility? Do you mean to kill us as you did Travis? Doctor Hornsby will be returning here shortly. It would be best if you were gone."

Danaher snarled. "Good. The sooner Hornsby arrives, the better. Now stop chattering and answer the question. Where is Simpson?"

Where is Mitchell?

"He went out."

"You're lying. Again. Come with me, Baroness. We're searching the house. He's here, I know it. And I aim to find him."

CHAPTER TWENTY-SIX

MITCHELL WAS PARTWAY up the stairs with the tea tray when he heard muted voices. At first, he thought Drew had arrived earlier than planned, or perhaps Corrine's brother had returned. But something told him—his intuition, perhaps—that this was not a social visit. A regular visitor would have pulled the front bell. Mitchell hadn't heard anything, and in the kitchen, where the servants usually worked, he would have. Slowly and carefully, Mitchell retreated to the kitchen and laid the tray and his cane on the counter.

Then he ascended the stairs as quietly as possible, grimacing as his leg ached from the effort. He inched closer, keeping his back to the wall. Mitchell could make out part of the conversation. A decidedly male voice asked where Mitchell was, and Corrine answered, "He went out."

"Come with me, Baroness. We're searching the house. He's here, I know it. And I aim to find him."

The sitting room door swung open, and Mitchell quickly ducked around the corner to avoid being seen.

"I do not have keys for the top two floors," Corrine lied coolly. "There are two unrented flats."

"Then we'll search the bottom two first. What's below this floor?"

That voice. Now that Mitchell could hear it clearly, there was no mistaking Danaher's menacing, gravelly tone. *Blast it.* The revolver Malone gave him was in his bedroom. How to fetch it? It would not be easy to climb more stairs without his cane.

"The kitchen and storage area," Corrine replied.

"Take me down there, Baroness. Lead the way. No sudden moves, now. I've got this pistol pointing at a vital organ."

Mitchell descended the stairs as quickly as possible, grabbed his cane, and slipped into the storage room, wedging himself between a pile of crates and boxes. At least he had a weapon of sorts. Thankfully, the sharp pain in his leg had subsided a little.

"A tea tray for two? There is someone else here!" Danaher snarled.

"I was down here earlier and boiled water for tea," Corrine replied calmly. "Feel the kettle. I left the tea to steep. I told you I'm expecting Doctor Hornsby to return very soon. I thought I would have tea ready for him."

Mitchell smiled, admiring Corrine's fast thinking and composed demeanor.

"The sooner I get the money—any money—I will leave this bloody city. What's in there?"

"The pantry."

"Open it."

"It's locked. I don't know where the key is."

Danaher growled in response. "And what's through there?"

"Storage."

The footsteps grew closer, and Mitchell held his breath as the door banged against the wall.

"See? It's nothing but boxes and crates," Corrine stated.

Danaher kicked a stack of boxes, and they tumbled to the floor. The crash had the sound of breaking dishes. It was lucky the boxes were nowhere near him.

"Damn all toffs and this barony!" Danaher sounded testy and exasperated, which meant he was losing patience. "I visited that stingy skinflint of a father ten years ago. Do you know what he gave me? Two hundred pounds! And more than two hundred thousand pounds are in the accounts—maybe more. You look gobsmacked, Baroness. Did your husband never tell you the extent of his wealth? If he left you next to nothing, then he fleeced you good and proper."

"I'm sorry your father never acknowledged you or gave you the proper life you were entitled to. But legally speaking, you have no claim on any of the money. According to British law, illegitimate children have no claim on estates or inheritances. I do not think that is just, but it is the law. Gilbert Addington should have set up a trust for you and seen to your education and well-being. I'm sorry he didn't, but that is no excuse for you to come and terrorize me. I can do nothing. Women mean less than nothing when it comes to wills and legacies."

"You talk a good game, Baroness. In fact, you talk too much."

Mitchell peeked around the corner of the boxes to see Danaher pushing Corrine into the kitchen area. He could rush him, but with the revolver digging into Corrine's back, he couldn't take the chance he could move swiftly enough to disarm Danaher before he pulled the trigger. Mitchell would have to wait for a better opportunity.

"That door leads outside?" Danaher barked.

"Yes."

"It's locked."

"I know nothing about how it's locked as I've never used this entrance," Corrine stated.

"Right, Baroness. Why would you use a servants' entrance?" he sneered.

"There are keys on that hook," Corrine said. "Maybe one of them opens this door or the pantry."

Mitchell slowly headed to the door of the storage room. Danaher had left it open. He heard the sound of keys jingling. Peering into the kitchen, he saw that Danaher and Corrine had their backs to him. Danaher was distracted as he removed keys from their hooks.

Mitchell did not hesitate. He moved forward, tucked the cane under his arm, picked up the tea tray, and flung it as far as possible. The sound of broken china and the silver tea service clattering across the tiled floor created enough of a distraction that he was able to jump Danaher when he wasn't looking. Mitchell raised his cane to hit Danaher on the head, but he turned slightly, and Mitchell caught his shoulder instead. Danaher yowled in response. Mitchell didn't hesitate. He swung again, this time hitting Danaher's hand. The pistol skidded across the floor, and both men lunged for it.

Corrine kicked it across the room, then chased after it just as Danaher rolled on top of Mitchell, punching him in the jaw. Mitchell saw stars and was momentarily knocked senseless.

Danaher scrambled to his feet. "Is this the leg that caught my bullet?" Danaher stomped on Mitchell's injured leg, sending a radiating wave of hot pain through the limb. "Too bad I didn't aim a little higher!"

Mitchell groaned and, with his good leg, kicked Danaher's legs out from under him. He hit the floor hard. Though he could hardly see straight through the haze of agony, he grabbed Danaher by the hair and smacked his head against the tiles.

Danaher groaned but grabbed Mitchell's arm, about to bite him.

"Enough!" Corrine cried. "I have this revolver pointed right at you, Danaher. Do not move."

Mitchell pushed Danaher away, then struggled to get to his feet. It took a moment or two, but he managed it. "Well done, darling," Mitchell said proudly to Corrine. "You kept him talking and distracted him enough for me to get to him."

"That is what I was hoping to do. He picked the rear door lock. That's how he got in. He knows about the loan money. My father told him."

Mitchell frowned. And her father never warned her? Miserable bastard. "Here, I'll take the gun. Drew has a telephone in his study. Ring the Marylebone station and ask for Mahone. The operator will connect you."

"Right away." Corrine hurried toward the stairs. Then she

stopped and blew him a kiss before ascending the stairs. God, how he loved her.

"You're a blasted pain in my arse, always interfering in my business," Danaher grumbled. "Addington shot first."

"Tell the police when they get here. You're not as bright as I gave you credit for. You should have left the city when everyone believed you dead. But instead you stayed, all because of money."

"That old sod owed me!" Danaher yelled.

"Shut it. I don't want to hear anymore." And he didn't, for his leg throbbed like the very devil.

POLICE OFFICERS AND detectives swarmed the bottom flat of Gloucester Square. They stood in the sitting room arguing over who would take possession of Danaher. F Division, Paddington, was there because Drew's home was located in that particular district. Inspector Stanhope was there from Mitchell's division, wanting Danaher for the kidnapping and fraud charges in Notting Dale. Ultimately, Mahone, from Division D, Marylebone, won the first pick as murder trumped all the other charges.

Two uniformed officers escorted Danaher toward the door. Danaher was cursing everyone within earshot. Two more uniformed police followed behind, along with the police and detectives from the other divisions.

"As far as other charges—" Mahone stated, "—the kidnapping in Notting Dale and his other criminal activities, everyone will get their turn."

"Will he be charged with murder?" Corrine asked. "He claims my husband fired first."

"I just came from speaking to his son. He awoke this morning. Cillian claims they came to collect money owed, but the safe was empty. He says Addington pulled the gun from the safe and fired. We'll get to the bottom of it. But my guess is that Danaher will end up in Newgate. Anyway, I have your initial statements. We will require a more detailed version of events in a few days. I will be in touch." He held out his hand to Mitchell. "Well done, Sergeant and Baroness. You make quite a formidable team."

Mitchell shook it. "I am relieved Danaher is in custody."

"Good afternoon, my lady. Doctor Hornsby." Mahone touched the brim of his hat and departed.

"Well, that was quite the scene to come home to," Drew murmured as he sat on the sofa. "Danaher here? In this flat? Unbelievable. Who would have thought he was desperate enough to seek out Corrine like that? The late baron should have gone to the police when Danaher first showed up at his door," Drew concluded.

Corrine came to stand beside Mitchell. She slipped her arm through his, and when he looked at her, Corrine gave him a warm smile. "Drew is correct. Travis should have gone to the police. Mr. Dobson, his solicitor, practically begged him to. Why he thought he could handle Danaher himself, we will never know. I did not know Travis at all; that is plain."

Mitchell patted her hand. "He thought he was protecting the barony, I suppose. It was rash—and dangerous. And he paid with his life."

"Excuse my personal question, but has something developed between you?" Drew gave them a knowing smile.

"I think it has always been there," Corrine smiled in return. "We love each other. Is that wrong, considering Travis's recent burial?"

Drew shook his head. "I do not know much about love, only what I have witnessed within my family. I am of the opinion that when it happens—embrace it. As a doctor, and you, Corrine, as a nurse, know that life is far too short. Revel in your feelings. The American poet and philosopher Henry David Thoreau said it best. 'There is no remedy for love but to love more.' Love more, my friends."

Corrine ran to Drew and threw her arms about his neck,

kissing his cheek affectionately. "You are the dearest of friends. Thank you. Let's celebrate Danaher's arrest. And love and all that entails. Let's take supper at The Crowing Cock, the three of us."

"I agree. But let me examine Mitchell's leg before we go. Are you still in pain?" Drew asked, concern in his voice.

"Yes, it aches more than usual, but I can stand on it. Still, it wouldn't hurt for you to have a look at it before we leave."

"I will go and change," Corrine said. "I have a gray gown I can wear to show half-mourning, and I do not care if I am whispered about—blast society. In a little over a year, it will be a new century. I am eager to get on with my life. And that life includes Mitchell."

Mitchell remained silent. Had she overstepped, bringing their mutual feelings out into the open when they hardly had time to acknowledge them? Her emotions could no longer be contained. Corrine wanted the world to know how much she loved Mitchell. How she yearned for him—utterly ached.

A smile crept across his handsome face. "Yes. Celebrate. I could not agree more."

Corrine squealed with happiness, then jumped to her feet, ran to Mitchell, and threw her arms about his neck. He laughed, and the sound of his joyous laughter caused her heart to swell to near bursting. Mitchell slipped an arm about her waist and spun her about the room.

"But your leg!" Corrine cried worriedly.

"I don't feel any pain, not while you are in my arms."

Drew stood. "On that note, I will go change for dinner."

Corrine and Mitchell laughed. Then Mitchell slowly lowered her until her slippered feet touched the floor.

Corrine stood on the tips of her toes and whispered in his ear, "Come to me tonight after supper. I want you."

"God, yes." Mitchell kissed her passionately. Deeply. "You had best change for supper or I will be making love to you on this sofa."

The thought of it thrilled her to her toes. "Is the door unlocked?" she murmured.

Mitchell reached into his pocket and tossed her the key.

She caught it. "The key to your heart?"

"Oh, my darling," Mitchell replied huskily. "You had that weeks ago."

Corrine chuckled as she hurried down the hallway. She could not wait for tonight.

Chapter Twenty-Seven

THE SUPPER WAS delicious, and the company was enjoyable. Liam Hallahan came to see them briefly and offered his best wishes for their upcoming marriage. When they returned home, Drew went inside, stating he had research to do. Corrine slipped Mitchell her key before heading upstairs.

How long to wait? Thirty minutes? An hour? Mitchell was nervous as hell. He hadn't been with a woman in more than five years, and he had certainly never been with one he loved more than his life. His few previous encounters were brief—sex, not making love. To Mitchell's mind, there was a difference. He had no doubts about his lovemaking ability, even with his leg still not up to snuff, but was unsure he could adequately show how much he loved her.

And he did. *Oh, God, how I love her.*

Thirty-five minutes later, Mitchell slipped the key in the lock and entered the darkened flat. "Corrine?"

She glided toward him, a luscious silken and lace silhouette in the moonlight. Corrine took his cane from him and tossed it aside. Then she removed his wool and suit coats and dropped them to the floor. Her evocative scent of roses and vanilla inundated his senses, making him dizzy with passion. He pulled her close, burying his face in her neck, draping kisses down her slender neck and across her collarbone. She had her hair down, and Mitchell reveled in the feel of it.

Corrine sighed softly as his hands traveled over the curve of her hips until he cupped her rear, bringing her against his aching erection. "I do not have much experience, darling," he whispered as he ground his hips against her. "And it has been five years since the last of my four encounters."

Corrine curled her tongue about his earlobe, wrenching a moan from him. "I have once, many years ago. I was lonely, and it happened so quickly, it barely left any impression on me."

Mitchell smiled as he kissed her cheek. "Then we start with a fresh slate."

Corrine grabbed his hand, pulling her toward her bedroom. "The sooner we get started, the better."

The room was softly lit, giving enough illumination for him to see her nightgown more clearly. She looked beautiful in the shamrock green sheer confection that accentuated her luscious curves and generous breasts.

Corrine walked around him in a circle. Her fingers trailed across his rear, over his hip, until they reached his aching erection. She grasped him tight, eliciting an agonizing moan from him. Mitchell had never been this aroused before. He fumbled with the buttons on his waistcoat, so Corrine assisted him. The garment hit the floor, along with his shirt. She caressed him, exploring, kissing every inch of skin.

"Mitchell," she rasped seductively. "I want no barrier between us."

Mitchell grasped her chin, tilting it upward until she caught his gaze. "Are you sure? I have a sheath."

"None."

Mitchell smiled. "No sheaths, then. I want you. I always will." He kissed her, his hands exploring her curves, caressing her breasts. As Corrine moaned in reply, he flicked his thumb across her erect nipple. Without breaking the kiss, they divested Mitchell of the rest of his clothes. He kicked his trousers and small clothes aside.

Corrine stepped back, giving him a thorough inspection,

which caused him to grow harder. "Oh, you are well put together. In all ways," she whispered.

Mitchell looped his arm about her waist and pulled her close, nuzzling her neck. He stepped back, heading toward the bed, bringing Corrine with him. Laughing, she playfully pushed him down, pulled her silk nightgown over her head, and rolled in next to him. Mitchell couldn't stop touching her. His hands were everywhere.

And when he slipped his hand between her legs, he moaned. "Wet. Gloriously wet."

"And much to explore. But now? Make love to me."

Mitchell did not need any further invitation. He rose above her. The anticipation had him trembling from need. How long he had waited for this. *There. Perfection.* Mitchell closed his eyes. He felt—complete. Alive. *Home.*

THE FEEL OF him filling her had Corrine's heart beating furiously. Mitchell held still, as if savoring their joining. She moved her hips slightly, and a guttural groan escaped him.

"I could stay like this forever," he ground out, his voice husky.

"As could I," Corrine purred as she thrust upward. "However, I want this."

"Always tell me what you want, in bed and out of it."

"Oh, I shall."

He started slow, with long, even strokes as they explored each other, kissing and caressing. Corrine gently nipped his shoulder, causing another of those glorious growls. The rhythm built, the pace quickening, and Corrine met each thrust with equal enthusiasm. Her desire was all-consuming. Before long, she was panting, yearning… She was so close….

"Come for me, darling," Mitchell groaned.

That was all Corrine needed to hear. She let herself go and cried out his name. All she could see were colors swirling in her vision as her body trembled and shook with the intensity of her climax.

At her release, Mitchell's body grew rigid. His teeth clenched, and he threw his head back in complete surrender.

They held each other for several minutes as their breathing regulated, and then Mitchell laid back down, pulling her into his embrace. "My God," he rasped with awe.

"I agree. More?"

Mitchell chortled. "Oh, yes. Much more. And we have the entire night."

"And the rest of our lives."

They hadn't discussed a future together. But it was implied. Implicit. Understood. Whatever word fit. Corrine wanted no other man.

The heart knew.

Mitchell smoothed her hair from her forehead. "All of it. Forever."

THE SUN POURED into the bedroom, rousing Mitchell from his slumber. He should have returned to his room before the sun peeked over the horizon, but he could not tear himself away from Corrine. She was curled up next to him, her head on his shoulder, breathing softly. Last night, they'd shown each other how much they cared, with their bodies as well as their words. And they had agreed to a future together. Mitchell had never been happier in his life.

And he was desperate for the future to start *now*. He kissed her forehead, and Corrine stirred. He loathed to wake her as she looked so contented and peaceful. He understood the feeling.

"My darling" he whispered, kissing her forehead again.

"Oh, I like it when you call me that," she replied sleepily.

"I know I should be on bended knee, but I prefer it here, in bed, with you in my arms. I can't think of a better way to propose to you. Marry me, my darling. You are everything I never thought I would find, and I do not want to waste another moment. I need you. I love you. You are life itself."

Corrine looked up at him, her eyes shimmering with emotion. "Oh, yes. And we will do it right away—before the year is out. We will arrange it somehow. I cannot imagine drawing my next breath without you by my side. I love you so very much." She leaned over to kiss him passionately. Then she sat up partway, braced by her elbow. "People will say it happened too swiftly. It's only been a matter of weeks! How shocking! And so soon after her husband's death! But I do not care about any of it. I never sought society's approval, and I am not about to start now."

Mitchell smiled. "Hear, hear. I completely agree."

"You will think me forward, but last night, when you took a hansom to the Gransford town house to fetch Wright and the carriage to take us to supper, I had an interesting and illuminating conversation with Drew. He is well versed on many topics."

"Yes, so I noticed," Mitchell teased.

Corrine kissed his nose. "I asked about marriage and the quickest way to get it done. I thought of a registry office, but can you believe all the paperwork can take seven to ten days? Drew said the swiftest method is still the old way. A special license."

"Married in a church? I am not one for regular church-going."

"Neither am I, but that should not matter to a true man of God."

Mitchell smiled. "Let me guess. Drew knows of the very man."

Corrine laughed. "Of course, he does! He gave me the name and the church—a friend of his father's. Remember, Viscount Hawkestone was a vicar for a few years. I say we get dressed and go at once to make plans. It will be a simple ceremony, with

Drew and my brother as the only witnesses."

Mitchell caressed her cheek. "And here comes the reality of the situation. I'm a detective in the Metropolitan Police. My income will not provide the lifestyle you were born into, regardless of financial struggles. You are the daughter of a viscount, the widow of a baron. Marrying me will be a step down into the middle class. Where will we live? In this tiny flat?"

"Or we can rent the upper flat until we make further decisions. Very well, a dose of reality. I have ten thousand pounds still left of the marriage settlement. We can live comfortably on the interest and your salary with proper investments."

"That's right. I'd forgotten that Chambers said it is yours."

"There is a good chance I will lose the monthly stipend as a dowager, but the dividends from that settlement money will more than make up for it. We can buy a modest house somewhere, get your parents' furniture out of storage, and make a proper home. And you will continue to recover until you can return to work." Corrine took his hand and kissed it. "I do not care for the trappings of the supposed upper crust; it has only brought me misery. I want *you*, my love. Wherever we live, it will be home. Our home—filled with love. And if we can manage it—children."

Mitchell pulled her to sit upright on him, her knees on either side of his hips. "I adore this position. Remember from last night?" Mitchell would never forget it. *Not ever.*

"Oh, yes. I rather like this, too," she murmured huskily as she slowly lowered, taking all of him. "In fact, I love it."

"Then, ride me, my darling."

CORRINE SMILED AS she entered the kitchen. "Enjoy your holiday, Mrs. Evans."

"Aye. And you and all, my lady. Blimey, I nearly forgot." She bustled over to the icebox. "A delivery from The Crowing Cock. Here's the note."

Corrine opened it and read it.

For your Christmas Eve repast: A roast beef pie with assorted root vegetables, shallots, leeks, mushrooms, and red wine sauce. Also, smoked trout with saffron cream. Mince pies and fruitcake. As a thank you for all you have done and as a celebration for your future. Enjoy the holidays.

Liam Hallahan

Corrine was genuinely touched. It reinforced her first impression of Liam: gruff exterior but hidden depths that he did not show to just anyone.

"This is from a friend," Corrine said softly. "He owns the restaurant and sent us a meal for tonight."

"Nice of the man," Mrs. Evans remarked. "I'll reheat it for you after I've finished my cooking. Is that all right, my lady?"

"Perfect."

Later that evening…

A TABLE AND chairs had been set up in the sitting room so Drew, Mitchell, and Corrine could gaze at the Christmas tree while enjoying their meal from Liam's restaurant. Mitchell cut into the beef pie. "This is absolutely stunning."

"I completely agree," Drew replied. "And the fish course was lovely, too. What a decided advantage it is to have a talented chef in our group. Perhaps someday, he will think of us as friends."

"And brothers?" Mitchell said.

"It is possible. Why not indeed?" Drew replied.

Mitchell raised his wine glass. "To The Duke's Bastards. May we always rise above Chellenham's loathsome legacy."

"Hear, hear," Drew and Corrine replied in unison.

"On that note," Mitchell said after sipping the wine. "Corrine and I wish you to stand up with us. We are asking her brother, Jeffery, tomorrow."

"Of course I will. Gladly. When is the happy occasion?"

Corrine smiled. "New Year's Eve morning. We took your advice and met with the vicar at Bow Church in Stratford. Reverend Wilton was very accommodating and will be procuring the special license from the bishop. Afterward, we have decided to take a trip. Perhaps for a month or a little longer. But we are unsure how far to travel considering winter has arrived."

"First, congratulations. And a honeymoon journey is just what you both need after the events of the past few months. I may know of a place."

Mitchell laughed. "We hoped you might."

"Within the Hornsby family, we have a few cottages scattered about Great Britain. There is one in Pevensey Bay along the southern coast. It's a lovely spot near a delightful seaside village. It is only five miles from Eastbourne. You can rent a horse and carriage for the month when you get off the train. People in the village also work at the cottage when we use it. There is a cook and maid; they are a mother and daughter, and the son looks after the horse and grounds. If you decide to go there, I will send word to the family to prepare for your arrival."

Corrine clapped her hands together with delight. Seeing Corrine so happy caused Mitchell's heart to swell with joy. A month cloistered away in a seaside cottage? It sounded like heaven. "We will take it," Mitchell murmured. "Thank you. Your generosity has overwhelmed me from the moment we met. You are a good friend—and brother."

Drew flushed, the first time Mitchell had seen an unguarded emotional reaction from him.

"I would not have been able to get through the past several weeks without you. I will never forget it," Mitchell continued.

Corrine raised her glass. "A Happy Christmas to us all. Oh,

listen! I hear carolers!"

Corrine ran to the front window and looked outside. Eight people of various ages stood on the front walkway, singing. "It is one of my favorites."

"I will go and let them in." Drew disappeared into the hallway.

The carolers sang "Hark the Herald Angels Sing," then a beautiful rendition of "Coventry Carol." Corrine held out the mince pies and cake platters while Drew and Mitchell gave everyone two shillings each, much to the gasps and joyful thanks of the carolers. After wishing them a Merry Christmas, the vocalists sang the boisterous "Gloucestershire Wassail" as they exited the room. Drew escorted them to the door.

"Wassail! Wassail! All over the town. Our toast it is white and our ale it is brown. Our bowl it is made of the white maple tree. With the wassailing bowl, we'll drink to thee."

Their harmonious voices faded as they moved farther along the street.

"They were wonderful," Corrine enthused.

Drew entered the room. "A note was delivered just as I was about to close the door. On Christmas Eve, no less. It's addressed to you, Corrine."

Corrine tore it open. "I am to avail myself at one in the afternoon on the twenty-eighth at Mr. Dobson's law office. The new baron will be there." She folded the note and placed it in the envelope. "It is just as well. It's best to get things settled. I will also tell them of my impending marriage. Will you come with me, Mitchell?"

"Of course. I am forever at your side."

"I will have to send a message to Mr. Chambers. He should be there as well."

"On that note, literally speaking, let us finish our meal," Drew suggested.

Mitchell could not remember enjoying just being with people more. Knowing Danaher sat in a prison cell certainly added to the celebrations. But it was Christmas, and he had not participated in many holiday festivities since his parents passed. He'd met with some of his fellow policemen for a drink on Christmas Eve, but the next day, he usually worked or found a pub that was open and had a hot pot and a pint of stout.

From this day forward, all that would change. He had a new lease on life and would recover and return to his career. But the most important thing?

He had someone to love and someone who loved him in return.

A Merry Christmas, indeed.

CHAPTER TWENTY-EIGHT

CORRINE HAD TO admit she felt apprehensive on the journey to the solicitor's office, and Mitchell must have sensed it as he took her gloved hand, laced his fingers through hers, and held it, squeezing it gently and assuredly along the way. Mr. Chambers was to meet them at the office.

All she wanted to do was to put this entire Addington marriage debacle behind her. How it ended—with Travis's murder—was still difficult to comprehend. After introductions, Corrine and Mitchell sat at the round table in the conference room, and Mr. Chambers sat on her right. She cast a glance at the new baron. He was quite handsome, with the same shade of golden-brown hair as Travis's. He and Mr. Dobson sat in front of piles of legal-looking papers.

"How was your journey, my lord?" Corrine asked politely. There was no harm in starting this off on the right foot.

"Tiring, I must say. But swift. I have been in this office since nine this morning. There was quite a lot to hash out. I am still not used to the 'my lord' business. That will take time to adjust to as well. My late father mentioned once we had peerage relations in London, but I thought no more of it, for he stated there was no chance we would ever inherit. Now, here I am."

Corrine could hear a slight Irish lilt to his speech. "Have you lived in Ireland your whole life, my lord?"

"On and off. My mother is from Ireland. We had no dealings

with the Addingtons in London. None at all. What is the connection again, Mr. Dobson?"

The solicitor consulted his papers. "Through your paternal great-grandfather, my lord."

"Right. Anyway, here we are. My bride's parents are over the moon to have a baron for a son-in-law, at any rate."

"Before we delve into matters," Mr. Chambers interjected. "We want to inform you of a loan the late Travis Addington made to her ladyship's father right before his death." Mr. Chambers explained about the loan, Corrine's unreliable, reckless father, and how Mitchell had recovered most of it. He slid a paper across to Mr. Dobson. "A promissory note, not worth the paper it is written on."

She and Mitchell had met with Mr. Chambers yesterday, and he concurred it was time to mention the loan.

Mr. Dobson read it, then handed it to the baron.

"The loan was to be paid back in full if you divorced? How extraordinary," the baron murmured.

Mr. Chambers held nothing back. He told the baron of the dire situation that had prompted her to accept the marriage proposal and the marriage settlement and how most of it had paid her father's considerable debts, and the rest propped up the viscountcy. Corrine had asked Mr. Chambers not to mention Travis's loathsome heir proposal. It had no bearing on the legal matters.

But something was bothering her. She turned to Mr. Dobson. "I have a question. After paying my father's debts and giving the viscountcy a stipend, some of the marriage settlement remains. Mr. Chambers said it was mine. Is that true?" Corrine held her breath as she waited for the reply.

Mr. Dobson folded his hands on the desk. "I recently took on all of Baron Addington's legal work, not just his will. I have seen the marriage settlement agreement, and yes, the money is yours."

Corrine exhaled in relief. "At the end, we were estranged. And the loan to my father—complicated matters. We have eighteen thousand pounds in our friend, Doctor Hornsby's safe. As for the rest of the loan, my younger brother is trying to collect the remaining funds from my father. I truly had no idea about the loan."

"Thank you, my lady, for telling us. You could have kept the money and not said a word," the baron said. He gave her a warm smile.

"Speaking of Danaher," Mitchell said. "He confronted Corrine a few days ago." Mitchell gave them a condensed version of the events.

"My God!" Mr. Dobson exclaimed. "Mahone sent word the criminal had been arrested, but I had no idea of your involvement. I'm relieved you are both safe."

"As am I," the baron said. "Mr. Dobson informed me about Danaher this morning. I am doubly relieved he is in custody."

"Thanks to Mitchell." Corrine took his hand. "We are to be married on the morning of the thirty-first."

Mr. Dobson raised an eyebrow but remained silent.

"May I offer my congratulations to you both?" The baron smiled. "That makes what I proposed to Mr. Dobson all the more relevant and timelier. Mr. Dobson?"

"Right." The solicitor rifled through his papers. "First, with your marriage, that means legally, the monthly stipend will cease."

"I assumed it would," Corrine replied.

"You will no longer be a dowager baroness, but you are permitted to use the honorary 'lady.' As in 'Lady Corrine Simpson.' I believe Baron Addington would agree."

The baron nodded. "I do."

"I will allow the baron to address the loan shortly. The residence on Carol Street is not entailed, and the baron and his wife do not need it. He wishes to offer the property to you, with all the furnishings for—"

The baron held up his hand to silence the solicitor. "For nothing. We agreed on a low figure, but after hearing about what you have endured, allow me to gift the property to you. Mr. Dobson said it had not belonged to Travis Addington for very long. He paid the mortgage in full less than two years ago. Mr. Dobson tells me it is well-appointed and respectable. If you would rather sell it and live elsewhere, you can. Regardless, the house is yours, along with the contents."

Corrine and Mitchell exchanged astonished looks.

"We accept," Mr. Chambers said quickly.

"Will you live at Wimpole Street, my lord?" Corrine asked.

"No. I will not bring my bride to a house where a murder took place. Mr. Dobson says I can lease it until I manage to remove the property from the entailment. The case must appear before the Court of Chancery, which may take some time. Meanwhile, I will locate and purchase another residence within London. I imagine we will also stay at the country estate in Aldershot."

"Thank you, my lord, for the residence. We truly appreciate it," Corrine smiled. It was more than generous. It was thoughtful and kind. Would they live there? That was a discussion for another time.

"As to the loan," the baron stated. "Return the money from the safe, and I will forgive the remainder of the credit. Whatever your brother recovers, he may keep to boost the viscountcy's finances. Mr. Dobson will craft the legal papers and confer with Mr. Chambers. I would politely suggest your brother invest that money and build the coffers. Mr. Dobson has some ideas on further adding to one's financial legacy. You may wish to consider it as well, my lady. If I am not overstepping the bounds."

"Not at all. I will inform Jeffery. Thank you again, my lord."

"I believe that is all we must deliberate over for now. Is that correct, Mr. Dobson?" the baron stated.

"It is. Mr. Chambers and I will work together to craft the legal papers needed as soon as possible."

"I will stay for a while," Mr. Chambers said. "No time like the present to get started."

The baron stood, as did Corrine and Mitchell. Mitchell held out his hand. "Thank you, my lord, for your kind and just consideration."

"Well met," the baron replied, shaking Mitchell's hand. "And Lady Corrine, when my wife arrives, will you visit us, along with Sergeant Simpson? I know no one in London and would like us all to become acquainted."

"We are going on a month-long honeymoon journey to the south coast, but yes, when we return, I would be pleased for us to become acquainted. I will contact Mr. Dobson once we are back in London."

Once outside the office, Corrine exhaled shakily. "I cannot believe what just happened."

"Nor can I," Mitchell replied. "The late baron's house? Have you ever been inside it?"

"No. Can we live there? We have the next month to discuss it."

"In bed, of course. I'm hoping we are snowed in for the duration."

Corrine laughed, then slipped her arm through Mitchell's as they headed toward the Hornsby carriage. "I said all would work out."

"That you did, Lady Corrine. It appears the Addington barony is in good hands. At last."

After assisting each other into the carriage, Corrine settled into Mitchell's warm embrace. It was over. And wherever she settled with Mitchell, she'd be home.

EPILOGUE

And finally, on New Year's Eve morning…

MITCHELL AND CORRINE stood before Reverend Wilton on a bright wintery morning at the Bow Church. Nearby were Drew and Jeffery Edgeworth.

They had invited Corrine's brother over after meeting the solicitors and the baron. To say he was relieved about the loan would be an understatement. Edgeworth had collected all but eight hundred pounds from his viscount father and agreed that prudent investments would be wise. He promised he would consult with Mr. Dobson and Mr. Chambers.

As for Corrine's father, the viscount had grudgingly agreed to sit on the board of The Strand Bank, and while it had taken some convincing, Mrs. Robson had decided to marry him. They would be moving into the Baker Street viscount residence sometime in January. Edgeworth was considering finding other lodgings.

Corrine was still not sure she could ever forgive the viscount for his thoughtless actions through the years, and especially for not warning her about Danaher. The wounds were still too fresh. Jeffery had told them their father was scared—Danaher had threatened him and his family. Regardless, it still hurt Corrine, and that cut Mitchell to the bone. Mitchell thought the man was unworthy of Corrine's concern and affection, but ultimately, it was her decision whether she wanted her father in her life.

He would do anything to protect her from any more strife. And so he'd suggested they stay at the cottage for two months instead of one. Corrine had readily agreed. They would need that time to rest. And to be alone. Mitchell had much to consider, like his future with the Metropolitan Police. He wanted to return to work, but when? And doing what? He also needed to come to terms with finding out about the man who'd fathered him and what that entailed in the future. Yes, they both needed time to reflect—and revel in each other's company, physically and emotionally.

When they returned from the honeymoon trip, Corrine agreed to meet Mrs. Robson and her son, James. Corrine was also eager to reestablish her girlhood friendships with Celia, Countess Winterwood, and Selena, the Duchess of Barnsdale. She had already written them letters, as she hoped that come spring, Celia could make a trip to London and stay either with the duchess or with them. Mitchell agreed to the visit, for he would do anything to see Corrine smile.

Mitchell only wanted to focus on Corrine—his lady. She looked lovely, wearing a white-gold gown and holding a bouquet of snowdrops and primroses. Mitchell had been alone and lonely for more years than he cared to count. Corrine had changed all that. First, with her tender and compassionate care while he recovered from his injury, and then by asking him to take on her case. He'd loved her the moment he laid eyes on her. And that was even before he'd seen her courage, generosity and goodness. She deserved to be happy, free from stress. And so did he.

They exchanged rings, the solemn words reverberating in his mind. *"I give you this ring as a symbol of my love, and with all that I am and all that I have, I honor you."*

For all the days of his life.

Author's Note

Unwanted children have been abandoned for centuries. In Britain, it wasn't until the Adoption of Children Act of 1926 that adoption had legal status. Before then, it was informal, if it happened at all. Most of the children found jobs in factories or apprenticeships; others wound up on the streets. An unmarried woman could not name a man as the father of her child on the birth certificate unless she gained an affiliation order against him, so most children had no idea who their fathers were.

I enjoy pouring over old maps of London and researching various aspects of the Victorian era. Several streets and businesses I mention are real, but some are fictional, as are the street numbers. Many Victorian-era pubs, like The Victoria, are still in operation in London.

Many of Drew Hornsby's observations have been well-researched, as have the Victorian menus I have mentioned. Eating out became very popular in the late Victorian age, with numerous pubs and restaurants opening throughout the city.

All the information regarding marriage and divorce in the 1890s is accurate. It wasn't until The Matrimonial Act of 1923, where adultery became the sole ground of divorce by either a husband or wife, that a woman gained the same rights as a man to obtain a divorce.

I hope you enjoyed Corrine's and Mitchell's story. But there are more adventures on the way. Watch for Corinne's chum, Celia, to find her happy ending in *The Chef and the Countess*. Coming soon...

About the Author

A multi-published author from the East Coast of Canada, Karyn Gerrard loves to write historical romances. Tortured heroes are an absolute must. She whiles away her spare time writing, reading romance, and drinking copious amounts of Earl Grey tea.

Karyn's been happily married for a long time to her own hero. His encouragement and loving support keep her moving forward.

Catch up with me on social media:
Website – www.karyngerrard.com
Facebook – facebook.com/karyn.gerrard
X – @KarynGerrard
BookBub – bookbub.com/profile/karyn-gerrard
Amazon – amazon.com/stores/Karyn-Gerrard/author/B0052XUPQE
Instagram – @karyngerrard